25p

DIMSIE GROWS UP

Dimsie Maitland has left school, and the future seems anything but promising. Her father has recently died, and her plans for a medical career have to be abandoned when she sees how much her mother now needs her companionship – especially as their new home is to be in a remote lochside cottage in Scotland.

But the enterprising Dimsie thinks up an alternative career for herself – as a "herb doctor", growing and using herbs for medical purposes.

And her sympathy and sunny temperament soon win her friends among her new neighbours: young Lintie, the orphan; Miss Withers, Lintie's guardian; even the Ogre, the misanthropic author. Her schoolfriends, too, come to stay – Pam, Erica and Jean, all co-members of the Anti-Soppists League at Jane's. To Dimsie's horror, however, she discovers that Pam appears to have turned into a Soppist – she has fallen in Love!

But gradually Dimsie comes to understand what has happened to Pam – for she herself falls victim to the same disease, thereby learning both the problems and the pleasures of "growing up".

D1585215

DIMSIE GROWS UP

DORITA FAIRLIE BRUCE

JOHN GOODCHILD PUBLISHERS
WENDOVER

John Goodchild Publishers,
70 Carrington Crescent,
Wendover,
Buckinghamshire,
HP22 6AN

First published in this revised edition 1984
© Copyright Dorita Fairlie Bruce's Executors 1984

Cover illustration by Gordon King
Cover design by Graham Andrews

Set in 11 on 14pt Times by John Buckle (Printers) Ltd., Gt. Yarmouth
Printed by Nene Litho, Wellingborough, Northants.
Bound by Woolnough Bookbinders, Wellingborough, Northants.

British Library Cataloguing in Publication Data
Bruce, Dorita Fairlie
  Dimsie grows up.
  I. Title
  823'.914[J]   PZ7

ISBN 0-903445-91-3

CONTENTS

CHAPTER 1

Prologue

A wild spring storm tossed the trees round the Lodge, hurling young leaves and torn twigs about the lawn which was usually so trim, beating against the blank uncurtained windows, and whisking out of sight a scattering of straws and scraps of paper – the trail of a departing furniture van. Along the foot of the chalk cliffs and on the tiny beach of St Elstrith's Bay the waves broke thunderously; but to Dimsie Maitland, moving through the empty rooms inside the Lodge, there was, for once, no exhilaration in the sound, but rather something unspeakably desolate. The sea had always reflected her mood, and tonight it did so still; but desolation was something new to Dimsie, and she did not yet understand how to cope with it.

Wandering into the room which had been her father's study. she knelt on the dismantled windowseat and gazed out into the gathering shadows of the garden. She had had no time to be miserable during the past week, since she had packed her mother off to Scotland and had herself settled down to pack and dispatch the contents of their home, with the "daily" to help her. Constant hard work had kept depression at bay till the last van was gone, and Susan, duly paid off, had departed for her home in the village. All

Dimsie had to do now was to lock the door and make her way across the familiar downs to a square white house surrounded by wooded grounds – her old school, the Jane Willard Foundation, where she was spending her last night before going north to take up an entirely new life.

"I say, Dimsie! are you there? Ugh! how creepy and forlorn it all seems in this half-light! I had to run down to the Post Office for some stamps, so I thought we might as well walk back together, if you're ready to come."

The speaker stood hesitating in the doorway, golden curls blown out by the wind and blue eyes gazing rather doubtfully at Dimsie.

"Gracious, Rosamund! how you startled me!" exclaimed Dimsie, springing to her feet. "I suppose those men left the door open. I didn't hear you come in. Yes, I'm quite ready, and very glad to see you. I was rather dreading the walk back alone."

Rosamund Garth slipped her arm sympathetically through Dimsie's as they went out of the house, and battled down the drive against the gale.

"It isn't the place, of course," said Dimsie, as the gate banged behind them. "If – if my father had been alive I shouldn't have minded a bit going back to live in Scotland, but now——"

"I know," Rosamund nodded. "This upheaval must come as a sort of climax on the top of everything else. It's almost a pity you did not go at once, immediately after he died, when you were both too numb to feel anything else much. To have waited nine months must make it worse."

"We *had* to wait," said Dimsie, "until things were sorted out and Mother could decide what to do."

They had reached the turn into the valley road which wound between the downs in the direction of the school, and

Dimsie, stopping short, shook herself abruptly.

"I will not give way to the miseries," she told Rosamund fiercely, "so don't encourage me, Rosamund. It's fatal! *Everything* depends on me now – Mother, and our new home, and our future existence. Things are going to be difficult, I can tell you, for we're not at all as well off as we used to be, and it won't help matters if I get into the habit of moaning."

"The habit certainly isn't of very long standing," returned Rosamund, with gentle sarcasm. "I think you might be forgiven for indulging in it a little, tonight. It isn't good for people always to keep a stiff upper lip."

"Yes it is," said Dimsie firmly. "It's the only way to get along at all sometimes. Are you really coming up to London with me tomorrow?"

"I think so. Primrose and her husband are back in Hampstead now, and I'm due there in any case. Miss Yorke only asked me down, this week, on your account, you know."

"I know. It was very good of her, and you've been such a help, coming down to the Lodge every day and helping me with the packing. Miss Yorke was brilliant to think of it, and to know that I'd rather have you just now than any of the others."

Rosamund looked pleased.

"Would you really?" she asked. "More than Pam?"

"Yes," Dimsie answered, after a moment's thought, for she was always strictly honest. "Pam, fond though I am of her, would be too bracing at present. I want someone soft and sympathetic like you, though later on Pam will come in very handy."

"I wonder what she's doing now," mused Rosamund, as they turned into a path which skirted the Jane Willard playing-fields and climbed through a belt of wood to the garden above. "Somehow I'm rather disappointed with Pamela. I thought she'd do something spectacular when she grew up, but it's two years now since we left school, and she has only won a tennis championship and taken up golf."

"What about yourself?" asked Dimsie slyly.

"Oh, I know! But then I never was brainy like the rest of you. My gifts are purely social, and I use them to the best of my ability. Pam ought to soar above golf and tennis though. Look at Mabs being a journalist in a London garret, and really beginning to get on too! She was having tea with the Gordons – Jean told me in her letter yesterday – looking rather thin and starved, but full of hopeful prospects."

"Oh, Mabs will get on!" declared Dimsie with conviction. "She's the sort that does. If I spend tomorrow night at Jean's on my way up, I shall hear all their news. Erica ought to satisfy your ambitious soul, Rosamund; she seems to be getting on splendidly with Mr Gordon."

"Yes. Jean told me that he says she is the best secretary he has had since he first went into Parliament. If he becomes the next Prime Minister it will give Erica lots of experience in politics before she tries to stand for election herself."

"Plenty of time for that yet," said Dimsie. "After all, Erica's only twenty. Did Jean mention her own work? She hasn't written to me for ages."

"Oh, she keeps on sending her poems to publishers but she says they behave in very much the same fashion as Noah's dove. She doesn't seem at all discouraged though. If she had been, she would have written to you fast enough; we all rely on you when we are depressed about anything – we always have. Whew! I'm glad to get out of that storm at last. Are you going up to Miss Yorke now, Dimsie?"

Dimsie nodded as they closed the hall door behind them and crossed the brightly lit hall.

"Yes, I'll run up to the study now, and have a chat before tea. You come too when you have taken off your things. That's the biggest disadvantage of going north, Rosamund. I shan't be able to run up to Miss Yorke any more for casual chats."

"Never mind," said Rosamund, as she turned off into the senior common-room. "You'll be able to come back for long visits."

Dimsie shook her head; she had a better idea of her family's financial state. Things were going to be very different now, for money would be much tighter than in her father's lifetime. She and her mother could not have afforded to stay on in St Elstrith's Lodge, and both had considered it a piece of luck when the tenants of their old family home in the West of Scotland had given up their lease just at the most convenient moment.

She explained this now to the headmistress of Jane's, as they sat together with chairs pulled close to the study fire, and Miss Yorke studied Dimsie's face with keen far-seeing eyes. She knew, despite the present weary droop of her shoulders, that Dimsie was strong enough mentally and physically for what lay ahead of her. Not many girls of nineteen had so much character in their faces; the sensitive mouth was strengthened by the determination of the chin, but Dimsie's chief beauty lay in her brown eyes.

"You'd love Twinkle Tap," she was saying now. "Yes – isn't it a strange name? The village people pronounce it 'T'inkle Tap', which sounds funnier still. I think it must have been called that first of all because you can see its light far off as you come up the water after dark. The ancestor who built it was a sailor, and perhaps he liked to see its windows twinkling when he came sailing home up the loch at the end of his voyages. There are lots of strange stories about it."

11

She stopped abruptly, and gazed into the burning logs as though she saw pictures of the low rambling house on its hilltop, looking across a grey sea-loch to the amethyst mountains which rose, mist-capped, on the farther shore.

"I remember it quite well," she went on, "though we have never lived there since we took the Lodge; even before that we spent our winters in Glasgow, and only went to Lochside for the summer. Of course it will be very quiet there, but Mother won't mind that, because it is sheltered and warm, and not so damp as most West Coast places. Fortunately too, she's much better than she was."

"Is it a large house?" inquired Rosamund, who had joined them, and was roasting her knees on a stool on the opposite side of the fireplace.

"Oh, no! quite small, but very old and quaint – you'll see when you come to stay. But you will have to bring a bicycle – there's no bus, and no shops nearer than Dunkirnie, which is a good way round the point at the foot of the loch."

The housekeeper brought in the tea things, and set a plate of muffins on the brass trivet beside Dimsie, who promptly impaled one on the prongs of a toasting-fork, and held it to the blaze.

"Not many more cosy teas here for me, Miss Yorke!" she sighed. "But never mind! I'll give you lovely scones when you come to T'inkle Tap. Promise to spend the whole of next summer holidays with us."

"That's greedy," scolded Rosamund, getting ready to butter the muffins as Dimsie finished toasting them. "Think how many people besides you want Miss Yorke. Tell us more about Twinkle Tap. I'm getting quite interested."

"There's a marvellous garden," said Dimsie dreamily, "all made up of odd bits carved out of the hillside. The sunsets there are glorious, and there are two tall sentinel pines on each side of a green gate——"

"That gate must have been repainted scores of times since then," broke in the practical Rosamund. "Probably it's red now, or yellow – and the pines are most likely blown down, for a house in that position would catch all the gales. No, Miss Yorke, I'm not trying to wetblanket her, but you know how she hates it if things or people don't come up to her expectations, and it's years since she saw the place. Don't go counting on green gates or pinetrees, Dimsie, because you mayn't get them, and then you'll be disappointed. Of course the sunsets are safe enough."

"I shan't be disappointed," said Dimsie firmly. "If it isn't as charming as I remember it, then I must manage to prefer it as it is. Here's another muffin for you, Rosamund."

"But, my dear," interposed Miss Yorke, who had been listening silently to their chatter while she made the tea, "what are you going to *do* up there? How are you to go on with your medical studies?"

The cloud which had lifted a little from Dimsie's face settled down again, and she answered quietly:

"That's all over, Miss Yorke. Mother sent me on a letter this morning from my father's executors. We shan't be penniless – we shall even be quite comfortable if we live quietly at Twinkle Tap – but I can't be a doctor now; the extra expenses of training are out of the question, even if I got a grant."

There was a moment of dismayed silence; her old school had looked forward to a brilliant career for Dimsie; then Miss Yorke began:

"I had no idea it would come to that. I am so sorry——"

Dimsie interrupted her, trying to smile.

"Don't be sorry," she said quickly. "I have been

trying to put it out of my head as much as possible, and there's another idea – of course I don't know – it may be quite impossible."

She helped herself to a lump of sugar from the basin which Rosamund held out to her, and stirred it absent-mindedly in her tea.

"Tell us about it," suggested Miss Yorke encouragingly, while Rosamund listened with silent interest.

"Well, there's a herb garden," explained Dimsie, and her face lit up again at the thought of it. "It has got flagged paths edged with dwarf lavender, and great thick bushes of grey southernwood – appleringie we call it up there – and clumps of marjoram and sage – and oh, you should see the wonderful blue of the succory flowers on their tall spikes! If I shut my eyes, I can picture it now against the darkness of the yew hedge."

"Of course!" exclaimed Miss Yorke. "I thought the description seemed familiar – your cousin Daphne once sent me a sketch of it, and I have got it still somewhere. She told me it was planned first by your great-grandmother – isn't that right?"

"Our great-grandmother twice removed," Dimsie answered. "Some of the plants and shrubs that she put there are growing still, though they are twisted with age. She made the herb garden so that she might grow her own remedies to heal her neighbours both rich and poor. My father used to tell me the story, and how the garden was her pride and joy as long as she lived. It has been sadly neglected recently, but what I want to do – if I can – is to restore it to its former usefulness, and I am sure Great-grandmother's spirit will bless my efforts."

"She ought to be very pleased with you," declared Rosamund, while Miss Yorke asked:

"Isn't there some tradition that she still walks among her lavender? It's so long since Daphne told me about it that I may be inventing that part of the story, but I have an idea that she told me something of the sort."

Dimsie laughed.

"Oh, we always *say* so, but I don't think anyone has ever met her in reality. What do you think of my plan, Miss Yorke? Do you suppose I could get books about herbs and learn to grow them – properly and scientifically, I mean?"

"And treat the neighbourhood for its ailments, and poison half of it?" suggested Rosamund sceptically.

"I hadn't thought of that," exclaimed Dimsie. "I only meant to start a little herb farm if I could, and supply chemists for my own profit. Your idea is much more altruistic, Rosamund, if I could manage it."

"What? Poisoning people?" asked Miss Yorke, laughing.

"No," said Dimsie. "I was treating that part of her remark with the contempt it deserved. But herb doctors need no degrees or University training. I could study at home. After all, I suppose that's what Great-grandmother did, and think how she helped people in her day."

"My dear girl!" exclaimed Miss Yorke, somewhat alarmed at the trend of the conversation, for she was aware of Dimsie's enthusiasms and her unquenchable desire to help people which had first put the idea of a medical career into her head; "don't tamper with matters of that sort about which you know nothing whatever – at present anyhow."

"But I can learn," urged Dimsie, eyes sparkling. "How did all those people in the past get their knowledge of herb medicines? It was on them that the world depended for its cures in those days."

"Humph!" said Miss Yorke. "Of course no doubt

Providence did watch over those early experiments in medical science, but even so, there must have been a good many accidents. Nowadays our knowledge has advanced beyond your herb medicines or rather it has incorporated the best of them in modern prescriptions.''

"I'm not so sure it's an advance,'' said Dimsie, and jumping to her feet, she crossed to a hanging bookshelf with whose contents she was evidently familiar, for her hand went straight to a small brown volume, well worn, as all Miss Yorke's books were.

"Listen to this from Apocrypha,'' she went on. "It's in Ecclesiasticus. 'Of the Most High cometh healing . . . The Lord hath created medicines out of the earth . . . and He hath given men skill that He might be honoured in His marvellous works.' Now, doesn't that clearly mean herbs? Aren't they God-given remedies for illnesses?''

"Surely any remedy is that, if it's a remedy at all?'' interposed Rosamund.

"I think so,'' agreed Miss Yorke. "But perhaps there is something to be said for Dimsie's point of view. Anyhow, grow your herbs and use them the best way you can. I believe,'' she added, looking thoughtfully at Dimsie, "that you have a passion for healing, wherever you find the need for it, and that certainly is a gift from the Most High. But remember you also require the gift of skill. Be content to go slowly, and don't do anything impulsive. Was that a knock at the door? Molly Lamond, I suppose. I promised to see her after tea. Come back again later, you and Rosamund. This may be our last evening together for a long time.''

CHAPTER 2

Travelling Under Difficulties

Dimsie stood on the platform at Euston and watched the hurrying crowds. Her ticket and her seat were taken, her luggage was on the train and there was nothing to do now but wait for departure time. She had come early to avoid the inevitable rush, and Jean Gordon, her hostess of the night before, who had accompanied her to the station, had been obliged to run off to a dinner party, having (as she put it) "seen her through the worst".

Dimsie disliked trains, and had no desire to get in before it was necessary; she would have many hours in which to tire of her corner of the carriage before Glasgow, for her chances of sleep were poor, and it was dull travelling alone. She almost wished she had accepted Jean's offer to come north with her; but that had meant delaying a day or two till Jean was clear of her many engagements and ready to start, and Dimsie was anxious to get back to her mother as soon as possible. The Gordons had a place not far from Twinkle Tap, on the other side of the loch, and Jean, who loved it, tried to escape there as often as she could, so the two looked forward to seeing something of each other from time to time.

"Thank goodness I shan't have to make this trip often!" thought Dimsie, as she watched the latecomers searching feverishly for seats. "It isn't even as though Glasgow were the end. Directly I've grabbed some breakfast there will be another train to catch, and then the ferry for Lochside. Just look at all that luggage!"

She watched a man, who walked with a limp, pushing a load of luggage on a trolley which he had apparently commandeered. He paused opposite her to mop his brow, and replied to some inaudible speech of an agitated lady beside him.

"My dear madam, it's a pleasure. Glad to be of help. Let's see if that van there will take your trunks. There actually seems to be a guard in charge, which is hopeful."

Something about his deep, good-humoured voice attracted Dimsie, and she turned for another look at its owner. Tall and well-built he was full of vigour and vitality despite his limp. As she gazed after him, he looked back for a moment straight at her, as though drawn by some magnetism in her look, and she had a glimpse of a strong, not particularly good-looking, face, and a pair of humorous blue eyes which smiled as they met her own.

"He looks nice," she thought, as she retraced her steps towards her carriage. "That pile of luggage belonged to the protesting lady, I suppose, and to those other people who were following him so closely. I like a man who will take all that trouble for strangers – especially when he happens to be disabled himself.

She stepped in, removed the suitcase which had been keeping her seat, and pulled out her mother's latest letter from the pocket of her coat. The household seemed to be settling down at Twinkle Tap, and had quite established itself during the week since its arrival. Mrs Maitland was exploring old familiar haunts which she had not seen for years, while her niece Daphne was putting the house in order. Housekeeping was not easy, they found, in a place where the nearest shop was three miles away across the hills.

"Daphne is far more domesticated than I am," wrote Mrs Maitland, "and she manages wonderfully. I believe she would manage even on a desert island. It is very good of your Aunt Isabel to spare her to us for so long."

Dimsie read and smiled. Her mother's spirits were evidently reviving, away from the recent sad associations at St Elstrith's, and Dimsie knew that later on she would love to potter round among the villagers and renew old ac-quaintanceships. Dimsie guessed that between her mother and Daphne there would be little left for her to do after a week or two; but surely, with the help of the herb garden, she would discover something positive to do. She *must* discover it, for she knew that keeping busy was very necessary for her.

"If I don't work," she thought, "I shall think, and if I think too much I shall begin regretting and longing for what I can't have. There's no sense in regrets. I shall never have money enough for my medical training, and if I had – there's Mother to look after. It was so different when Father was alive, for they were everything to each other, and they wouldn't have missed me badly enough to matter."

Just then her eye fell on a postscript.

"Daphne thinks it may interest you to know that there is no doctor nearer than Dunkirnie. She feels there is a splendid opening for you and your herb garden."

Dimsie laughed, and leaning back in the corner she closed her eyes.

"I wonder!" she thought. "I wonder!"

It was only three minutes to starting-time, and the compartment was beginning to fill up rapidly. Dimsie watched lazily and without special interest till the lastcomer limped in and took his place between the nondescript occupants of the opposite seat. It was the man with the humorous eyes who had been pushing the luggage truck, but now his vitality seemed less obvious, and there was a weariness about his expression as he folded his arms and settled down to get what sleep he could amid the rattling throb of the train, as it gathered way and plunged from glittering London into the warm darkness of a May night.

One by one the other travellers dropped asleep in uncomfortable attitudes. Some unfortunate late arrivals arranged themselves as best they could with the help of bags and suitcases. Dimsie tried at first to read, then gave it up in despair, finding the lamp impossibly dim, and sat instead gazing out at the mysterious shapes of the black landscape; every now and again bracelets and diadems of jewelled lights flashed past as the train roared northwards through villages and little towns.

She glanced across at the man with a limp. In sleep he looked sad and the lines on his face looked deeper in the flickering overhead light. Dimsie realized that he was a disappointed man, and wondered if his limp had something to do with it.

She must have fallen asleep, for the next thing she knew was a loud jarring of the brakes as the train came to a standstill, and a confused noise of shouting outside.

"Oh, what is it? Has there been an accident?" she asked out loud, still uncertain whether she was awake or dreaming. She was answered by her opposite neighbour, who said reassuringly:

"No, no! Probably a signal against us. Except for the moon everything is pitch-black outside – no lights anywhere – looks as though we have stopped in the middle of a moor."

"So we have, sir, and I can tell you why," growled a heavy-looking man who stood in the corridor beside the doorway. "This is a wildcat strike, and we shan't get much farther tonight. I heard some talk of it at Euston – but I took no notice. Five minutes to midnight," he added, pulling out his watch.

"Barty, go and see if it's a strike and what we can do," came in a woman's fretful tones. "Remember we must get to Moffat by morning."

"Barty", galvanized into energy, disappeared into the corridor, and a draught of chill night air proved that the outer doors were open. A hubbub of questions and exclamations arose down the length of the train. In the moonlight Dimsie saw knots of people collecting on the embankment, and her own compartment was emptying rapidly. "Mrs Barty", evidently unable to sit still, followed her husband, who was talking and waving his arms by the track. Presently the man with the limp got up also, then paused and half-turned to Dimsie curled up in her corner.

"I say!" he began. "Excuse my asking – but have you any friends on the train? In another compartment perhaps——"

She shook her head.

"No, I'm on my own. I'm going to join my mother in Scotland."

He hesitated, then blurted out:

"If there's anything I could do to help, please ask, won't you? They're bound to fix up some means of getting to the nearest point of civilization. We can't all sit in an abandoned train till the strike clears up. I was just going to see what we can do.

"Oh, let me come with you!" cried Dimsie impulsively. "I don't like being here alone."

"Come on then," he said, and reaching up to the rack he lifted down her suitcase. "We may as well take as much as we can carry, for it's sure to be a matter of grabbing any opportunities which come along and the rest of the luggage will have to fend for itself. No – I can manage yours easily as well as my own – it's far too heavy for you. My name's Peter Gilmour, by the way.''

"I'm Dimsie Maitland," said Dimsie as she followed him down the steps and up the embankment, where a narrow white ribbon of road cut across the blue-blackness of the empty moor. The passengers were collecting there in a straggling line, uncertain which way to turn or what to do.

"Where are we?" queried Dimsie of Peter Gilmour. She was shivering a little, but more from excitement than cold.

"I don't know," he answered doubtfully. "Judging from the time I should say we must be somewhere in Lancashire, but I couldn't swear to it in a court of law."

As the moon emerged from a bank of clouds, two men slunk up behind them and stopped for a moment to gaze along the road.

"It oughter be 'ere by now, Bill, that blinkin' car,'' grunted one of them. "Coming from some place over to the right it were. Don't see no sign of it, d'you?"

Bill mumbled a response, and they slouched off again to stop farther on where the people were fewer. Gilmour touched Dimsie's arm, and chuckled.

"That's done it!" he exclaimed. "Do you know who those gentlemen are?"

"No," she answered.

"Why, the train driver and the guard! Here they've stranded about a hundred and fifty innocent people in the middle of the night, without any visible means of transport, and they have the nerve to expect a car to carry them away in comfort! But I begin to see a glimmer of hope now. Come along.''

Picking up the baggage again, he set off at a good pace along the road in the direction in which the traindriver had been looking for his car, while Dimsie kept up with him, curious to see what would happen next, and feeling convinced that her positive companion would find a way out. It was usually Dimsie's job to sort things out when emergencies arose, but this particular emergency was a little beyond her, and there was something about Peter Gilmour which inspired confidence.

They had not left the train far behind when they came upon the massive Barty standing dejectedly by the roadside with his hands in his coat pockets, while his wife crouched on a suitcase at his feet, sobbing, her face in her hands. This, at any rate, was a situation which Dimsie could deal with. Going forward, she knelt on the dusty wayside grass beside the woman, and made sympathetic noises, while Barty turned to Gilmour.

"Pretty kettle of fish!" he exclaimed bitterly. "Any idea of our whereabouts? We've got a little girl – our only daughter – dangerously ill up at Moffat in her grandmother's house, and my wife and I were sent for this evening. They're going to operate within the next twenty-four hours, and here we are – stranded!"

Peter looked sympathetically down at the poor mother, while Dimsie tried to comfort her.

"If I could reach the nearest town with a garage- ——" began Barty miserably.

"Can you drive?" asked Peter abruptly. His eyes were fixed on something the others had not noticed – advancing headlights moving swiftly over the white road.

"Yes," answered the big man dully.

"Look there!" and Peter pointed ahead. "That car is coming to pick up the train crew – or it thinks it is. I

23

reckon you and your wife need it more, so, if you will kindly follow my directions, I hope – er – to practise a little piracy."

The car was nearly upon them now, and before the others could ask him what he intended to do, Peter had limped straight into its path, and stood there signalling to it to stop. The driver (its only occupant) took it for granted that this was one of his friends who, growing impatient, had walked out to meet him. Slowing down, he stopped a few yards ahead.

"Couldn't get here before, mate," he said sulkily.

"I've no doubt you did your best," Peter answered coolly. "Now just hop out of that my lad, since you have come. We need your car, and – as you can see – I've got a gun trained on you."

This last piece of information was as great a surprise to Peter's party as it was to the man in the car. Dimsie had seen him put the baggage down beside Mrs Barty and had noticed him pulling something from the pocket of his coat, but neither she nor the other two had imagined such a *coup* as this.

"Quick!" she cried to Barty, grasping the situation in a flash. "Get your wife into the back seat! We haven't a moment to lose, for the railwaymen will guess there's something going on when they see the car standing still." And grabbing the suitcases she pushed them in beside the poor dazed woman, whose husband had half-lifted her into the car. The driver, meanwhile, put up his hands, and stumbled open-mouthed on to the road, where he stood still, covered by Peter's gun, while Barty replaced him at the wheel.

"Turn the car round as quickly as you can," directed Peter. "I'll keep this character's hands up till you're round."

Apparently the train crew had suspected nothing

from the stopping of the car, probably supposing that the driver had pulled up of his own accord to answer some question regarding the neighbourhood in which the unfortunate travellers found themselves adrift; but when the car slewed round in the opposite direction, a shout went up, followed by a yell from the driver.

"You deserve to be shot for that," said Peter calmly, "but I'm a humane person."

And lowering his gun he sprang up beside the big man at the wheel as nimbly as his limp would allow him. Behind them they could see dark figures running. Barty stalled the engine. The shouts increased, and Barty, the sweat standing on his brow, tried frantically to restart the car. If it refused to go – if their pursuers caught up with them – they would be overpowered easily and their chance would vanish – the one precious chance of reaching Moffat by morning. To the strained nerves of its occupants the car wasted minutes instead of seconds before it responded to Barty's efforts and leaped forward down the moonlit road with a jerk which threw Dimsie and "Mrs Barty" into each other's arms. At the same moment Peter pocketed his gun and leaned back with a sigh of relief.

"We shall be all right now," he said hopefully. "Exceed the speed limit all you can, and you'll get your wife there in time yet."

"Thanks to you," returned the burly man in a voice which trembled surprisingly. "Not that we can ever thank you, all the same. May I know your name? Mine's Pritchard – Bartholomew Pritchard."

"Mine's Gilmour," replied Peter briefly. "I'm a doctor, and I used to be a surgeon – if you care to tell me anything about your daughter's case as we go along, I might be able to relieve your anxiety."

It was typical of Peter that he never doubted the poor anxious father would mention some hopeful circumstance which he might pounce upon and emphasize to console him, and – as often happened in Peter's experience – he was justified.

They came to a signpost on the edge of the moor, and pulled up to read it, Pritchard interrupting his unhappy rambling tale to help in deciphering the letters by the dim moonlight. It gave them a useful clue to their whereabouts, and scrambling in again, the big man swung the car into a wide hard road running northwards.

"I know where I am now," he declared confidently. "Been this way before. It's merely a case of hard driving, regardless of the police, till our petrol gives out – which won't be just yet, judging by the supply in the car. Those strikers evidently meant to go a good distance."

"We shall be able to get more when we need it, I suppose," said Peter.

"Oh, yes! We shall pass plenty of towns with heaps of garages," and Barty plunged again into the description of his daughter's illness.

"Why, you know!" exclaimed Peter at the end of it, "that operation is perfectly simple nowadays, and there is scarcely any danger at all. Once, I grant you, it was not an unusual thing to lose cases through it, but that was before the cause was properly understood. I should imagine your daughter has every chance of pulling through."

"Do you think so? Do you really think so?" Barty's heavy face lit up. "I must tell her mother what you say. It may comfort her a bit."

Presently he inquired:

"What d'you mean by saying you used to be a surgeon? Given it up now, what?"

Peter stared straight ahead of him at the glare which the car's headlights threw on the road.

"Not exactly," he replied jerkily. "It gave me up. Had an accident which affected my hand."

"I'm sorry," said Bartholomew Pritchard.

They crossed the Border as dawn was coming up over the eastern hills, and stopped for petrol outside a garage which looked too pretentious for the little village in which it stood. There was some talk of breakfast, but the Pritchards were so obviously anxious to get on that Dimsie hastily declined, and Peter at once did the same. They each had eatables of some sort in their cases; so biscuits, sandwiches, and chocolates were pooled, and Mrs Pritchard was coaxed to eat her share, the whole party growing very friendly over the strange impromptu meal and their adventures.

"I'll drive the rest of the way," Peter volunteered, "if you'd like to sit with your wife; at least, if Miss Maitland doesn't object to joining me in front?"

"Oh, I'd like that!" cried Dimsie, enthusiastically. "And I've just passed my test – but under the circumstances perhaps I'd better not drive."

"Oh, no! please don't," begged Mrs Barty, with unflattering nervousness. "I mean – if there was any delay——"

"There won't be," said Dimsie reassuringly. "I shouldn't dream of trying it, Mrs Pritchard."

With Peter at the wheel, they rushed off again through the fragrance of the dewy May morning, with the low light of the rising sun lying level along muirs faintly washed with green among the dark patches of the heather, and the earliest larks soaring upwards in song. It was eight years since Dimsie had last seen Scotland and her heart leapt at the sight of the towering hills flecked here and there with the white gleam of a waterfall, the rough grey dykes, and the conical haystacks so different from the cottage-shaped ones she had grown accustomed to in England. In fact it was all different, a difference which spelt Scotland at every mile, and Dimsie suddenly discovered that she was intensely Scottish. The unusual depression which had brooded over her like a cloud for the last few months disappeared, the speed of the car exhilarated her, and she laughed softly to herself for no reason whatever.

"This is better than a stuffy old train after all," suggested Peter, glancing at her with an amused smile, as the telegraph poles slipped by them on a long straight stretch of empty road.

"Much!" agreed Dimsie emphatically. "But it has been an *extraordinary* journey, hasn't it? Indeed it's thanks to you that we have had any journey at all since midnight. Do you generally carry a loaded gun about with you on the offchance of a sudden emergency?"

He laughed as they topped a long brae and rushed down into the dip beyond.

"No, it's not one of my ordinary habits. But that gun was not loaded at all, as it happens. It belongs to a friend in Glasgow, and was being repaired in London, so I collected it for him on my way to the station."

"Not loaded?" Dimsie laughed. "If only that man had known! Then it was all bluff."

"Entirely. I was so disgusted when I thought of that poor woman behind there and her sick child."

"By the way," he went on, as they slowed down before sweeping through a drowsy grey village flushed with the fruit-blossom in its gardens, "may I ask where you are going? Can I drive you anywhere after we have dropped the Pritchards at Moffat?"

"Not exactly, thanks," said Dimsie with some hesitation. "My home is at Lochside – a little village near the head of Loch Shee which you probably have never heard of."

Peter's eyes crinkled surprisingly, and he seemed about to say something; then paused and apparently changed his mind.

"You're wrong," was his actual reply. "I know it extremely well."

"Then I suppose you've fished there," said Dimsie. "People do, I believe, in the summer. Anyhow, you probably understand the difficulty of getting to it by road."

"I might run across to Gourock," he said, after a moment's thought, "but there's no guarantee that the ferries will be going when you get there."

"Where are you going yourself?" inquired Dimsie.

"I? Oh, to Glasgow – at present. I've got friends there who are going to put me up."

"So have I," said Dimsie. "At least, I mean there's an old school friend who would put me up, and it's the nearest spot to Loch Shee under existing circumstances. So I shall come to Glasgow with you, if you will be kind enough to take me."

CHAPTER 3

Pamela at Home

They left the grateful Pritchards at Moffat in good time; then came the run to Glasgow through smiling spring country. Their journey was uneventful, except that now and again they stopped to offer a lift to some hitchhiker or stranded traveller who looked wistfully at their empty rear seat. By noon, when the car drove through the outlying suburbs of the grey smoky city, they had become almost old friends, and Peter said at last:

"I suppose you will push on to Lochside as soon as you can find a means of getting there? So it's no use planning to see anything of you while you are in Glasgow?"

"Not a bit," agreed Dimsie promptly, "I shall get home as soon as I possibly can, and there's sure to be an emergency service to Dunkirnie, if only to fetch the stranded holidaymakers back to town. Dunkirnie is just across the hills from Lochside, or round the foot of the loch, whichever way you like to look at it – but of course I forgot, you know it. And oh! what about my luggage? Shall I ever see that again?"

"Well," said Peter, driving more cautiously as the traffic thickened, "I was about to suggest that you might give me some particulars by which to identify it, and then I could make inquiries at the railway station this evening, when I go to see about my own. It may be a few days before it turns up, but as I am staying on in Glasgow I shall be on the spot to pick it up when it does appear. Then, by that time (if the boats are running again, as I hope they will be) I might bring it down to you, and hand it over in person. That is, if you will allow me the pleasure?"

"Pleasure!" echoed Dimsie. "It sounds much more like a great deal of trouble. But of course I shall be extremely grateful, and Mother will want to thank you for rescuing me from a nasty predicament. I hope you realize how grateful I am. But for you, I might be still in the wilds of Lancashire."

Peter laughed.

"Not a bit of it! I happened to be on the spot, but someone else would have turned up if I hadn't. It's a theory of mine that whenever you're in trouble, something always turns up. Up this turning? Oh, I see! Well, I've enjoyed the journey, strike or no strike."

"So have I," answered Dimsie. "By the way, what do you mean to do with the car?"

"Hand it over to the railway people with full particulars, and trust to luck that its rightful owner may see it again some day."

They swerved round into a little street of low houses tucked away in the shadow of the University tower; the streets and terraces which surrounded it were tall, severe, and stately, with area railings and long flights of spotless steps leading from door to pavement; but Hawthorn Place boasted strips of front garden shut in by the trees from which it took its name, and they softened the little houses half-hidden behind them. There were other trees, some planes and a few birches in their green spring foliage, but the rosy blossom of the hawthorn was the real colour, while here and there a drift of tiny crimson petals eddied on the grey stones of the pavement.

They pulled up before one of the small iron gates, and Peter jotted down the details of the luggage in a black notebook which he pulled from his pocket.

"I'll see to all that," he said briskly. "Sure you'll be all right now? Then *au revoir,* and an easy run home tomorrow!"

He handed out her suitcase, and stood while she opened the gate and ran up a mossy flagged path, edged with box and cheerful (if somewhat grimy) daffodils. On the doorstep she paused to wave her hand, after which he limped into his seat again and drove off to the city, and Dimsie found herself being ushered into an eccentric-looking room furnished almost entirely with curios. She gazed about her disapprovingly, as the "daily" went off to summon Pam.

"Pam might have done better than this," was Dimsie's mental comment. "It's all very exotic and, no doubt, valuable, but no one could call it comfortable. Perhaps she can't help it though. Perhaps she isn't allowed a free hand, with no mother, and such a peculiar exploring sort of father."

There was a sound of flying feet on the stairs, and across the hall, and the door burst open.

"Dimsie! What luck! I might have been out, or away from home, or anything! *Why* didn't you let me know you were coming?"

"Because I wasn't," returned Dimsie, extricating herself with difficulty from Pamela's hug. "This is all a mistake owing to the train strike, of which I presume you have heard. I ought to be home by now, but as a matter of fact I would have been still stranded in the middle of England if it hadn't been for a most enterprising man and a car which he stole at the point of an unloaded gun."

"Just sit down," said Pamela firmly, "and explain yourself. Evidently you have been having one of those thrilling adventures which you always have and I never do. Tell me all about it – from beginning to end. Of course you're staying to lunch?"

"More than that," said Dimsie, subsiding into the depths of a dingy Chesterfield. "I want to say the night, if I may? or till the boats are running again for Loch Shee."

"Wonderful!" cried Pamela with enthusiasm. "I hope they won't run again for *days*. Oh, Dimsie, I *am* glad to see you! It's so dull here all day long, with only myself to talk to."

"But why?" asked Dimsie in astonishment. "Where's everybody? You're not living here alone?"

"More or less. Jim is with his ship, you know, and Edgar got a job in Singapore and went off three weeks ago, and Father is dashing about preparing for another of his exploring trips."

Dimsie sat up suddenly.

"Oh, Pam! is he going to take you *this* time?"

Pamela shook her head.

"No," she said, with a touch of something very like despair in her voice. "I don't believe he *ever* means to. And I'm simply longing for it more an ever this time. I suppose it's in my blood, but funnily enough Father doesn't seem to understand that. Now, get on with *your* story, Dimsie; you haven't told me a word of it yet."

Dimsie did as she was told, and Pamela heard her to the end, attentive and absorbed.

"I wonder who the Gilmour man can be," she said, when Dimsie had finished. "I like the sound of him."

"He was fantastic!" returned Dimsie enthusiastically.

"You should have seen him dealing with the driver of that car. Very few people would have had so much sense. But what have you been doing with yourself all this time? Any more championships? I saw your photograph in the paper after that last match at St Andrews."

"I haven't gone in for anything since," replied Pamela, with a touch of listlessness very foreign to the energetic person Dimsie remembered. Dimsie looked at her in silence for a moment with a puzzled expression; then she said impulsively:

"Come back with me to Twinkle Tap and stay as long as you like. If your father is so busy, he won't mind, and when you are bored there's always good fishing on the loch, and a golf course at Dunkirnie."

Pamela brightened up.

"I defy anyone to be bored with *you* about. Besides, I love the country; it's only in town that there is nothing to do. But do you really mean it, Dimsie?"

"Do I usually say things unless I mean them? I shall be glad of your help in the herb garden. You know, Pam, I can't be a doctor now." She paused to clear her throat. "There isn't enough money now, that's all. No – don't sympathize – I can see you're just on the verge of it, and I've made up my mind to do without sympathy – for the present. I'm going to get down to something else straightaway, and that's herbs."

"Herbs?"

Dimsie nodded.

"I mean to work with them, and grow them, and read them up, for I feel that some day I could be a herb doctor. Miss Yorke doesn't altogether approve, and Rosamund thinks I'll be run in for poisoning people, but I don't see it necessarily follows."

Pamela looked at her doubtfully from the other side of

the fireplace. Dimsie's eyes were very bright, and her lips were set in a determined line which Pam knew of old; apparently her mind was made up, despite both Miss Yorke and Rosamund.

"But aren't herb doctors a sort of quack?" asked Pamela.

"Certainly not! Now, Pam!" cried the would-be herbalist hotly, "do get out of the habit of yielding to oldfashioned prejudice – indeed you don't know how old-fashioned! Two hundred years ago, of course, if you understood too much about the healing properties of herbs, you were burnt at the stake for witchcraft. They didn't know their Apocrypha, those old eighteenth century magistrates. And, for the matter of that, I don't suppose you do either.

"Not with reference to herb doctors," confessed Pam cautiously.

"I thought not. Yet there's a passage in Ecclesiasticus which seems to have some reference to the subject: 'For of the Most High cometh healing . . . He hath created medicines out of the earth.'"

"I have read that," said Pamela, "but it never struck me before that it meant *herbs*."

"What else could it mean?" demanded Dimsie, preparing to argue. "They 'come out of the earth,' don't they? And they're used in most medicines. What else can the verse refer to?"

"I don't know. You may be right. Anyhow I can't contradict you."

Dimsie sank back into the shabby cushions on the Chesterfield with a grunt of disappointment.

"I should think not, indeed!" she said. "But I rather wish you would, all the same. I can see many long and heated discussions ahead of me, and it would be useful to practise

35

on you. Can't you see, Pam, that it's obvious? My reasoning is that Nature has been given a remedy for every hurt. There's a dock growing near each nettle patch, for example. Yes, I know what you're going to say," as Pam opened her mouth. "We do make use of herbs to a large extent, as it is, but they are usually distilled with alcohol, which causes them to lose half their effectiveness. Besides, I want to go farther. I believe plenty of illness which is now treated unsuccessfully, might be cured if its particular antidote could be discovered among the medicines which come out of the earth. Anyhow I mean to try."

"But how?" Pamela's interest was aroused. "Do you propose to start a practice without any sort of qualifications, and experiment upon your wretched patients willy-nilly?"

"Only if they are quite happy about it, of course. But the experiments will not be too risky because I mean to study the whole thing thoroughly first. That's the beauty of being a herb doctor." Dimsie leaned back, nursing her knee with clasped hands, her face glowing with enthusiasm. "You don't require qualifications – at least, I mean none of the stupid exammy kind – it's all learnt by study and experience. That's how it was done by my great-grandmother twice-removed."

"And how many people did she kill in the course of acquiring her knowledge?" asked Pam cruelly.

"Not many – or they'd have drowned her as a witch; they very nearly did, you know, but her grateful patients rescued her. You're adopting the same unenterprising attitude as Miss Yorke and Rosamund, but I don't mind," said Dimsie approvingly. "Anything's better than saying you can't contradict me, for that gives me no scope for argument at all. Besides, it will be so enjoyable in future years when I'm being hailed as a benefactor of mankind, to see you looking small and foolish."

But Pamela resented this charge of lack of enterprise, feeling that it did her an injustice.

"I *shan't*," she said. "You're quite wrong. I shan't look foolish because I entirely approve of everything you have been saying, and I mean to back you up through thick and thin – even to helping you to fly the country when there's a warrant out against you for poisoning someone. Come and eat! You must be hungry after your exciting journey."

Professor Hughes did not appear at the meal, and his daughter said that he was probably lunching with a friend in Edinburgh, whose brains he had gone to pick regarding his impending trip.

"He didn't mention it at breakfast this morning, but the idea probably grabbed him later. The rail strike? Oh! he dashes about everywhere on his motor-bike. He likes to feel independent of everything and everybody."

"Then he won't mind your coming home with me," said Dimsie, "as soon as the boats are running."

Pamela propped her elbows on the table and laughed.

"Mind? It will be the greatest relief to him! He doesn't know what to do with a daughter, and half the time he solves the problem by forgetting her existence. You see, I was quite small when Mother died, so they packed me off to Jane's straightaway, and in the holidays I usually had invitations, or aunts took me in. I say, Dimsie! I've just had a great idea – but I don't know what you will think of it."

She paused, and looked at her friend doubtfully across a bowl of hyacinths.

"Let's hear it," said Dimsie, but rather vaguely.

Her busy mind was already turning over schemes to relieve Pamela's loneliness. With Dimsie, to see a difficulty was to tackle it immediately and she had grasped at once what this dried-up life must mean to Pam, who had been one of the most sociable people at school.

"Once you have left school," thought Dimsie, "situations are not nearly so easy to handle, but the same principles must apply in a broader sense, once one has learnt what to do. Given a lame dog and a stile, commonsense ought to show some way of getting one across the other."

She came to with a start to hear Pamela saying plaintively:

"Of course I knew you wouldn't *jump* at it, but you needn't treat it with quite so little interest."

"I wasn't," said Dimsie hastily. "I didn't exactly hear what you said – that's all. What was I treating with little interest?"

"My great idea," replied Pamela flatly. "I only thought, if Mrs Maitland didn't mind, I might come to you as a paying guest while Father is away exploring. I could help in the herb garden, as you said, for you can't run a big thing like that singlehanded."

"It hasn't got to be a big thing yet," corrected Dimsie cautiously, "but you would be a fantastic help, Pam, and I'd simply love to have you. So would Mother, for you have been a favourite of hers ever since you first stayed with us at St Elstrith's. It's better than a great idea – it's just plain commonsense – the very commonsense I was looking for myself, and you've supplied it."

"What *do* you mean?" asked Pamela, staring at her in astonishment, but Dimsie laughed and shook her head.

"Nothing. May I have some more pudding, please? I don't think you'll find it dull with us, because there's the fishing and that golf course at Dunkirnie. Rosamund might be bored, or Mabs, or Eric, but you're different. Let's pack after lunch, Pam. You never know how soon the boats may start again, and you will want a lot of luggage for such a long stay."

Pamela laughed.

"Thanks! but I shall only want enough to go on with, this time; I can come back for more when Father is ready to start, and the house has to be shut up. It will be a great relief to him. He said only this morning that he didn't know where I could go while he was away, but he supposed something would turn up – and it has!"

Dimsie said nothing, but her face grew severe, for Professor Hughes was not the sort of father to whom she was accustomed. Pam's schoolfriends had always known that she ran wild with her brothers during the holidays, and was allowed to do things at which their own parents would have held up their hands in horror; but for that they had considered her rather lucky than otherwise. It had never struck them that there was anything forlorn about her life nor had any such idea ever occurred to Pamela herself until she left school and had time to think about it.

CHAPTER 4

Twinkle Tap

After all that, Dimsie went home alone the following day, by the one solitary ferry which was still plying between the city and Dunkirnie, leaving Pamela to follow at her leisure in a week's time. The boat was not uncomfortably crowded on its outward voyage, but a seething mass of stranded holidaymakers awaited it at Dunkirnie pier, and Dimsie was very grateful that she was leaving it there. She decided to walk home across the hills, because it was one of those halcyon days when spring is quietly turning into summer, and the woods are a glory of blue hyacinths. Dimsie remembered a short cut across the golf course and, having taken it impulsively, was relieved to find that she had not forgotten the way. Presently it brought her out upon the main road again by the rim of a little loch partly overgrown with waterlilies and flags, and there, on a large boulder, her bicycle lying beside her on the dusty grass, sat Daphne, with a broad shady sunhat hiding her black hair.

Dimsie encircled her mouth with her hands, and yodelled on a note peculiar to the Jane Willard girls; then running down the slope, she landed with a spring at her cousin's side.

"Daph!" she cried. "I've had *such* a journey! Did

Mother get my message last night? I hope she wasn't worried."

"She probably was," said Daphne calmly. "But you know what Auntie is – if she worries she worries to herself." She made room on the rock beside her for Dimsie. "You must need a rest if you've walked from Dunkirnie. Sit down and tell me what has been happening."

Dimsie obeyed, while Daphne nibbled grass and followed her tale with close attention.

"Pamela was right," she declared, when it ended. "You certainly have got a remarkable knack for getting mixed up in adventures. It used to be the same at school, where adventures don't generally happen. And when is this super man coming down with the luggage?"

"I can't possibly tell you that. He has to get it first, and then the strike will have to calm down. That's why Pam didn't come with me today as we planned at first. She could have got *herself* here, but not all she wanted to bring."

"She could bring yours along with it when she does come," suggested Daphne, "if your friend got it as far as Hawthorn Place. It would save him the trouble of a trip down to these outlandish parts."

"Oh, no!" said Dimsie cheerfully. "It will be no trouble to him – he said so. He said he'd like to see me again, and I told him I should be delighted. Why are you looking like that, Daphne? He really was extremely nice."

"He may have been," conceded Daphne in peculiar tones, "but after all, you *are* grown up now, Dimsie, and you really ought not to be so friendly with strange men."

"I wasn't," said Dimsie, quite unmoved. "It was true that I should be delighted, so why not say so? He looked very pleased, and I am sure he was taking endless trouble on my behalf. I really can't be prim and proper even if I am grown up."

41

Daphne accepted this statement philosophically.

"No," she agreed. "I don't suppose you can. Never mind. You'll learn. Meantime we'd better get going. Auntie and I heard of this Dunkirnie boat, and guessed you would contrive to get across by it, so I cycled up in this direction, thinking I might meet you."

"You timed your ride very well," said Dimsie. "Can you lend me some things, Daph, till my luggage comes? I have got practically nothing in my suitcase, and that's left in Dunkirnie to be sent over with the milk lorry."

"We'll see what we can get in the village as well," said her cousin, and picking up her bicycle she wheeled it out into the road. "You'd better ride, for you must be tired, and I can keep up with you on foot. So Pamela is coming to stay with you while the Professor is away? Auntie will be delighted; she has been worrying about the lack of companionship for you."

"She needn't," said Dimsie calmly as she rode at a pace to suit her cousin's brisk walk. "She knows I can be company for myself; but she'll be pleased about Pam, all the same, because she's fond of her, and that's a good thing, seeing Pam wants to come as a p. g. for eighteen months – all the time Professor Hughes is away, in fact."

Daphne looked slightly taken aback.

"As long as that? You seem to have fixed things up pretty well between you. Do you think there's any danger of Pamela being bored in this out-of-the-way place?"

"Oh, no! I shan't let her. She'd find it far more boring to stay with her relations in England. I'm worried about Pam just now, Daphne, and I want to keep her under my beady eye, to cheer her up if necessary. No, I don't know what's wrong, so it's no use asking me. Tell me, who lives at Lochside now?"

"I really don't know," replied Daphne, breaking into a trot as the bicycle speeded up. "You see, we have hardly had any time for seeing people in the ten days since we came here; it has taken very spare moment to put the house in order. Auntie met Mrs McIvor in the village one morning, even more fearfully and wonderfully arrayed than she used to be, and she was coming up to see us soon, but luckily we've been spared so far."

"And who has got that house below us with all the trees – Laurel Bank?"

"It has recently been taken by a mystery – a young man, suspected of being an author; but very few people have seen him, as he never ventures outside his own grounds. Rumour (alias Mrs McIvor – it would be!) says that he wears a brown velvet mask, and hates everybody."

"Wow!" exclaimed Dimsie. "*That* will interest Pam. But why does he wear a *mask*? That's *incredible* in this day and age!"

"I don't know why," said Daphne. "I leave that to you and Pam to find out. *Now* do you know where you are?"

The road, making its way through a wood of birches, had reached the crest of a short hill and Dimsie dismounted to look in silence down the vista which opened before her between the feathery green of the branches on either hand. Below her lay Loch Shee, a sheet of silvery water which mirrored here and there the green hills towering opposite, their higher slopes clothed with dark firs. A break in the trees on her left showed the blue Highland peaks which rose beyond, soft and mysterious, with the bloom of distance upon them. A single brown sail like an autumn leaf drifted up the loch towards the small village at its head.

Dimsie drew a long sigh of contentment, then turned a beaming face to meet her cousin's smile.

"It's *very* good to be home again, Daph!" was all she said, but Daphne was satisfied.

"Sure you won't hanker after St Elstrith's?" she asked, to set all final doubts at rest.

"Oh, no!" replied Dimsie briskly. "You see it's no good hankering after something you can't possibly have, and besides, I'm realizing more each minute that this is really *home*. And I mean to be fantastically busy. Come on! I can see the garden wall topped with grasses and snapdragons just as it used to be."

And she set off for the green door in the lichened wall – a door which was guarded by pines still, for all Rosamund's gloomy prophesies.

The house stood on the extreme brow of the hill with only a few ancient firs to shelter it from every breeze that blew; and the narrow flower garden growing round it was fenced about by a low hedge of escallonia with its pink flowers and sweet sticky leaves; the beds were filled with such hardy plants as might be expected to stand buffeting and exposure, though there was little in bloom save some large bushy clumps of well established wallflowers; up the side of the house climbed a huge fuchsia, soon to be covered with small scarlet bells.

Mrs Maitland was waiting for them at the door, having heard their steps and voices as they came round the house, and Dimsie, relinquishing the bicycle, sprang hastily forward to greet her. Her mother was a small, dainty woman, youthful despite her white hair, fragile-looking but full of restless energy. Her eyes were brown as her daughter's, but otherwise there was very little resemblance between them.

Tea was ready in the low-ceilinged wide-windowed dining-room, and here, over scones and heather honey, Dimsie once more told the story of her journey.

"My dear, you were very lucky," exclaimed her mother, "though I am very thankful I didn't know what was happening. Your telegram got here very nearly as soon as you would have done yourself, and of course we read about the strike in the morning paper. I feel very grateful to that nice man – did you say his name was Gilmour?"

"Yes," said Dimsie. "Though of course Barty helped with the driving."

Mrs Maitland laughed.

"He certainly acted with great promptness, and I expect Barty and his wife were even more grateful to him than I am. Anyhow, I am getting quite curious to meet this highhanded deliverer of yours."

The end of the strike, which came three days later, brought news from Daphne's home which hastened her departure, already overdue, and Dimsie and her mother were alone at Twinkle Tap when Peter Gilmour arrived with the missing trunk. Dimsie encountered him by accident on the brae leading up from the pier, where he was helping a grinning small boy to push the box along on a wheelbarrow.

"The porter down below there hasn't quite realized yet that the strike is over," he announced cheerfully, pausing to greet her. "At least he isn't to be found at present, so I chartered Jimmy here in his place, and we have been getting along like a house on fire. Now, Jimmy, my lad, it's level going from here to the gate of Twinkle Tap, so I think you can carry on by yourself. And how are you?" turning back to Dimsie, "after all our excitement the other night?"

"Oh, very well, thanks!" said Dimsie cheerfully. "I always am. And Mother has been simply longing to see you ever since she heard all about it. I am sorry she is out just now – down in the village somewhere – but of course you must stay to lunch. Come in and have some cake and milk

45

just to keep you going, and then I'll show you the garden till Mother comes back."

"Show it to me now," suggested Peter, limping after her through the green door, his hands thrust into his jacket pockets. "If you are really going to be kind enough to give me lunch, I daren't anticipate by starting in on cake and milk at twelve o'clock, but I am rather keen on gardens."

Dimsie looked pleased.

"Are you?" she asked. "I'm glad. I thought you were too nice not to be keen on things like that. Come along then. It's not very tidy yet, but we're getting on, Geordie and I."

Chuckling to himself at her frankness, Peter followed her down a steep path to the small orchard where apple-blossom flung a glow across the bent grey branches, and a few late tassels lingered on the flowering currants below. He had never before met a girl quite like Dimsie, and her unexpectedness was very refreshing.

"Our garden is three hundred years old," she explained, "and the people who first planned it seem to have taken in a bit of the hillside from time to time whenever they felt inclined. The flowerbeds are above us round the house, but we can only grow hardy things there. This sloping patch was made the fruit garden – I suppose because it lies on the sheltered side."

"I see you've got plenty of vegetables," said Peter, looking about him keenly, "but not a single herb. I'm rather interested in herbs."

"People aren't as a rule," said Dimsie, looking pleased again. "They think they're dull. But we have plenty of herbs, and they are *my* department. I'll show you."

She led him down some worn stone steps at the righthand corner of the orchard, skirting a high clipped yew hedge of uncertain age and venerable appearance; at the foot of these they came upon a little wicket gate in the hedge which let them through into the next section of this curious garden – a long narrow shelf running round an outward curve of the hill overlooking the loch, and which was shut off from the view of the house above by a sheer bank on which there were some ancient larches. Along the outer edge of the shelf ran an old wall of lichened stone, and the farther end was closed by a dark hedge of privet. The whole strip was taken up with wide beds of various herbs divided by flagged pathways, and the damp warm air was filled with strange aromatic perfumes.

"You probably want to stand still and sniff," remarked Dimsie, pausing to look round at her companion. "I always do."

He gazed about him in genuine pleasure.

"I've sometimes dreamt of such a place," he said, "but I hardly hoped to see one in real life – and I've seen some herb gardens in my day. But this – why, it must be hundreds of years old!"

"I told you – three hundred, to be exact," said Dimsie dreamily, moving across to an old stone bench set in an angle of the wall beside a clump of junipers. "It was planted by an ancestor of ours to please his wife, who was very learned in herbs. He built the first Twinkle Tap, which somehow got burned down in a skirmish with the Clan Campbell during the '45; that crow-stepped gable and the rooms beyond are all that is left of it. Old Simon Maitland would hardly know it now if his ship came sailing up Loch Shee again."

"Was he a sailor?"

"Yes – a sea-captain from the North who married a West Coast girl, and settled in her part of the country. She seems to have been in advance of her times, for she was almost a doctor. Tradition says she cured half the ills of the neighbourhood with drugs grown in this very garden."

He looked at her curiously.

"Is that what *you* mean to do?" he asked.

Dimsie's eye lit up. "Oh, I want to!" she exclaimed, with a catch in her voice. "You can't think how badly I want to! You see, I was to have been a doctor, but since I can't I've been thinking about things, and it seems as though this might be – almost as good – not quite, of course."

And suddenly, to her own amazement, she found herself telling Peter Gilmour all that she had told Pamela a few days before. He listened quietly and without comment, looking at the purple peaks beyond the loch where a faint mist was blurring the sharpness of their outline; but Dimsie felt that he was following all she said with intense interest, and when she stopped he turned and looked at her with a quiet considering gaze.

"People will call you a quack, you know," he said, but there was no joking in his voice. "I have heard of that great-grandmother of yours; she's something of a legend about here, and I believe she narrowly escaped drowning as a witch."

Dimsie nodded.

"Yes, I know. That was how they greeted the discoveries of science in those days, but surely they know better now. Not," she added, laughing, "that *I* presume to have *discovered* herbs, but perhaps – perhaps if I study I may find out things about them which haven't been known or practised before. I should *hate* to be called a quack, though," she added frankly, smiling up at him as he stood beside her, his hands still deep in his pockets.

He returned the smile with a shake of his head.

"The worst of it is," he said, "that they'll call you that, no matter how widespread and many your cures may be. You must found a school of herb medicine, and train up a generation of students to follow in your footsteps. Then you may be acknowledged years hence as a great and wise physician."

She joined in his laugh for a moment, then answered his teasing seriously.

"I don't know that I should ever be fantastically keen on that side of it," she said, "even if I could have gone on with my profession, and worked hard enough to make a name. Being famous isn't the point, somehow."

Peter leaned his arms on the wall.

"No," he said. "You're right there. The chief point is to cure disease, by whatever method you can. Healing is a great work. It has always appealed to me – enormously."

Dimsie glanced up at him swiftly.

"But aren't *you* a doctor anyway?"

He shook his head.

"Not altogether. That's to say, I have taken my degree, but I have never practised. When I was at college I was very keen on surgery – hoped to make my mark at it some day. Then this happened to my hand."

He pulled his right hand from his pocket and held it out to her, and she saw what she had not noticed before, that his two middle fingers were missing, leaving an unsightly stump.

"Oh, I am so sorry! I can't tell you how sorry I am!" she cried.

"It's all right," he said, "I only showed you because I wanted you to see that I could understand how you felt about giving up your chosen profession. I don't know what prevented *you,* but it isn't a bit of good moaning about it, is it? Most likely Providence has got something more important for each of us to do."

"I hope so," said Dimsie eagerly. "And I hope it's

49

herbs for me. You wouldn't like to take them up too, I suppose? Or have you found something else to do? I expect you had to, when you lost your fingers."

"Oh, yes!" he answered. "I went back to college again, and studied for further medical qualifications. I expect to start in general practice very soon now, but I want to study a bit longer first."

Dimsie hooked her hands about her knees, and looked up at him.

"Isn't it strange," she observed, "how dreams come true for the wrong people? You have become the thing I want most of all to be, yet you're not a bit satisfied."

"It is odd," he admitted, "but I'm afraid life's a bit puzzling at times. I know a man – my best friend – and he fell in love with a girl who seemed to love him too, though he couldn't afford to marry her. Then suddenly things got better and he was just on the verge of proposing when something happened which ruined everything. That's the sort of thing which puzzles me a good deal at times. Why are we allowed to climb so near the top, only to slip back again with a crash?"

Dimsie nodded.

"It is confusing," she agreed, "but of course it must come out all right somehow. I suppose your friend is quite sure he can't ask the girl to marry him now? Sometimes, people don't see the way out of their difficulties even when it's so straight in front of them so that it seems almost impossible for them to miss it. They need somebody else to point it out."

"That's true," he agreed, "but I believe he has looked at it from all sides, and I can't see any solution myself."

"Then Providence must have something better planned for him too," said Dimsie with matter-of-fact conviction, getting up as she spoke. "You'd better help him to find it; I should think you would be rather good at that." She regarded him critically for a moment, then turned towards the gate.

"Come and meet my mother. She should be back by now, and you are just the sort of person she likes, because you are interesting to talk to. You must come and see us again if you are ever in Lochside."

"Which I hope will be often," he said. "I didn't tell you before, but I've got a friend down here whom I look up frequently. He has been rather under the weather lately, and I like to keep an eye on him. If you and your mother will let me stop off at Twinkle Tap sometimes it will be a very great pleasure."

CHAPTER 5

A Garden of Herbs

"Dimsie! The post is in, and there's a letter for you from Jean."

Pamela, with the afternoon sun glinting on her brown hair, stood at the gate of the herb garden, and waved an envelope.

"Come and open it," she said. "I want to hear her news."

Dimsie propped her hoe carefully against the trunk of a gnarled and ancient crabapple tree, and stepped out of the bed in which she had been working.

"Are you sure it's from Jean?" she asked. "I was expecting to hear from that wholesale chemist in Edinburgh, whom I wrote to last week. He ought to want some nice fresh digitalis, and my foxgloves are particularly healthy. I've got a positive hedge of them against that bank over there."

"Well, if the chemist uses pale green envelopes with the fancy initials 'J. G.' on the flap," said Pam, "this may perhaps be his. But even then I think I know the writing."

"I'd rather it was the chemist," said Dimsie ungratefully. "And I've told Jean before she ought to give up that pale green paper of hers. She may imagine it's poetic, but as a matter of fact it's merely 'soppy'. I'm beginning to fear that

Jean has escaped very much from our influence since we left school."

"She *ought* to be all right," observed Pamela, "with Erica to keep an eye on her. But probably Eric hasn't much spare time, and Jean is left to do things by herself. Anyhow, let's hear what she has got to say."

Dimsie tore open the "poetic" envelope, and glanced down the sheet inside.

"Not much in that," she said, handing it across. "She's coming up to Kilaidan tomorrow, and we shall probably see her the next day. She's sick of London and the social round, as usual, and wants peace to sit in the heather and write poetry. She forgets the heather won't be out for another six weeks at least."

"Where is Kilaidan?" asked Pam, when she had read the hurriedly scrawled note. "I never stayed with Jean up here, you know – only twice in London."

"Haven't I shown it to you?" exclaimed Dimsie. "Why, it's just across the loch there, up at the head, and the Gordons' house is among those trees at the point. The ferry crosses to Kilaidan always after calling at our pier. Oh, and that reminds me! How did this letter arrive so soon? It's only half an hour since I saw the boat coming in."

Pamela looked rather embarrassed.

"I went down to the Post Office and fetched it," she confessed. "Shall I help you with that weeding now, Dimsie?"

Dimsie gave her a quick look, then turned to take up her hoe once more.

"I shall be very grateful – only don't pull up the balm again in mistake for nettles; apparently you can't tell the difference with gloves on, and I'm rather keen on that balm."

"What does it do besides smelling nice?" asked Pamela, anxious to divert attention from her own unusual hurry to meet the mail, for she felt there had been something behind Dimsie's look of query.

"It contains a kind of healing oil. I am going to cut it all down at the end of August, and extract the oil – though I don't quite know how at present. I only know that is the time to do it, and I shall find out the process later. I mean to make tea from some of it; that's simple enough anyhow, and it's very good for colds or headaches."

"I hope it's all right," said Pamela uneasily. "You've got a rather casual way of approaching these mysteries which makes me rather nervous. It's all very well to grow the stuff and pack it off to dispensaries where they do the rest, but when it comes to making tea of it yourself – well, a little knowledge may be a dangerous thing."

"Now, Pam!" said the student herbalist, in an injured voice. "You promised to believe in me, and you might know I shan't be careless. It ought to give you all the more confidence that I don't pretend to know *everything* right off. Wait till you catch cold next winter, and you'll be only too grateful for my balm tea."

"Perhaps," said Pam dubiously. "If it doesn't taste too disgusting. What about that clump of succory over by the yew hedge? Had I better get a stake and tie it up? That wind last night has knocked it about a lot."

"Thanks," said Dimsie. "It's safer than letting you weed. Not that I blame you, seeing most herbs *are* weeds."

She bent over her work again, secretly watching Pamela on her way to the toolshed, and noticing a lagging dejection in her manner. Dimsie's concern had not lessened since Pam's arrival at Twinkle Tap. There was some subtle change for which she could not account; the cheerful adventurous

54

Pamela of their schooldays only showed occasionally on the surface now, and below there were strange new depths which Dimsie had not so far been able to fathom.

"There's something odd about Pamela," she thought, weeding industriously among the mixed gusts of perfume which rose from marjoram and hyssop. "She dreams far more than Jean, these days, and she is always hoping for some letter which never comes. I wish she would tell me what's wrong, but I can't insist as I would have done three years ago." She straightened herself with a sigh and threw a handful of chickweed into the garden basket. "That's one of the great drawbacks to growing up – you can't tackle things straight out, because everything is so much more complicated. You have to respect people's reserve instead of forcing their confidence, even when you know it would be for their own good."

Outwardly Pamela seemed happy enough, and was a very pleasant addition to the household at Twinkle Tap. Her violin was a great delight to Mrs Maitland, who was musical and enjoyed practising with her, while Pam was always ready to work in the garden under Dimsie's orders; at other times she boated on the loch, or cycled over to the golf course at Dunkirnie, where she was getting very good. Occasionally Dimsie went with her, but not often, for her herbs took up a lot of her time; there had been so much neglect to put right, so much replanting to be done, that her hopes of a favourable crop that season depended largely upon the amount of work she could put into it meanwhile. And in the evenings, when her mother and Pamela played duets on piano and violin, Dimsie pored over herb books ancient and modern, taking copious notes, and trying hard to fit herself to be at least as useful as her "great-grandmother twice-removed" whose record had inspired her.

55

A quaint little portrait of this lady hung beside the west window in the sitting room. It was only a foot square, and showed her sitting on a low stone wall in a very full grey gown with pink flowers; her hair was darker than Dimsie's chestnut colour; but she had the same steady dark brown eyes, and there was a general resemblance between the two faces which Pamela noticed and commented upon at once.

"So that's the lady who walks," she observed, but Mrs Maitland had answered with unwonted sharpness.

"Don't talk nonsense, Pamela!" she exclaimed. "I dislike silly jokes of that sort. It is to be hoped the poor thing has something better to do, after her busy life, than to haunt the scene of her past labours."

Pamela stopped at once, but Dimsie took up the argument.

"I don't know," she said dreamily. "Great-grandmother loved the herb garden when she was alive – probably it had lots of happy associations for her – isn't it rather natural that her spirit should want to visit it again from time to time, to see if it is all as tidy as she left it? I shouldn't be at all frightened if she came walking down the flagged paths, some evening, as they say she does, with her little high-heeled shoes clicking."

"Well, *I* should, my dear – I should object to it very much indeed!" said Mrs Maitland decidedly. "Pamela, come and try over that 'Berceuse' with me before we go to bed. You both have talked quite enough nonsense for one evening."

But Dimsie, weeding her beds on the afternoon when Jean Gordon's note arrived, was to hear more of her ancestress, and from an unexpected quarter. When it was nearly time to stop work and get ready for supper, Geordie, the boy who helped the gardener, arrived with his wheelbarrow to remove the pile of rubbish from the corner where she had been emptying her basket, and Geordie was in an unusually expansive mood.

"Eh, but ye maun hae been gey busy, Miss!" he exclaimed admiringly, as he surveyed the result of her work. "I doot thae yerbs wasna kep' mair tidy even in the Grey Leddy's day."

"What do you know about the Grey Lady?" asked Dimsie abruptly, while Pamela, gathering up twine and scissors, came nearer to listen.

George looked taken aback.

"Ou – juist as muckle as we a' ken," was his ambiguous reply, and he bent down for an armful of weeds, throwing them on to his barrow with the air of one who has no desire to be questioned further. But Dimsie was not to be cheated.

"Well, that's precious little as far as I'm concerned," she remarked, sitting down firmly on the parapet beside him. "Have you ever seen her, Geordie?"

"No me!" he answered in hasty alarm, throwing a half-glance over his shoulder. "I'm no a Hielandmon to see things – forbye I dinna come doon here at the hoor she walks."

"When's that?" pursued Dimsie, while Pamela waited eagerly.

"I canna tell ye," declared Geordie doggedly. "Sandy would be awfu' riled we' me gin he heard us talkin' aboot *her*."

Sandy was the gardener, and a person of great importance at Twinkle Tap.

"Maybe he would," said Dimsie, with persistance, "but you see *I* choose to talk about it, and I am not afraid of Sandy."

George eyed her respectfully, and reflected that this

was perfectly true. Miss Maitland had set Sandy utterly at defiance with most of her doings in the herb garden since her return home, yet nothing serious had happened, and her plants still flourished exceedingly. Geordie plucked up courage.

"Weel," he said cautiously, "I canna speak frae me ain expeerience, ye ken, but there's them as has seen her when they've been doon yonder on the shore in the gloaming. She's aye sittin' on the wall glowering oot tae the mooth o' the loch – but ye canna see onything verra distinct, and mebbe it's juist a bit mist rising up frae the damp yerb-beds."

"Maybe," agreed Dimsie calmly. "Is that *all* you know, Geordie?"

He flung on the last armful of weeds, and picked up the handles of his barrow.

"Ay," he said, "that's a'. They say doonbye," he added, anxious to give his audience as much sensation as he truthfully could, "that she walks because there's something she's wantin, but what it is naebuddy has been able tae jalouse. Could ye no find oot yoursel', dae ye think, Miss Maitland?"

Dimsie turned her head, and stared meditatively down the loch, very much as the ghost was supposed to do, and for a moment she said nothing; but George waited hopefully, and Pamela watched her curiously. What was teeming inside her brain now? Presently Dimsie looked round again, and smiled encouragingly.

"It's just possible I might," she replied. "I'll think about it. Now take those weeds down to the rubbish heap, Geordie, and top them *right* on. You made rather a mess on the path yesterday, and I can't have Sandy complaining to me *every* day, you know."

George accepted his dismissal with a grin, and

disappeared through the gate in the yew hedge, whistling "Annie Laurie" under his breath, while Pamela perched herself beside Dimsie on the stone coping.

"What do you think of that?" she asked with awe. "Do you believe it, or is the whole thing village gossip?"

Dimsie shook her head doubtfully.

"I don't know," she confessed. "We have always known the legend of the Grey Lady, but my father said he never saw her, and I haven't yet spoken to anyone who has. Though it wouldn't surprise me if she wanted to come back, poor thing! and see how her garden grew, for by all accounts it was the thing she cared most for in life – except perhaps her son."

"More than her husband?" asked Pamela.

"Well, she didn't have very long with him. He was lost at sea four years after their marriage, and they say she would never believe he was gone, but went on hoping and watching for him to come back again. Rather tragic, wasn't it?"

"I don't know," said Pamela, in a curiously repressed voice. "Don't you think it was better than being quite certain that he would *never* come back again? At least she could still look forward to *something*. I think I shall go up and get cleaned up now, Dimsie. It must be nearly supper time."

"Do," said Dimsie approvingly. "I'm sure you look dirty enough for anything; so do I, if it comes to that. Gardening isn't clean work, but it's very healthy. We'll set the jaded Jean to it as soon as she arrives – have her over by the day, and give her the dirtiest jobs as an entertainment. It may help to counteract the poetry."

She lingered behind to nip a few dead bells off a promising bush of comfrey which grew close to where they had been sitting, and her face was very sober.

"Poor Pam!" she thought. "There's something very

much the matter – I wonder if she can possibly be in love. Oh, dear! those are the tiresome sort of things that happen when people grow up, and *I* can't help her, because it's never happened to me, thank goodness! I suppose they will *all* be doing it soon, especially Rosamund – it would be exactly like her; and she, at any rate, will want my advice just from sheer force of habit. It's all very depressing."

But Dimsie was never depressed about anything for long, and started to smile quietly to herself as she climbed the worn steps to the upper garden.

"Miss Yorke needn't have feared I wouldn't find enough to do at Lochside; even without my herbs there's so much to do cheering people up. First Mother (though she's so determined to be cheerful she hardly gives me a chance) and then Pam's peculiarities, whatever may be the cause of them; and Jean arriving tomorrow, clearly in a very 'soppy' state from too much poetry – I can't think what Erica has been doing to allow it; too absorbed in her own work, I suppose, to keep an eye on Jean. Oh, and then there is Peter Gilmour! I should like to help him if I could, because he's been disappointed but doesn't make a fuss. Those are not the easiest kind of people to help, though; one knows better what to do with the lame dogs that hold up their paws and whine."

She considered all this as she made her way upstairs to her bedroom. Dimsie's lame dogs had always been legion in her schooldays, and she was bound inevitably to find someone in need of the support she was so ready to give. Such people were not slow in finding her.

As Dimsie changed into a smoky-grey dress after throwing off her gardening clothes, some association of ideas reminded her of Geordie's tale.

"Why there's Great-great-grandmother too!" she

exclaimed aloud. "Poor thing! haunting the garden for three hundred years because she wants something that 'naebuddy can jalouse'! I wonder if it's really that, or whether she just can't keep away from the sights and scents she loved so much. If it's that, I can sympathize with her, but if there's anything she wants, I'd like to be able to help. What with Mother, Pam, Jean, Peter Gilmour, and the ghost – I must write and tell Miss Yorke that life in the country is simply teeming with interest."

She ran a brush through her hair, and went down to dinner, humming happily to herself, to find that Pamela seemed to have cheered up and was chatting gaily to Mrs Maitland. Dimsie, with approval, watched her eat an excellent meal, and decided that her earlier fears were imagination.

"Whatever is the matter with her? She certainly *can't* be in love, that's one blessing!" she thought. "Nobody who was *really* in love would take two helpings of rhubarb pudding, and any other trouble I'm sure I can deal with in time, if she'll only let me try. It's very puzzling, of course, for I never knew Pamela keep anything from me before, but I must just wait until she is ready to tell me. It isn't 'done' to go poking your nose into other people's problems so long as they are anxious to keep them to themselves. After all, it's a free country, and everyone has a perfect right to their own problems – kindly remember that, Dimsie, you nosy thing!"

CHAPTER 6

The Rescue of Waggles

Two mornings later Jean crossed from Kilaidan by the ten o'clock ferry. She was met at the pier by her friends, Dimsie brimming over with news and questions, Pamela rather quieter than of old, but obviously glad to see her.

"We saw the ferry put out from Kilaidan and guessed you'd be on board," explained Dimsie, "so we came down to meet it. Did you have a good journey yesterday?"

"Quite ordinary," replied Jean. "Nothing like yours, of course – but it's worth anything to be back again. London is stifling just now, and full of idiots. Luckily for Erica, she seems to enjoy it as much as Father does, but I had a craving for hills and peace and sea air."

"You needn't think you've come up here to lead the Simple Life and write sonnets though," said Dimsie briskly. "Has she, Pam? Pam and I are much too busy to allow it. So Eric is enjoying herself, is she?"

Jean nodded, her grey eyes twinkling.

"Fantastically! I believe she writes all Father's speeches for him now; anyhow they've improved tremendously recently. And Mabs has got a permanent job, you will be pleased to hear. She's to do the gossip column regularly for 'Home Fires'. The editor says he never met anybody with such a natural gift for collecting news."

"*We* could have told him that," remarked Pamela wisely. "And what about Rosamund? Have you seen her?"

"I met her at a party last week, and she sent her love. I asked her to come up with me, but she is having far too good a time – looking sensationally pretty too." Jean laughed over some memory which she evidently meant to keep to herself, and Dimsie eyed her severely.

"I hope a good time doesn't mean flirting?" she asked suspiciously. "I never feel we can absolutely rely on Rosamund."

Jean chuckled again.

"Well, why shouldn't it?" she asked. "As a matter of fact it does." She looked at Dimsie with an amused glance. "It's bound to happen, especially with Rosamund – and why not?"

"You *can't* say we're not old enough now," added Pamela swiftly.

Dimsie marched on up the sloping road from the pier with her chin in the air.

"It's all so – so 'soppy'," she said with disgust. "I did hope we could escape it – but I knew Rosamund wouldn't."

"The Anti-Soppist League must die a natural death now we've left school," Jean said. "When one grows up there are other things in life."

"How exactly like a poet!" blazed Dimsie, swinging round in sudden wrath. "At any rate *I* shall go on anti-sopping if I'm the only one left who does! What's the use of learning to be sensible at school if it all goes to the winds directly we leave? I loathe sentimentality!"

"Hang on!" exclaimed Jean, staring at Dimsie in genuine amazement. "None of us has done anything very sentimental so far, and if Rosamund does flirt a little now

63

and then, you admit yourself that it was only to be expected. If there is safety in numbers, I can assure you *she's* all right."

"What about your poems?" inquired Pamela, trying to change the subject. "Have you had any accepted lately?"

"None," Jean replied. "They always come back addressed in my own horrible handwriting with a polite rejection slip. But the other day," she looked more cheerful, "the regrets were *written,* not printed, and so charming that my spirits scarcely drooped at all."

Dimsie looked interested.

"That must have been almost as good as an acceptance," she observed sympathetically. "I can just imagine what a difference it would make."

"Oh, it did!" cried Jean. "If editors only knew, I'm sure they'd spend a little more time refusing things carefully, and not use those horrid curt slips."

"Well," said Pam thoughtfully, as they paused to look back upon the view of the loch behind them, "it seems to me simply putting temptation in their way to enclose that self-addressed envelope. Stamps you must enclose, but think how easy it is for harassed editors to put your Manuscript straight into the enclosed envelope and post it back if they haven't got time to read it at the moment. Whereas they might think twice if they had to find an envelope and address it."

"Oh, Pamela!" exclaimed Jean, shocked at such cynicism. "They always *say* they are panting for fresh talent."

"I know," said Pamela, "but they get such a lot of it."

They branched off to the right at the top of the brae, Dimsie having an errand at the village shop, whose rounded windows leant over the pebbled pathway, displaying besides their ordinary wares shoes and stationery, crockery and soap. Jean, when she came north, always found the shop's contents much more irresistible than the garish displays of Oxford Street, and insisted upon diving in now for fresh supplies of "strippit ba's" (known in English as bullseyes); after which they retraced their steps past the low slate-roofed houses of the summer visitors standing behind their trim hedges of fuchsia and escallonia. There was one larger than the rest, near which they slackened speed as they passed, gazing curiously at the blue curl of smoke which rose from one of its chimneys above the encircling trees. There was little else of the house to be seen, for the thick branches shut it in completely, and it was screened by a high yew hedge.

"It looks very discouraging to casual visitors," remarked Dimsie. "I wonder how he is, poor man! You heard about him, of course, Jean?"

"No – who? I heard some stranger had taken Laurel Bank, but I don't even know his name."

"You *ought* to be interested then," said Dimsie, "because he's an author – at least people say he is, but you never know. Anyhow he lives there all alone except for a housekeeper, and the villagers find her very tiresome and ungossiping. It's specially trying for Mrs McIvor; she can get no information whatever."

"Serves her right – horrid old woman!" was Jean's comment.

"He never goes out," pursued Pamela, taking up the tale, "and they say he actually wears a *mask*. It all sounds very thrilling and mysterious. I wish we could come across him. I didn't know such romantic people existed nowadays."

"They don't," said Dimsie, dampingly matter-of-fact. "If we knew him, we should probably discover he was a most ordinary person with quite a simple explanation for his mask. You and Jean mustn't let your imagination run away with you. It only leads to disappointment in the end – at least so Rosamund says, though personally I've never found it so."

"Well, it certainly makes life more fun in the meantime," said Jean, "if you hope for the best. Hullo! what's the matter here?"

From round the corner of the Laurel Bank garden came sounds of woe apparently kept in check by tremendous efforts at self-control. Dimsie dashed into the little side lane, and there in front of her stood a small girl in a shabby outfit, crying hard, while she bent forward, hands on much-darned knees, and tried to peep through a tiny gap low down in the yew hedge.

"What's the matter?" asked Dimsie soothingly. "Can I help? Whose little girl are you?"

The child stood up, rubbed her hand across her eyes, and stared doubtfully at the unknown lady; her tearful gaze next wandered to the other two who had halted behind.

A glance showed them that she was no village child, though her clothes were very worn and mended; but they couldn't get her to say anything – she seemed struck dumb.

"We'd better go on, Jean," said Pamela at last, when their coaxing had proved useless. "Leave her to Dimsie; she'll sort it out if she can, but the poor little thing is overwhelmed by so many of us. Follow when you're ready, Dimsie. You'll find us somewhere about."

Left alone with one questioner to face instead of three, the child soon found her tongue.

"I'm not *anybody's* little girl," she replied suddenly. "I'm the Lintie."

"But won't you tell me your real name? Are you lost?" She shook her head.

"There isn't room to get lost in Lochside," she

answered, "and I haven't any realer name than Lintie, except a horrid long one called Carolyn. Can you make yourself small enough to look through that hole?"

Dimsie eyed it dubiously.

"I'm afraid not. Why? Have you dropped your ball through it?"

The Lintie shook her head again.

"I haven't got a ball. It's Waggles, my dog. He will go in there whenever we pass, and – and now I'm afraid he'll never come back – not any more ever!"

"Oh, nonsense!" exclaimed Dimsie quickly, seeing the eyes fill with tears again. "You've only got to call him. See – I'll whistle, and you call. He's sure to hear."

"No," said the Lintie, "he isn't. The nasty man who lives in that house doesn't like Waggles going into his garden, and he said next time I wouldn't get him back – and this *is* next time! And I've called, and I heard Waggles yelping, but the Orge's got him so that he can't come back, and he'll p-probably be – be murdered——"

This time the tears did flow again, and Dimsie, kneeling on the dusty path, put her arms round the little shaking figure, rather horrified at this description of the mysterious author.

"I'm sure he won't. Why, Lintie, he's only a man who lives in that house; there aren't any ogres nowadays. There hasn't been one for ever so long – hundreds of years. Suppose you stop crying, and I'll go with you to the front door, and we'll ask him to give Waggles back to us."

The Lintie considered this while she scrubbed her eyes with a small handkerchief rolled up into a damp ball. To her mind (knowing the Ogre whose existence this bold lady denied) the idea of demanding Waggles's return was a very forlorn hope. Still it might be as well to try it; certainly no stone, however improbable, should be left unturned. So she slipped a hot little hand into that of her new friend.

"All right," she said, "we'll go and try if you like. But he is an Ogre, 'cos I've seen him, and he's got a false face all brown. Nobody but an Ogre would have that."

"I expect he's only a rather nasty man," said Dimsie loftily, "who put on the false face to frighten you. I must say I'm surprised at him, but you needn't be afraid, I don't like people who try to scare little girls, and if he does it again, I fancy he'll be afraid of me!"

The Lintie, greatly cheered by such bold words, chuckled with delight.

"Oh, I hope he will! I'm not frightened for myself, you know – at least, not exactly – it's only 'cos of what he might do to Waggles."

"What kind of dog is Waggles?" asked Dimsie, relieved to see that the tears were stopping.

"A very beautiful kind of dog," replied the Lintie earnestly. "Mr Danks, the pier-master, gave him to me when my Daddy died out in the Garden of Eden. He said it was a great pity I shouldn't have something belonging to my very own, and Miss Withers said she didn't care, so long as he didn't bring his great muddy paws into her clean house."

"Who is Miss Withers?" inquired Dimsie as she fumbled with the latch of the gate.

The Lintie looked puzzled.

"I don't know," she answered. "She's just Miss Withers. She lets rooms to people in summer, and dressmakes the rest of the time. I lived with her after Daddy went away, 'cos we happened to have taken her rooms then, and the Garden of Eden wasn't a fit place for a little girl, though I wanted badly to go and look for the angel with the flaming sword. You see, there was nowhere else to leave me 'cos I'm rather different from other children through never having had a Mummy all my life."

Dimsie, remembering a time when she had supposed herself to have no mother, tightened her grip on this curious child's hand, and they went up an untidy path to a dilapidated porch; the whole place had a grubby uncared-for appearance which offended her and she eyed the dingy brasses with great distaste. There was no reply to her ring, but from some outhouse they could hear the melancholy wails of an imprisoned Waggles. Dimsie seized the knocker, and banged vigorously on the blistered door.

"It's not a bit of use," said the Lintie, growing doleful once more. "You can see it isn't. They don't mean to pay any attention whatever you do."

"We'll see about that!" said Dimsie indignantly. "At least we can find out where Waggles is," and seizing the child's hand again, she set off down an overgrown shrubbery path which led in the direction of Waggles's disconsolate wails. A sharp bend brought them in sight of a small garden shed, and at the same moment a tall broad-shouldered figure strode down an intersecting path and barred their way.

"The Ogre!" breathed the Lintie, clutching Dimsie's hand very tightly. Looking up, Dimsie saw a brown velvet mask out of which a pair of steely eyes confronted her, while an irritable voice exclaimed:

"Now then, what are you two children doing in this garden? It's quite enough to have the place invaded by all the mongrels of the village, but when it comes——"

The angry outburst ceased suddenly as, on looking more closely at the elder of the trespassers, he realized his mistake; and Dimsie, drawing herself up to her full height, answered with icy dignity:

"I think if you stop shouting for a moment, you will

69

see that I am not a child to be bullied or shouted down. I rang and knocked at your door without getting any reply, so I was obliged to invade your garden in search of this little girl's dog, which you appear to have stolen."

The Ogre fell back a step, obviously amazed at the fierceness of this unexpected attack.

"Stolen!" he repeated helplessly, while Dimsie went red, feeling that she had allowed her angry sympathy with the Lintie to make her say more than she had intended. But she stood her ground nevertheless; it was preposterous that any grown man should upset a defenceless little girl for no reason at all.

"Yes, certainly – stolen! What else can you expect me to believe when I can hear him yelping inside your shed at this very moment?"

The Ogre wheeled round abruptly, and looked in the direction of the shed.

"Is that where he is? He must have rushed in after rats or something, and the door has banged shut on him – it has got a habit of doing that. As for stealing him – I wouldn't take the beast as a gift!"

Here Lintie suddenly flared up in her turn, anger overcoming her nervousness. This insult to Waggles was more than she could stand.

"He's *not* a beast!" she cried. "He's an angel! And you said I would never get him back if he came in here again – you know you did!"

To have her own bad example so quickly followed completed Dimsie's embarrassment.

"Lintie!" she said quickly. "I am afraid we have both made a mistake after all, and Waggles has got into this mess by himself. I am very sorry," she added, turning to the Ogre awkwardly, "if I said more than I should, but – I thought you

70

had locked the dog up, and the little girl was very distressed."

The Ogre shrugged his shoulders resignedly.

"I admit the case looks bad against me," he admitted. "The tiresome animal is never out of my garden, and I may have threatened him in self-defence, but I assure you he shut himself into the shed. I heard him squawking and was trying to find him when I found you instead. I suppose the best thing I can do to convince you of my good intentions is to set him free at once."

It was very evident from his gruff tones that he hoped by doing so to rid himself the sooner of his unwelcome visitors. Dimsie felt that her attempted apology had not been met halfway, and watched in stony silence while he fumbled with the stiff fastening of the shed door, and Waggles whimpered inside. Losing patience finally, the Ogre gave the latch a clumsy wrench, the door burst open, and out sprang the prisoner, to jump all over Lintie, as full of joy at their reunion as though they had been parted for months. Waggles was evidently a gentleman of demonstrative feelings.

CHAPTER 7

The Ogre's Den

Having got what they had come for, Dimsie prepared to leave at once, but a sudden spatter of hail and rain came down before they had left the shrubbery, and with two strides the Ogre was upon them once more.

"You can't go home in this," he exclaimed with disgust. "You'd better come inside."

"Certainly not, thank you," replied Dimsie, more freezing than the hail. "I shouldn't dream of trespassing more than I have done already."

"Nonsense!" he answered curtly. "You haven't got an umbrella, so there is nothing else to be done," and seeing from her face that she had no intention of giving in, he swung the astonished Lintie up under his arm like a bundle of rags and made for the house, and Dimsie had to follow, gritting her teeth together in helpless rage.

They made their way in by a side door and through a small dark hall into an untidy study reeking of tobacco smoke. There was a shabby armchair pulled up to the fire, and a writing-table littered with loose papers, but otherwise the room seemed to be mostly furnished with bookcases of every size, shape, and dimension. So much Dimsie's eye took in before she exclaimed angrily:

"I don't know why you should force me to take shelter when it isn't the least necessary. I don't *want* to come in."

He set the breathless Lintie on her feet once more, and turned round, but the baffling mask hid his expression, though Dimsie had an uneasy suspicion that he was laughing at her.

"Don't be childish!" he said. "I know you didn't want to, but you couldn't leave the kid to her fate with a bad tempered villain like me."

If he expected her to contradict him politely, he was unlucky. Dimsie thought he was rude, if not actually unkind, and she saw no reason to contradict him. Moving across to the window, she stood there, watching the heavy rain as it beat down among the laurels and shrivelled rhododendrons, and wished earnestly that it would clear up and set her free from this objectionable person with his brown mask, which was probably an absurd affectation. The Lintie had done well to call him an ogre – the term suited him exactly. What was keeping the child so quiet? She glanced over her shoulder to see Waggles and his mistress side by side on the hearthrug, her arm round the place where his waist ought to have been had he possessed one, on her lap a large children's annual open at a brightly-coloured picture; several more annuals were lying beside her on the floor.

In her astonishment Dimsie looked unintentionally at their host, but meeting the sarcasm in his eyes, she promptly turned back to stare at the hail again. How did books of that sort come to be in such a house – in such a room? Obviously there were no children at Laurel Bank, and it was doubtful if there ever had been.

"You idiot!" she told herself. "Of course he must have bought them to give away – though he hardly seems friendly enough to give anybody anything."

The shower slackened and stopped as suddenly as it had started; the sun shone out again in a pale turquoise sky; piled-up banks of purplish clouds drifted northwards, and the little white pellets of hail on the lawn and the path changed to glistening drops.

"Come, Lintie," said Dimsie, turning back into the room, her head held very high. "We can perfectly well go home now if this – this gentleman will be good enough to allow us."

The Ogre's eyes twinkled again.

"My name is Orde," he announced abruptly, "Kenneth Orde – and I believe you are Miss Maitland from Twinkle Tap? So now we are introduced."

"Yes, I am Dimsie – I mean Daphne Maitland," said his guest, colouring a little over the slip by which she had given him the undignified pet name made up long ago from her initials, D.I.M. "The rain is quite finished. Come, Lintie."

Lintie looked up vaguely from the page she was devouring.

"But I don't *want* to go home," she declared unexpectedly. "I'd rather stay here a little longer. I never saw so many lovely books in all my life before."

Waggles thumped an approving tail on the floor. It was not the books he cared about so much as the warm and comfortable rug, and besides he had long wanted to get inside this house. Once in passing he had observed a tasty kitten on the lawn, and ever since he had hoped to meet it again. Certainly the kitten was not there at present, but if they only stayed there long enough it might appear.

"I'll tell you what, Lintie," said Dimsie, holding out her hand. "Up at my house – T'inkle Tap – there are books too, books which I had when I was little. If you come and see me one day, I will give you some for your very own, to take home with you."

The little girl's face shone with delight. Instantly she scrambled to her feet and followed her new friend through the hall into the porch, where Dimsie paused and turned stiffly to Kenneth Orde.

"Good afternoon," she said. "I am afraid we have wasted a great deal of your time when it really wasn't necessary," and she walked determinedly down the drive without a backward glance.

Lintie, however, was more gracious. Coming to a standstill on the doorstep she looked up at him with a wistful expression on her pale little face.

"Thank you very much," she said, "for not having murdered Waggles, and for letting me look at those books. I'm very much obliged, and so is Waggles."

The brown velvet mask at that moment hid a wonderfully soft and kind expression which perhaps the Lintie, with the quick intuition of childhood, guessed although she could not see it.

"That's all right," replied the Ogre gruffly. "Come again when you like. Bring the animal too, if you can keep him under control and stop his barking – not unless."

She held out her hand, which he shook formally, before she trotted down the path after Dimsie. Out in the road once more, they both stood still.

"*Now* you're all right," said Dimsie cheerfully. "We've rescued Waggles, and seen the inside of an ogre's den. Was it at all like what you had expected?"

Lintie considered the matter thoughtfully.

"Not a bit," she said at last. "It almost made me wonder if p'raps we may be wrong, and he isn't an ogre at all. I never heard of ogres having books like that in their dens."

"No," agreed Dimsie with gravity. "It seems unusual; but if you remember, I told you he wasn't really an ogre at all – though still that doesn't explain the books. Well, goodbye, Lintie! I must run, or I shall be late for lunch. Mind you ask Miss Withers to let you come to tea with me on – well, yes – Friday afternoon."

She nodded farewell, and sped up the brae at a cracking pace and reached the house to find Jean and Pamela waiting for her on the terrace path above the herb garden.

"Where on earth have you been?" they demanded together. "Did it need all this time to dry that child's tears? I hope you took shelter somewhere from the hail."

"Oh, I did!" Dimsie assured them. "I took it because it was thrust upon me, and very much against my will too! Come in to lunch and I'll tell you all about it. I suppose Pam will say I've been having another adventure. Anyhow I have come across the Author, which was what you were wishing for a little while ago – I came across him very much indeed! and I can tell you his acquaintance is nothing to write home about."

They went into the dining-room, where Mrs Maitland was already at the head of the table, and Dimsie had no reason to complain of the interest shown by her audience.

"Who is the child, Mother?" she asked, when she had finished. "You are sure to know, because you go so often to the village. What does she mean by saying that her father died in the Garden of Eden? And has this Miss Withers adopted her?"

"Practically, I think," Mrs Maitland answered. "(Help yourself to potatoes, Jean dear.) Miss Withers is a newcomer to the village since our day, and they happened to be lodging with her when the father got an offer of some post in the Middle East – engineering, I believe – and as it wasn't possible to take the child there, he seems to have left her in Miss Withers's care; apparently he had no relations who could, or would, take charge of her. I suppose he sent money home for a time, but then he was taken ill out there, and I don't know what has happened since. Anyhow, no one has turned up to claim the child, and I suspect poor Miss Withers has a hard enough struggle, now and again, to make both ends meet."

Dimsie looked admiringly across at her mother.

"Mother, you'd beat Mabs Hunter for general information! I can't think how you learn it all."

Mrs Maitland looked embarrassed.

"Oh, Dimsie dear! it sounds as though I encourage gossip, but the village people are always so ready to volounteer information before it's asked for if they see you are the least bit interested. Your Lintie came into the Post Office one day when I was there – a white-faced, dark-eyed little thing, with a yellow dog at her heels – and Mrs Adams insisted on giving me an extract from her biography. I confess I *was* interested, for she is such an unusual-looking child."

"And the Ogre?" questioned Jean. "Otherwise the Author? What about him, Mrs Maitland? Apparently he has got a story too."

"I'm afraid, on thinking it over," said Dimsie uncomfortably, "that I may have been rather rude to him. You see, the little girl was in such distress, and I know I did lose my temper a little——"

"I am sorry about that," said her mother gravely, "because I think he is rather an unhappy person just now. They say he is struggling to take up his work again, but is really not fit for it yet. Some sudden shock or illness seems to have upset his nervous system, and he is terrified of any dealings with the outside world at present."

"Poor thing!" exclaimed Pamela compassionately,

while Dimsie looked even guiltier than before. "But it won't do him any good to shut himself up like that. He would be more likely to get over his nervous trouble if he went about and mixed with other people."

Mrs Maitland helped herself to salad, and passed it on to Jean.

"This is a curious concoction Dimsie has grown," she said in parenthesis, "but you *may* like it. My dear Pam, I have suffered from a bad shock myself, and I know that you can't account for results, nor attempt to force people back into ordinary life till they are ready to return of their own accord. Yes, I know that isn't the commonsense way of dealing with such difficulties, but experience would show you (though I hope it never has to) that it is the only way which ever works. Of course, the poor man ought to have something to occupy him, but probably he goes on with his writing."

"What is his name?" inquired Jean.

"Yes, what is it? I don't believe I've heard it." said Pamela.

"You won't be much the wiser when you do," replied Mrs Maitland. "At least I have read no books by anyone of his name, but probably he uses a *nom de plume*. It's Orde, or something like that."

"It's Kenneth Orde," said Dimsie. "He told me so, this morning." She stopped abruptly, and nearly dropped the plate she was passing to Pamela as she caught sight of her face. It was only a fleeting look, not easy to describe, but Dimsie realized at once that Pam was on the verge of betraying herself in a way which she would afterwards regret, so she plunged gallantly into a flood of conversation about the first safe subject which occured to her – Jean's poetry.

"Why not put all your verses together and publish

them as a book?" she suggested wildly. "I'm sure they would pay. Everyone would buy them just to see what dreadful rubbish they were."

"Dimsie!" exclaimed her mother reprovingly. "Some of Jean's poems are very pretty indeed."

Jean's expression was a picture and Dimsie leaned back in her chair, feeling assured that everyone's attention was entirely diverted from Pamela.

"Poor old Jean!" she said with a laugh. "Mother, your *faux pas* was worse than mine, and she can't decide which of us has insulted her the worst. It's a terrible crime to call a poet's efforts 'pretty'. Jean taught us that years ago at school."

"I'm very sorry," said Mrs Maitland, with proper humility, though she looked as if she was trying not to laugh. "But seriously, Jean dear, why not take Dimsie's advice? About having them brought out in book form, I mean."

Jean shook her head mournfully.

"It isn't *done,* Mrs Maitland. In this case the piper would have to pay, and I haven't enough faith in my piping to hope that it would lure the pennies back again. The other day I sent some stuff to a man who was advertising for poetry, but he sent it back again by this morning's post. I haven't even opened the envelope – it's in my bag at the moment, where I crammed it before running down to catch the ferry."

"Then open it now," urged Dimsie. "Don't be pessimistic, Jean! After all, you never know."

"You'd know pretty well if you were me," retorted the blighted poet. "It's enough to make anyone pessimistic. I don't suppose your herbs ever come back declined with thanks. Oh, yes! I don't mind opening it. Perhaps he is one of those I was telling you about who enclose a personal note——"

79

She drew the envelope out of her bag and opened it with a listlessness which suddenly disappeared as she glanced at the contents. One or two typed sheets of verses slid unnoticed to the floor, where Dimsie rescued them, while Jean seized and scanned a large square sheet of paper lavishly printed with an office letterheading.

"Mrs Maitland!" she gasped, finding her voice again with a great effort. "Dimsie! Pam! look at this! He thinks very highly of the verses which I was kind enough to let him see, and he feels sure if I could send him a dozen more specimens of equal merit, we could come to terms regarding their publication. What a lovely man!"

"Terrific," cried Dimsie enthusiastically, grabbing the letter, and reading it in her turn. "And after our advice to you just now! Why, Jean, it's a clear call, as they say at missionary meetings. Here, Pam! just look at this!"

She had noted out of the corner of her eye that Pamela's self-control was returning, and felt it wisest to draw her back into the conversation; and Pam herself responded readily enough, if a trifle mechanically.

"It's marvellous, Jean! You will have to pick out twelve of your very best for him in order not to destroy the good impression."

Dimsie was frowning.

"Yes, indeed; that's most important – and no author is ever the best judge of his own work. Pamela, you and I must see to this. Otherwise we shall have her posting off a bundle of terrible rubbish that no self-respecting publisher would look at twice."

"Yes," agreed Pamela. "We shall come to tea with you tomorrow or the day after, Jean, and go over your stuff carefully. It won't do to run any risks."

"*You* didn't choose the three samples I sent him in the

first instance," Jean pointed out rebelliously, "yet he seems to have liked them. Perhaps I can gauge his taste better than you after all."

"I shouldn't wonder," agreed Mrs Maitland, rising from the table. "Don't let them interfere too much, Jean – it's quite possible that you know your own business best. And I don't want to be a wet blanket in the midst of so much enthusiasm, but I notice he only speaks of 'coming to terms'. Don't build too much on such a vague foundation. You may find that he expects you to pay for the cost of production after all."

"Oh, Mother, no!" cried Dimsie. "That would be terrible. Anyhow, let's go on hoping as long as we can, because it would be so splendid to see a book of Jean's in the shop windows. We will go to tea with her the day after tomorrow, Pam, because tomorrow I have got some urgent business to attend to."

CHAPTER 8

Dimsie Does Some Business

"The reason I can't go to Jean's tomorrow," explained Dimsie that evening, as she sat with her mother and Pamela beside the open window of the sitting-room, "is that I am going to take the early boat to town, and shall probably not return till the late one."

"What are you going to do in town?" asked Pamela, idly sorting out some loose sheets of music which lay on the wide windowseat beside her.

"Business," said Dimsie solemnly. "Jean may talk of my herbs not being declined with thanks, but something very like it has been happening this last week. I wrote to twelve different chemists in Edinburgh and Glasgow offering to supply them regularly with fresh herbs for dispensing purposes, and those who have replied at all, write to say that they are already receiving all they need."

"Well, it can't be helped, dear," said Mrs Maitland philosophically. "Both the chemists at Dunkirnie have promised to get some supplies from you, so that's a beginning."

"But it *must* be helped, Mother!" cried Dimsie excitedly. "Two little local shops will not exhaust all my supply – look at the size of the herb garden – and besides, it won't be profitable. I want to make enough, this season, to enable me to take in and plant a bit of the field beyond, so as to get a larger output next year."

"But those big city dispensaries must require such an enormous amount of stuff," argued Pam. "You couldn't possibly supply them – even one of them – not to mention twelve! I think it's very lucky they haven't taken you at your word."

Dimsie leaned forward earnestly in her seat, nursing her knees with clasped hands.

"You don't understand business, Pam. Of course I can't supply them with *all* they require – I don't suppose any *one* grower does – but I want them each to take as much as I can send them, and to be so delighted with the quality of my herbs that their orders will increase with the increase of my output. What I am trying to do is to start a herb *farm*."

Mrs Maitland laid down her needlework to listen with amusement.

"It never struck me before, Dimsie, that you had such a head for business," she said. "But why are you going up to Glasgow tomorrow?"

"Because I've marked down some of the big wholesale places for a personal call," replied Dimsie firmly. "They may not answer letters, but I hope they won't refuse to *see* me, and I hope to persuade them to try what I grow."

"Oh, Dimsie, you *can't*. It's like a commercial traveller touting for orders. And you won't persuade them to take what they don't want."

"Won't I?" Dimsie sounded very determined. "That's just what I'm going up for. I was afraid you mightn't like the idea, Mother, but you do see, don't you, that it's the only practical way of getting a foothold if I'm to succeed. And I *mean* to succeed. I have quite made up my mind about that."

"I'm afraid you have," sighed Mrs Maitland. "Well, anyhow I must come with you."

"Oh, no, Mrs Maitland!" protested Pamela quickly. "You would be worn out. But I can easily go instead. Do let me."

"Neither of you," said Dimsie firmly. "It's the sort of thing I must do alone. Mother don't you see? Do you suppose that any wholesale chemist or dispenser would take me seriously if I had Pam with me? It would give the whole enterprise an amateurish look at once."

"Why should I look more amateurish than you do yourself?" demanded Pamela indignantly. "You know people are always mistaking you for a child."

"Not if I dress up a bit," said Dimsie. "At least," recalling that morning's episode, "not often. And if they do, I soon show them how mistaken they are. Honestly, Mother, I can't have Pam with me unless she will stay outside."

"There isn't much use in that," said Pam disgustedly. "How can I lend weight to your interviews by remaining outside?"

"You wouldn't in any case," replied Dimsie. "That's just what I've been trying to explain to you. I shall be quite all right by myself."

She looked very businesslike as she walked out of the Central Station next morning, dressed in a plain grey suit and white silk shirt, and carrying a case of samples. No one who looked at her serious expression and purposeful face could have guessed the nerves which had possessed her during the short journey up from Gourock, where she had left the early boat. Though to her mother and Pamela she had made light of her errand, nevertheless it was not one about which she was particularly keen, and the polite refusal that she met with at her first attempt left her with clenched hands and tingling cheeks.

"Very sorry, but we are already in touch with growers who supply us with all we need," the head of the big druggists had assured her, and she found herself bowed out of his office and into the shop again before she had time to put forward any of the arguments with which she had come ready primed.

"I must do better than this," she told herself desperately after her third futile attempt. "I don't know why I can't talk to them as I meant to. It isn't as though I'm generally at a loss for words, and I don't think I'm shy. I never have been in my life before. How Erica would laugh at the idea!"

She was hesitating at the glass doors of a fourth pretentious-looking shop, when they suddenly opened, and a tall figure with a familiar limp emerged and almost collided with her before he realized who it was.

"Dimsie Maitland!" he exclaimed, beaming, as he shook her hand in a bone-breaking grip. "What a piece of luck! Have you come up to town for a day's shopping? But what's the matter? You don't look as cheerful as usual – rather like a bird with drooping feathers."

He scrutinized her anxiously, and Dimsie instantly made a brave effort to pull herself together.

"Or a dog with its tail between its legs," she suggested. "I didn't know it showed so plainly, but I've had a rather disappointing morning, that's all – nothing to worry about."

But obviously she was worried, and he continued to look at her with an anxious expression.

"I'll tell you what it is!" he declared with a sudden inspiration. "You're hungry! You must have had breakfast very early so as to catch the boat. Come along with me and have some lunch. Then you can tell me all about it."

"Thank you very much," said Dimsie with alacrity.

"I don't feel I *can* go into this shop," eyeing it with great distaste, "and begin all over again until I've had some form of sustenance – but I think it's mental consolation I need more than food."

"I'll give you both," he promised readily. "I'm extremely good at mental consolation and they do excellent curry at this place. Let's begin with curry and end with ices, just to even things out."

He was as excited as if he was planning a treat and Dimsie's spirits rose as they began their meal. He listened to her story.

"It doesn't sound so bad now that I'm telling it to you," she said at the end. "I've only been to three places, and probably my luck will turn after lunch; but the people I saw were so very definite and discouraging somehow."

"Stupid idiots!" exclaimed Peter, with a force which seemed out of proportion to the crime he was condemning. "But I don't believe you went to the right places, you know. Those are only ordinary shops after all, and you'd do better at some of those wholesale places farther in town. I'll tell you what! I'll take you to a place where I get most of the stuff I use for my own work, and we'll interview the manager together. I fancy you won't find him turning down an offer of good fresh herbs at reasonable prices."

"Oh, thank you!" said Dimsie. "But can you spare the time? I told Mother and Pam that I could manage beautifully alone, but now my confidence has been rather shaken, and it would be a great comfort to have some moral support."

"Then I am certainly coming with you," said Peter.

Fortified by curry and ices, and reinforced by a medical escort, Dimsie found things very different at her next interview. The manager seemed doubtful at first, but was evidently impressed by Peter's recommendations, to which

Dimsie listened with secret amazement. She herself was convinced that her plants were as fine and healthy as he claimed, but she had not known before that he had appreciated them to such an extent, both singly and collectively, on the one occasion when he had seen them.

"We usually buy in the market," said the manager, hesitating, "and our results have always been good, but since you think so highly of this lady's growing, Dr Gilmour, I might well place an order with her. If I could have her name and address——"

Dimsie gave it promptly, and answered a few questions as to her terms and the various herbs she grew, also the size of crop which she expected from each.

"I wouldn't have thought you had room for all that," remarked Peter with surprise, when they found themselves in the street once more. "Have you any more ground than that shelf running round the face of the hill?"

"Oh, yes!" said Dimsie. "That's the show part, but it widens out beyond the summerhouse into quite a respectable patch. I can't tell you how grateful I am for I don't think I could have done anything at all without your help."

"I don't know about that," he said, "but you are very welcome to the little I have done. I wish I could come farther with you," he added, glancing reluctantly at his watch, "but unluckily I've got an appointment out at Hillhead in twenty minutes. Do let me know how you get on. I'm extremely interested."

Dimsie said goodbye, and decided with renewed courage to make one or two further calls on her own before catching the Loch Shee steamer at the Broomielaw, which would carry her home in time for supper. She always loved the long, slow sail down the crowded river with its freighted docks and clanging shipyards, and her spirits rose in anticipation as she made her way along the grey, stifling streets; the city seemed very hot and airless today, very crowded with hurrying people, and long strings of slow traffic treading on each other's heels.

Apparently Dimsie's luck had not deserted her with Peter's departure, for at the next place she entered she was shown at once into a private office and asked to wait for a few minutes till a board meeting, which was finishing its business in the room beyond, should set someone free to attend to her. And she had not waited long before the connecting door opened, and at the tail of the small procession which filed through came a huge burly form treading with all the pompous importance of directorship.

"Bar – Mr Pritchard!" exclaimed Dimsie, springing to her feet and barring his way. "Oh, how is your little girl? I have so often wanted to know. Was the operation a success?"

"Good heavens!" cried Barty, startled out of his pomposity. "It's the lady of the train strike! Hello, Miss Maitland. What an extraordinary coincidence! My wife *will* be interested! Yes, thank you, it was perfectly successful, and the little girl's going to be better than ever. But what are *you* doing here? Want to see someone, eh?"

"I've come on business," explained Dimsie, seeing her chance. "I am trying to supply places like this with herbs which I grow in our garden at home and, as I can get no answers by post, I've come up to town today to pay some personal calls. Do you think there's any chance for me here?"

"Sit down," said Barty, pulling forward the easiest of the hard office chairs, and lowering himself into another. "Bless my soul! it's a small world – but my wife *will* be interested; she's often talked of you, and our race north that night. Now, let's hear all about it. Don't you go, Grayson; this concerns you."

Inspired by memories of Peter's impassioned address to the last man they had interviewed, Dimsie plunged into an account of what she intended to do, and Barty heard her out with most flattering interest. He was a director of many companies and chairman of most, and he had warm memories of Dimsie's kindness to his wife during their trouble, and was only too ready to use any influence he possessed on her behalf. Half an hour later Dimsie found herself bowed out of the door with a standing order in her pocket for various herbs, which was to be increased with the increase of her crop, if both sides were satisfied with the arrangement. Barty's car was standing at the kerb, and he insisted on running her along to the quay, where she arrived in excellent time for her boat.

"So that's a beginning, and a very satisfactory one too," she sighed contentedly, as the ferry beat its way out into the open Firth past Craigendoran Pier, and the purple peaks of Arran came in sight to the south-west, towering majestically above the headlands and islands. "Now it's up to me to keep it going, and if hard work is enough, I shall do it."

CHAPTER 9

Advising a Poet

The following afternoon Dimsie and Pamela rowed themselves to Kilaidan, and found Jean waiting for them at the small stone jetty which formed the private landing-place for Kilaidan House.

"It isn't a bit of use you coming," she said unhospitably, "because I've decided not to send my things to that man after all."

"And why not?" demanded Pamela, a trifle breathlessly, as she pulled the boat in and made its painter fast to the iron ring in the heavy flags.

"Because it's no good," answered Jean despondently. "I write such appalling rubbish."

"You do rather," agreed Dimsie candidly, "when you're left to yourself and not supervised, but that's exactly what Pam and I are here for. We'll see you *don't* send him rubbish."

"But I'm not going to send him *anything*," persisted Jean. "I've quite made up my mind."

Dimsie took her by the arm as they turned up the path which led to the house.

"That's all nonsense, you know," she said soothingly, "all nonsense and the poetic temperament. You can't throw away what may be the chance of a lifetime in that airy-fairy fashion. Neither Pamela nor I would allow it for one moment, would we, Pam?"

"I should think not!" agreed Pamela severely. "Don't let's have any more nonsense, Jean, but lead us straight to your poems, wherever you keep them. If there's much to read through before we decide, it will take us all our time, allowing an essential interval for tea."

"I think the best plan," said Dimsie briskly, "will be for us to read them aloud in turns. It will save time since we must both give our vote."

"Oh, no!" cried Jean, horrified. "Whatever you do, don't do that! I can't bear to hear you murdering them."

"It strikes me," said Dimsie with dignity, "that you are amazingly rude when Pam and I have taken the trouble to come over here this afternoon on purpose to help you. At great personal inconvenience to ourselves too, wasn't it, Pam?"

But Pamela was honest.

"Well, actually, no," she said. "As far as I'm concerned I'd rather read the worst that Jean can do than break my back over those weeds of yours in this heat. Is this where you work? Genius must have been burning, if untidiness is anything to go by."

Jean had led them round the large rambling house to a French window, through which they stepped into a room that certainly justified Pamela's sarcasm. It was small, shabby, and comfortable, but the round table in the middle was covered with notebooks of varying shapes and sizes, besides loose sheets of paper, many of which had overflowed on to the floor. On the mantelpiece stood a big silver-framed photograph of a young man wearing the Gordon tartan. Both visitors recognized it at once, for a smaller copy had stood on the chest of drawers in Jean's cubicle at school. It was the portrait of her brother who had died abroad very suddenly three years ago, when Jean was still at the Jane Willard.

Dimsie fell upon the confusion at once, and began to stack the notebooks in order, while Pamela collected and attempted to sort the loose sheets.

"Imagine bringing all this with you from London!" she exclaimed. "You must have needed an extra trunk or two. Anyhow we can do nothing till we have got it reduced to some sort of system. We'd better go through the notebooks first, Dimsie, and tackle the papers afterwards, when Jean has put them in order a bit. Only she can tell which page belongs to which."

Jean sat down with an air of resignation, and began to arrange the pile which Pamela dumped before her.

"I ought to have thought twice before coming up here," she said plaintively, "with you two living just across the loch. I might have known I should never be allowed to call my soul my own."

"I should think not indeed," returned Dimsie promptly, "if this was to be the result! It's lucky you came where responsible people could look after you. Erica must have simply left you to your own devices in the most careless way."

"Do you suppose," added Pamela, "that if I had allowed you to call your soul your own when we shared a study at Jane's, anybody else would ever have been able to get into it?"

"I don't *want* people marching around in my soul," retorted Jean flippantly. "But if you mean the study, I'm sure you made as much mess as anybody with hockey sticks and rackets and cricket-bats all over the place."

"Now, now, children!" interrupted Dimsie. "We can't waste time squabbling. I'm sure you were both equally messy in those days, though I can't say I remember it. What about those verses on Goatfell, Pam? I should be inclined to let them pass, wouldn't you?"

For the next half-hour Jean's two visitors alternately read and argued over the merits of different poems, while the diffident opinions which she herself occasionally voiced were promptly overruled as being prejudiced.

"You can't possibly judge your own work," explained Dimsie kindly. "Just leave it to us, and we'll soon sort out the twelve best. I don't pretend to be much of an expert on poetry – I only know whether the stuff makes sense or not – but Pamela must know something about it because she's musical. Oh, yes! it *does* follow. I could prove it to you if I wasn't too busy at the moment."

"You're talking the most awful rubbish," said Jean resentfully. "Pam only knows a little less about poetry than you do yourself – and that's not saying much."

"We know what we like," declared Pamela, with finality, "and therefore we represent the general public for whom, I suppose, you wish to cater. What are you pulling such a face about, Dimsie? I – I rather liked that one."

"Of all the sentimental bilge!" exclaimed Dimsie in disgust. "It's the sort of thing Rosamund might have liked if we had let her – yes, I can just see Rosamund wailing over this, and Jean looking highly flattered – but *you* ought to know better, Pam! You never used to care about this kind of rubbish."

"What is it?" asked Jean, as she peered over Dimsie's shoulder, curiosity breaking through the pose of studied aloofness which she had been trying to assume for the last few minutes.

"I shall read it out loud to you," said Dimsie determinedly. "Yes, Jean – it's for your own good, that you may know exactly how feeble it sounds – a thing which perhaps you didn't realize when you wrote it down; I'm willing to give you the benefit of that doubt:

'In folded days – long laid aside
　　With sprigs of rosemary and rue,
And letters with old ribbons tied –
　　I loved and was beloved by you.

'What came between I cannot tell,
　　Nor how the breach betwixt us grew,
This only know I passing well –
　　It widened till our love slipped through.

'I should have donned white orange flowers,
　　(A woman's crown) when June shone blue.
I wept instead through lonely hours,
　　Unsought, uncomforted by you.'"

"It's not one of my best," admitted the aggrieved poet, "but it isn't as bad as you make it sound, reading it as though it tasted of rancid butter. At least it scans and rhymes properly."

"I don't believe 'tied' does rhyme with 'aside'," retorted Dimsie, "but that's neither here nor there. It's the sentimentality I'm complaining of, and the amount of it. People don't *do* such things in real life."

"Lots of people keep letters," argued Jean.

"But they don't tie them up with ribbons and waste good rosemary on them. You know what I mean perfectly well – it's this idiotic lovesick nonsense!"

94

Jean laughed cheerfully.

"Oh, Dimsie! you're so funny when you puff up like an enraged turkeycock! What's the use of fighting against human nature? You know when people grow up, they mostly do fall in love sooner or later."

"Well then, they needn't be so silly about it," answered Dimsie crossly, "like your woman with her old letters and widening breaches and orange blossoms! I shouldn't mind people falling in love so much if they would only be sensible, and get married, and not *talk* so much about it."

"But," said Pamela, in a peculiar tone, "people don't always marry when they fall in love."

"Then they should talk less still," retorted Dimsie. "Oh, you'd know what I mean if you only thought for a moment!" She went pink, and added: "It's not the sort of thing that ought to be taken lightly, and if people will write poems about it, they should be very careful."

"Oh!" exclaimed Jean, and a light of understanding broke cross her face, while Pamela turned to fumble among the papers before her as though seeking for one special sheet. She found it presently, and laid it quietly on the table before Dimsie.

"I think perhaps you will like this one better," she said. "It's called 'A Knight to his Lady'. Jean, I guess you must have written it down here. Did you?"

Jean nodded.

"I believe it's one of my best," she said awkwardly. "Yes, read it aloud if you like, Dimsie. I shan't mind, so long as you don't hate it too much."

"I'll try not to," said Dimsie; then she added, her tone changing as she glanced down the page: "No, I think I shall probably like this one."

And she read:

"I know – when I have fought that last strange battle
    Which all must lose, if they would greatly gain,
When I have yielded up my lance and sword
To Him Who gave them, my great Over-Lord
    And laid me down where I can hear no more
Through the green woods the lowing of the cattle;
    Nor curlews calling round the lochan's shore,
Nor the soft music of the summer rain –

"Your voice would reach me through the utter silence,
    Love of my life! whom here I might not claim!
Would echo through dim wastes where shadows creep,
Break in live melody upon my sleep;
    Though heedless of all other sounds I lay –
The wild clan-slogan, and the crashing violence
    Of falling claymore, and the trumpet's bray –
Your voice would reach me did it breathe my name."

There was a moment's pause when she had finished reading. Pamela stared dreamily out of the window, and Jean sat silent, wishing that she had not allowed Dimsie to read this special favourite; she felt she could not bear to have its faults dragged out and held up to ridicule by such a scathing critic with her caustic wit and unerring aptitude for putting her finger on the weak spot.

Dimsie swallowed hard, and she started to say something.

"Don't! oh, don't!" implored Jean in an agony of apprehension. "I know 'violence' isn't really right for 'silence,' but if I left out the 'o' and put in an apostrophe——"

"Don't be an idiot, Jean!" said Dimsie gruffly. "What does a little thing like that matter when the idea is so good?

Surely you *knew* I couldn't help liking that. It's worth all the other bilge you've written put together."

"Oh!" murmured Jean, shattered. "I'm glad."

"If everybody fell in love like that," went on Dimsie, "it wouldn't be so bad. Can't you see what I mean? If people would only wait till they can have the real thing – not play at it like Rosamund and some of the others. That's what is so – so 'soppy' – flirting and making silly jokes about it."

"Yes," agreed Pamela gravely. "I think you're right. People may burn their own fingers or other people's if they flirt."

Jean propped her elbows on the table and her chin on her hands.

"I *know* you're right," she said, "but there doesn't seem to be much harm in it sometimes. If you could see Rosamund! Neither of you has. Pam has been in the North ever since we left school, except for visits, and you have not been around much, Dimsie, because of your father. You know what Rosamund is like, with her golden hair and big blue eyes – a wild rose or a fairy princess – and when you see her at a dance or party, surrounded by men and flirting with them right and left, you'd as soon blame a pink sweet-pea for dancing in the wind."

Dimsie's serious face relaxed into a smile. She had been Rosamund Gath's special champion and protector from the first day of their meeting in the school dormitory.

"I know," she said quickly. "I can just imagine it! Well, I suppose there are exceptions. With Rosamund it is probably more of an art than a game."

"That's it exactly!" cried Jean, with delight. "Even Eric enjoys watching her, and *she's* serious-minded enough, goodness knows! But I think I understand what you mean now, Dimsie, and I will try not to write any more sentimental poems. It's time for tea now."

"We've wasted a lot of time talking," said Dimsie. "Never mind; we've found six which may do, and the 'Knight' makes seven. Perhaps you had better leave out that 'o' in violence. I don't see that it matters, but the publisher-man might."

"We can finish after tea," said Pamela, sweeping the still unedited works together on to one corner of the table. "It will be too late for weeding, anyhow, by the time we get home," she added hopefully. "Couldn't we stay to *supper*, Jean?"

The long gloaming of the North was beginning to fall when at last Jean's guests and critics decided that they had selected the most suitable poems and that she might be safely left to type and send them off herself.

"Mother will think we have been drowned on the return journey if we don't start now," declared Dimsie, pulling on her mauve sweater, and pausing to tidy her hair before the mirror which hung above the mantelpiece. "Do you know, Jean," she went on gazing at the silver-framed photograph in front of her: "your brother reminds me very much of someone, and I can't think who it is."

"You know that photo well enough," said Jean. "You saw it often at school."

"Yes, but it didn't remind me of anyone then. It must be somebody I have seen recently, and yet I haven't met so very many people. He must have been very good-looking."

Jean sighed.

"He was. I don't believe Father will ever get over it. You see, he hadn't been friends with poor old Derry for five years before he died, and there was no time to make it up, and I don't think Father can forgive himself. After all, Derry did nothing so very wrong, and Father was very hard on him, considering."

98

"What did he do?" asked Dimsie, deeply interested at once.

"Have I never told you about it? Why, he married when he was a student at college – married first and told Father afterwards. I don't know why he kept it quiet, except that he knew that he had no business to do such a thing, for he hadn't any money of his own. Father was furious about it. He continued Derrick's allowance, but refused to see the girl or take any notice of them at all. She died a year later and Derry was broken-hearted. He never came home or wrote to us, and then after a year or two he got a post abroad, and the next thing we heard was that he had died too."

Dimsie and Pamela listened sympathetically, and neither spoke much as they went down through the shadowy garden to the little toy quay where their boat was tethered.

"There's nothing one can say to a story like that," observed Dimsie slowly, as they said goodnight, "but you know how very sorry we are, Jean."

"Thanks – yes, I know," said Jean rather huskily. "Sometimes I think it wouldn't have been so bad if there had been a child left behind, to whom we could try to make it up. I know it would have been a comfort to Father."

She held the boat while her guests scrambled in; then loosened the painter, and tossed it to Pam, who caught it and coiled it out of the way.

"Let me row, Dimsie. I'd like to," Pam said, as they drifted out. "You can steer."

"All right," Dimsie agreed and having adjusted her rudder, she sat in dreamy silence, watching the yellow lights shine out in the small hamlets scattered up and down the shores of the sea-loch, as the stars were coming out in the deep blue above. The water was dark and still, sighing and whispering to itself as the boat slid through it with Pamela's rhythmic stroke. Somewhere, far up in the mystery of the great black hills, the bagpipes were playing, an almost unearthly music, very faint and far away.

The drift of the outgoing tide pulled them a little below Lochside, and Dimsie said, as she looked up at the hill where her home stood:

"It's easy to understand on a night like this how Twinkle Tap got its name. The windows shine out high above everything else, and on breezy nights, when the trees wave across them, they must twinkle like stars. It must have been this way that the sea-captain came home long ago and looked up to see his lady-love keeping watch for him among her herbs."

"Till at last he didn't come home any more," added Pamela, falling into Dimsie's mood. "Jean should write a poem about that, and how she waited for him in vain all those years afterwards."

Dimsie pulled the tiller-ropes so that their boat drove in nearer to the hill.

"And how she waits for him still, they say. Look, Pam! there is something grey and vague up there by the dyke where the stone seat is – just beside the junipers – don't you see it?"

Pamela rested on her oars, and glanced somewhat sceptically over her shoulder.

"It's only the mist gathering," she answered, "but of course you can understand how the stories arise. Anyone with a fertile imagination could make a ghost out of that."

Dimsie said no more, but devoted her energies to guiding the boat into their own landing-place, where Geordie awaited them, having watched their progress across the loch from some lurking-place of his own.

"Wull ye gan roon' by the road the nicht?" he

inquired, as they stepped ashore. "Ye'll no be gaun up through the gairden at this hoor?"

Dimsie laughed.

"Why not?" she asked. "It's the quickest way."

Geordie said no more but gave a significant shrug, as he locked up the boathouse for the night. As they took the stony path upwards through he trees, Dimsie said with a laugh which was a trifle unsteady:

"You know what he means, Pam? You're not afraid to pass the gate in the yew-hedge when it's growing dark?"

"Certainly not," said Pamela firmly. "Supposing the Grey Lady were there, would she harm us if she could? Apparently her one joy in life was to help everyone who needed her. Perhaps that's where you get your passion for lame dogs, Dimsie."

"Perhaps it is. I've always loved her and longed to be like her since my father first told me the story when I was quite little."

"I wonder," Pamela's voice came rather strangely out of the darkness which had deepened as they passed under the trees, "could you spare any sympathy for an experience you didn't understand?"

Dimsie caught her breath. Was she to have the confidence which she had been so careful not to force?

"Try me," she said simply. "I think I've got enough imagination."

There was a pause broken only by something which sounded suspiciously like a sob from Pamela; then she said:

"It's no good. I *can't* talk about it somehow – not quite, though I have never been so near it as just now. *I'm* a lame dog, Dimsie – about as lame as any on your list – that's all."

"I've known that ever since I saw you in Glasgow," Dimsie said in a troubled voice, "but I don't know how to get to you, Pam. That's what bothers me. It used to be so easy to help you all at school."

"It's much more complicated now," said Pam sadly, "but if anyone can find a way, it will be you, Dimsie. I *wish* I could talk to you – I'd like to. Probably I shall, some day, but not just yet."

"Pamela!" Dimsie came to an abrupt stop outside the gate of the herb garden. "Just answer me this one question, for anything's better than to have an uncertainty hanging over me. Are you or aren't you in love?"

There was a moment's pause, then Pamela turned away.

"I rather think I must be!" she answered, with a sound which was neither sob nor laugh but a little of both, and she fled up the stone steps to the house above.

Dimsie, her mind in a turmoil, waited before following, to gaze for a second across the low gate into the scented gloom beyond. The garden was empty of everything but its fragrance and a brooding sense of unutterable peace.

CHAPTER 10

On the Shores of the Lochan

Dimsie was up at half-past five, one morning the following week, and working among the dewy fragrant herbs. The post had brought her an order the previous afternoon from the dispensary to which Peter Gilmour had introduced her, and a hamper of herbs had to be gathered and dispatched by the nine-thirty boat. Pamela had made great promises of being up in time to help, but Dimsie heard no sound of stirring as she crept past her door, so did not bother to wake her up.

"Poor old Pam!" she thought. "I can easily manage by myself, and I expect she is often late going to sleep now that she has got something on her mind. I can't think what the mystery at Laurel Bank has got to do with it, for one thing is certain – it can't be the Ogre she loves, because nobody in their senses would fall in love with a man like that. It's a relief to be sure of that, but it doesn't help me to solve the problem of how he comes to be mixed up with Pam."

She plunged her arms into the green sweetness of balm and hyssop, rosemary and peppermint, cutting and bunching with swift fingers till the hamper which she had brought was nearly full; then she got busy on a blazing bed of marigolds, laying the golden heads close together till there was no more room in the basket. Then she carefully spread soft protecting

103

paper over the top, shut and fastened the lid.

"There, that's done!" she exclaimed, stretching her arms above her head with a sigh of content, and as she let them fall again the distant chimes from the little church at Kilaidan came faintly across the silver stillness of the loch. Dimsie counted the strokes.

"Only seven o'clock!" she exclaimed in astonishment. "I worked faster than I thought. Why, if I cycled quickly I could get the hamper into Dunkirnie in time for the eight-five boat, and that's a quick one. They would get the herbs at the dispensary a good two hours before they expected them, which would surely encourage them to think me prompt and reliable."

Dimsie picked up the hamper and hurried as fast as it would let her up the stone steps and through the kitchen garden. It took only a few minutes to get her bicycle from the outhouse where it was kept, and fasten the hamper on to the extra-large carrier behind her saddle. She stopped long enough to scribble three lines on a scrap of paper which she left on the hall-table for her mother or Pam to find, and then she was off, spinning along a mossy, wood-fringed track which was a short cut to the Dunkirnie road.

It was a wonderful morning for a ride, with larks singing above her, and peewits calling from the farther hillside. She met no one until she reached the outskirts of the straggling coast town, and freewheeled down a long hill to the pier. Here she handed over the basket and watched with satisfaction the ferry battling its way round the point from its last port of call. Altogether her morning had been well worth while, and she felt there was a good deal to be said for early rising when once the first horrible wrench was over.

She decided to return by the level shore-road, but only a little way along it misfortune met her in the shape of some broken glass – there was a sharp pop and her back tyre went flat.

Dimsie dismounted and inspected the damage. It was a very thorough puncture, and no amount of pumping would carry her even temporarily on her way. She went back to the nearest repair-shop, handed over her machine, and heard that it might, with luck, be ready for her in two days' time.

"I must take the short cut by the golf course" she decided, "but it means that I shall be extremely late for breakfast, and I'm hungry *now*. I shall buy some scones at the baker's and eat them beside the lochan. It will be rather fun after all – it's such a fantastic morning."

She bought potato scones, newly baked and thoroughly indigestible, and started on her long walk home, remembering with pleasure that the waterlilies would be in full bloom by now on the little loch, and deciding to breakfast as close to them as possible without actually falling into the water.

Apparently someone else had had the same idea, though she had crossed the road and made her way down almost to the water's edge before discovering that she was not alone in the world this morning, after all. From behind a clump of bog-myrtle bushes rose a tall figure, and Peter Gilmour's voice exclaimed:

"Good morning. You are up early today! Got such a thing as a spare handkerchief about you?"

"Why?" asked Dimsie in astonishment. "Where have you dropped from at this hour? Have you hurt yourself?"

He bent over a bundle which lay on the rough grass at his feet.

"No, but someone else has. This poor little dog was being hunted along the road by two horrible boys when – unluckily for them – I caught sight of the chase, and captured the lot; but not before they had thrown a sharp stone and gashed his back leg. And I seem to have lost my handkerchief."

Dimsie bent down to stroke and examine the exhausted dog, who feebly flopped his tail in gratitude.

"Why, it's Waggles!" she exclaimed. "I know him. He belongs to a little girl in the village, and she will be dreadfully upset about it. Poor little thing! Is his leg bad? Let me see."

She knelt down and examined the cut, still bleeding a little despite Peter's careful bathing.

"It must be tied up," he said, "but I wish we had some sphagnum moss for an antiseptic dressing. It doesn't grow round here though."

"But garlic does," said Dimsie, darting off to the marshy verge of the loch, while Waggles raised a tired yellow head to gaze after her in surprise.

"Garlic?" echoed Peter dubiously, when she returned with a small bunch of green-and-white. "Is that antiseptic? Well, the smell is enough to kill off any self-respecting germ! What do you propose to do with it?"

"I'll show you," said Dimsie briefly. "It's the juice that's good, you know. I'm not sure whether we ought to use leaves or flowers, so I brought both."

She crushed her handful into a bruised and pulpy mass, which she laid very gently on the clean wound, her patient watching with eyes which seemed to understand she was trying to help. Peter noted with approval how skilfully she bound her handkerchief round the dressing in a neat bandage to hold it in place, handling the injured limb in such a way that she evidently gave relief rather than pain.

"You'd make a fantastically good nurse," was his comment when she had finished.

Dimsie seated herself on the grass beside Waggles,

and stroked his rough coat with soothing fingers.

"I couldn't," she said. "It would mean going right away from home and leaving Mother. By the way," looking up at him with a teasing expression, "this is *your* case, and I calmy took it over without permission. I ought to apologize."

"Not at all," he answered. "I couldn't have done it without your help. You've forgotten this," and he held up his bad hand. "My bandaging now is so clumsy as to cause more pain than it cures."

Dimsie felt embarrassed and she looked away from him to where the wildfowl were skimming across the face of the lochan, leaving tiny rippling wakes behind.

"Oh!" she exclaimed. "I had forgotten. I am sorry to be so tactless! Though I expect you would have managed – I'm sure you could."

He shook his head.

"Besides," he added quickly, "you forget too I haven't your knowledge. The idea of using garlic never entered my head."

"I expect you don't read so much about herbs. I only hope I've applied it properly." Dimsie gave an anxious glance at the invalid, who was lying contentedly beside her, weak from loss of blood, and glad to rest in the safekeeping of people who seemed to be friendly. "What did you do to the boys?" she asked suddenly, and he was amused at the vindictive expression which crossed her face.

"To put it bluntly, I 'sorted' them out," he assured her grimly. "The stouter end of my fishing-rod came in very useful, and I think it will be some time before they torment a defenceless animal again. There's only one way to treat people like that, and I had great pleasure in doing so."

"I am very glad!" cried Dimsie fiercely. "If I had my way, all cruelty should be punished like that. I hate – hate –

hate people who ill-use children or torture animals! I hate them so much that I want to hurt them badly!"

He looked at her as she sat there, her chestnut hair blowing about her flushed face and her eyes flashing.

"I quite agree with you," he agreed quietly. "You haven't told me yet how you came to be wandering about here at a time when all respectable people are having breakfast."

Her face relaxed again and she laughed.

"That reminds me," she said, "I was coming down here to have mine. Will you share it?" and she produced her bag of potato-scones.

"Is it a picnic? I brought some cheese sandwiches myself," he said modestly. "Certainly, let us go halves. I have been fishing from an extraordinarily early hour, and those scones look very inviting."

Dimsie pushed them across to him.

"Help yourself. I bought them in Dunkirnie because I got a flat tyre and I knew I couldn't get home in time for breakfast. I cycled in with a hamper of herbs to catch the early boat – which reminds me to thank you again for going with me to those drug people. It was very good of you."

"Not a bit. I enjoyed it – and anyway I felt I was doing them a good turn too."

"But you never told me then that you were coming down to Lochside so soon. Did you suddenly feel you must have some fishing?"

"Not exactly. I came down for a couple of days to see a friend of mine who happens to be having a bad time – a chap called Kenneth Orde, who lives just below you at Laurel Bank."

"Oh!" Dimsie's chin went up, and her tone sounded supremely uninterested. Peter Gilmour watched her narrowly for a moment, then he said:

"Do you know you are a very inconsistent person?"

She looked round at him in surprise, her sandwich halfway to her lips.

"It's a fact," he persisted, nodding seriously. "For a wounded animal you are all sympathy and kindness, and eagerness to help, but you were fairly merciless, the other day, to a man who needs help if ever anybody did."

She went very red beneath the suddenness of this unexpected attack.

"I wasn't!" she cried indignantly. "Did he tell you about it? I was only – very distant with him, and he was extremely disagreeable. It was all about this very dog and the child he belongs to. Mr Orde had been bullying them both – at least I thought he had."

Peter Gilmour's eyebrows went up.

"But had he?" he inquired.

Dimsie stammered.

"Well, no – perhaps not exactly," she admitted, "but it looked very much like it, and anyhow he was – he was——"

"Grumpy and offhand," suggested Peter, to help her out. "I believe you there."

He stretched out his hand and broke a piece off a hawthorn bush which grew close beside him.

"See that spike?" he asked, holding it out to her. "It would have been a twig with flowers and leaves on it if circumstances hadn't stunted it into a thorn instead. Natural History fact. Bit of a parable too, when you come to think of it."

Dimsie remained silent. She was too honest to pretend that she did not understand him, and the rebuke went home. Peter said no more, but finished his scone and began to munch placidly at a cheese sandwich, while Waggles revived sufficiently to snap at an aggressive fly.

Dimsie herself was the first to break the silence.

"Do you know," she said in a very small voice, "no one has ever called me unsympathetic before, but you're absolutely right. I was almost positive at the time that I was being hateful, and now I'm convinced of it. What's wrong with him?"

"Several different things," said Peter slowly. "He had a serious accident six months ago – some chemical stuff exploded in his face. Appalling neuralgia is the trouble uppermost just now. Any noise is agony to him – such as the barking of this little animal for instance, when he got into the garden. But as for bullying either children or animals – why, it just shows how little you know about Kenneth Orde. He's particularly keen on kids – writes books for them, in fact."

"Does he?" Dimsie's eyes opened wide. "Then that explains all those annuals in his study. I suppose there were stories of his in them?"

Peter nodded.

"He writes for some of those things, but he does ordinary fiction as well – indeed he is rather well known under his pen-name. I'm hoping he will take it up again soon, but he hasn't been fit for work yet, though he intended to start on a novel as soon as he got settled here. I wish he could. If it wasn't too much of a strain, it would be the best thing possible. What he needs is occupation and plenty of cheerful company to keep him from brooding."

"But if he has got bad neuralgia—" began Dimsie.

"Oh, that isn't what prevents him from mixing with people," broke in Peter. "He is an absolute idiot about his face. Certainly it is badly scarred; that's why he wears his ridiculous mask. As if it mattered! As if anyone, knowing what a terrific person he is, would care twopence about his scars."

110

"Perhaps," said Dimsie, "he is afraid people might be sorry for him."

"Probably," said Peter. "But he has got to make a start sometime, with or without the mask, and that's where you come in, if you only would."

"I? How?" Dimsie looked rather startled.

"Well, if you would only be nice to him, you are just the sort of cheerful, no-nonsense sort of person who could do him an amazing amount of good, and make it easy for him to take up his job again. If he could come up to Twinkle Tap and meet your mother and your friend, and discover for himself that none of you see anything repulsive in his scars – well, it might break the ice all round, give him confidence to face other people, and help him overcome a lot of that morbid nonsense."

He looked pleadingly at Dimsie, who sat frowning, her way when working out a perplexing problem.

"It *is* very morbid," she said at last. "Do you know I can't help thinking there is more behind it than the accident, even though it did give him a terrible shock. I can't quite understand it if that is all."

Peter shot a quick glance at her, then snatching up a pebble he flung it far out into the lochan, startling a waterhen, who rose with an agitated flutter from the flags among which she had been paddling.

"You're right," he answered abruptly. "That isn't all – though I don't know how you discovered it. The rest I've no business to discuss, but I can tell you it's very bad. If ever a man needed a helping hand, it's Kenneth Orde. Will you do what you can?"

Dimsie heaved a sigh, as she looked away from him towards the blue hills towering up beyond Kilaidan.

"Of course I'll do anything I can," she promised, "but I

111

may not be much good, because I have never had any experience in helping people with that sort of trouble. It all seems so different from what I've been used to, but I should like to help – especially after being so horrible to him the other day. I promise I'll try."

"That's great!" exclaimed Peter. "Don't bother to do anything except make friends with him; that will be quite enough. I have to go back to town tomorrow, but I shall leave him with an easier mind if I feel I have got you to help."

She glanced at her wristwatch, and then sprang hastily to her feet.

"We've been talking here for ages!" she said. "I must dash home now, for there is a lot to do in the garden this morning. You can have no idea how fast weeds grow and flourish here unless you have tried to battle with them. I suppose it's the damp climate of the West. What about Waggles? Is he fit to walk that far?"

"Oh, I think so – on three legs. He has had a good long rest and his share of our breakfast. Besides, his mistress must be growing anxious, don't you think? I gather from what happened the other day at Laurel Bank that he is rather an important person in her eyes."

"Oh, very!" said Dimsie laughing, as she watched him packing up his rod. "I am only afraid that between Waggles and myself you haven't done much fishing this morning."

"Not much," he admitted, adding with a grin: "but I caught more than I hoped for, seeing I've got that promise from you. I hope you didn't mind my plain speaking just now?"

"Yes, I did," confessed Dimsie soberly, as they climbed the slope to the road, with Waggles hobbling contentedly behind. "I don't like you to think me un-sympathetic, but you were quite right all the same."

112

Peter adjusted his empty fishing-basket more comfortably on his shoulder, and kept step with her along the highway as well as his limp allowed.

"No, I wasn't," he contradicted. "I was a terrible liar really, and I don't mind saying so now that I've got my way. As a matter of fact I think you're a very sympathetic person when you get your sympathies focussed in the right direction."

CHAPTER 11

Dimsie Finds a Patient

Stress of business had compelled Dimsie to postpone Lintie's visit to her until a week later than the day originally fixed, but her mind being full of a variety of other matters she then forgot the invitation, and Friday afternoon found her curled up in a corner of the sitting-room settee immersed in a herb book from which she was taking copious notes. Pamela had gone golfing with Jean on the Dunkirnie links, and Mrs Maitland was reading aloud to an old bedridden woman in the village. On her way out she had looked into the sitting-room to say:

"You will be alone in the house, Dimsie, so if anyone comes don't get so absorbed that you forget to answer the door."

"Yes, Mother," replied Dimsie mechanically, without lifting her head from her work. As it happened she had not heard a word of her mother's speech, being absorbed in her book. Nothing less than a bomb would have roused her when she was studying, so it was hardly surprising that a timid knock at the front door went unnoticed; a second and louder attempt also met with no reply.

The budding herbalist scribbled on, her pencil flying over the lines of her notebook with little or no rubbing out;

for this was one of Dimsie's "good days" when the information she wanted seemed to leap at her, ready classified, from the printed page, and there was no time lost in long fumblings here and there for disconnected scraps of knowledge hard to fit in when found. She was compiling a handbook of useful facts and practical remedies, to which she could refer at once if, when an emergency arose, she had not already got what she wanted in her memory . . .

"Please I've knocked twice, and I couldn't reach the bell, so I just came in and found you. I hope you won't think it was rude."

Dimsie came slowly out of her concentration and, gnawing her pencil, she gazed with puzzled eyes at the intruder. The Lintie wore the same shabby clothes and there was a fresh darn on one knee, but she was carefully brushed and smoothed; and even wore a pair of cotton gloves, much too large and of a strong mustard colour.

"I hope," she said anxiously, disturbed by Dimsie's lack of response, "I hope it isn't a mistake. You *did* say Friday, didn't you?"

"Oh!" exclaimed Dimsie, thoroughly awake at last, and touched by the Lintie's look of distress. "Of *course* I said Friday – I remember now. And how is Waggle's leg? Did you bring him too?"

The Lintie shook her head regretfully.

"I wanted to, but Miss Withers said, was he asked? and I couldn't honestly say you'd remembered to ask him, so she said he must stay with her."

"What a pity!" said Dimsie, putting away her writing materials, and closing the big book with a snap. "Next time he must come too. Take off your coat, and then we must see about getting tea. You'll help me, won't you?"

"I'd like to," answered the Lintie; then her face

115

grew very red, and she stammered apologetically: "Please, if you didn't really expect me, and there isn't enough for tea, I – I shan't mind a bit going without. I can look at those books you told me about; that'll do just as well."

By a sudden intuition it flashed upon Dimsie that this strange, old-fashioned child did not always have enough to eat; otherwise surely food would seem a matter of course, whether she imagined she had been expected or not. Probably someone had to "go without" when guests arrived unexpectedly at Miss Withers's for tea. With this possibility in her mind she determined that the Lintie's meal should be a large one, the largest she could be persuaded to eat, and proceeded to rummage in the kitchen for homemade scones and cakes, and the choicest jams she could find.

"Do you like bramble or blackcurrant jelly best?" she inquired, while Lintie looked on with awe at such a display of plenty.

"I don't know what blackcurrant's like," she said simply. "We don't have them in our garden, but last year Miss Withers and I got lots of brambles up near the lochan, and she made jelly with them."

"You'd better have blackcurrant then," said Dimsie, stepping down from the chair on which she had been standing to rummage on an upper shelf. "It will be more of a treat for you. After tea you shall look at the books, and then we'll play games. It's too damp to go into the garden today, but we can have plenty of fun indoors, and my mother will help. I can hear her coming in now."

So the Lintie had the tea of a lifetime, and did full justice to it, only murmuring regrets now and then that Miss Withers and Waggles could not share it. The latter's leg, so she told them, was nearly healed now, and he was never allowed outside the garden alone for fear of meeting his former enemies.

116

"The nice man who brought him back," said Lintie, her eyes fixed solemnly on Dimsie, "told me to take him to *you* if ever he got hurt again, and you'd know what to do. So I shall."

"I hope you won't need to," said Dimsie, looking rather alarmed at this faith in her powers of healing.

After tea Lintie was introduced to various delightful new games, and threw herself heart and soul into the fun. Evidently playmates, even of the grown-up variety, were a rare delight to her. Miss Withers, it seemed, had no time to play, if she had ever known how (which Lintie apparently considered doubtful), and she had not allowed her charge to mix with the village children, so there was only Waggles.

"And that reminds me," said Lintie, in her quaint old-fashioned manner, "that I faithfully promised to come away at six. Do you think your clock is right?"

"I am afraid it is," replied Mrs Maitland, amused by her reluctance to go. "But you have still got five minutes to finish the game."

The Lintie laid down her cards unwillingly and with a lingering sigh.

"I shall need the five minutes for saying goodbye and getting started," she explained, "but I have enjoyed every bit of myself!"

Which was her own peculiar way of expressing supreme content.

Dimsie said she would see her home, and ran upstairs for her sweater, while Mrs Maitland helped the visitor into her coat. It was something of a struggle, for the coat was obviously outgrown, and in the midst of their combined efforts somehow – neither quite knew how – out of some part of the Lintie's clothes tumbled half a scone and a thick piece of homemade cake. There was a terrible silence, while the

117

colour rushed all over the little girl's face, and kindhearted Mrs Maitland racked her brains for some tactful way of carrying off the awkward situation.

It was Lintie who found her voice first, a very shaky voice full of great agitation.

"Oh, please!" she said, half-sobbing, "I'm not really a horrid greedy little pig, nor – nor a thief. It was part of the lots of things that you put on my plate, and when you'd put them there, that made them become mine, didn't it?"

"Of course! of course, dear!" agreed Mrs Maitland soothingly. "It doesn't matter at all if you prefer to keep them for later on. We should not have pressed you to take more than you could manage. It was my fault entirely, so you mustn't worry about it for a moment."

But Lintie was too honest to take advantage of that suggestion.

"But it wasn't your fault," she said, "'cos I could have managed it quite easily, only – you see – poor Miss Withers isn't very well, and she never has any cake – and the scone was for Waggles, to make up for being disappointed. And I'm afraid you'll think I'm terribly rude and never ask me again – but I couldn't *not* go halves with Miss Withers and Waggles."

Mrs Maitland hugged her.

"Certainly you couldn't, my love. You are a good unselfish little girl, and you shall come to tea with me regularly every week, and Waggles too. I should like to send a cake specially to Miss Withers, but I fear she'd think I was the rude person then, so I'd better not. But I'll tell you what I can do."

Lintie listened eagerly, and she started to smile again.

"I've got a bone in the larder which isn't of the slightest use to me, and I don't think Waggles would be hurt or misunderstand me if I wrapped it up in paper and let you take it home to him."

The Lintie beamed all over, and gave a little skip of joy.

"Thank you!" she cried. "Oh, thank you thousands of times! We don't ever have bones in our house, so you can just 'magine what a treat it will be for Waggles. He does get so tired of porridge all the time."

Here Dimsie came down to ask the reason for so much excitement, and went in search of the greasy offering for Waggles, returning with it safely wrapped up in a paper bag.

"I've had the most wonderful afternoon," observed Lintie thoughtfully, as she trotted down the brae with her hand in Dimsie's. "Isn't it funny to think that I might never have known you if Waggles hadn't shut himself in the Ogre's shed. I owe a lot to Waggles. Miss Maitland!"

"Well?"

"Don't you think that perhaps the Ogre isn't quite as nasty as he seemed at first?"

"I told you all along that I didn't think so."

The Lintie stopped short, and pulling her hand out of her friend's, regarded her with a shocked face.

"Oh, Miss Maitland! You talked to him 'zactly as if you thought he was the nastiest man you had ever seen!"

Dimsie had the grace to blush at this home-truth.

"Well, I told you he wasn't an Ogre, anyhow, and it was very wrong of me to talk to him like that. I'm sorry about it now."

"You can see he's really very nice inside, can't you?" asked Lintie, mollified by this handsome acknowledgement into taking hands once more, and conversation languished for the remainder of the walk downhill to Miss Withers's cottage. Dimsie was puzzling over a fleeting resemblance in the child which she could not place, and Lintie herself was too tired and happy to talk, full of dreams concerning future visits to Twinkle Tap in which Waggles might share.

Miss Withers opened the door in answer to their knock, a gaunt high-cheekboned spinster whose hard features softened at the sight of Lintie.

"Run awa' ben, dearie, and find the dog – he's been crakin' for you all the while. It was guid of you to bring her hame, Miss Maitland," she added to Dimsie. "I'd have fetched her mysel' but there was some work to finish for a lady over at Dunkirnie, and I havena been just verra weel forbye."

"I can see that," returned Dimsie, scanning the woman's haggard face with a look which she made as professional as she knew how. "Would you care to tell me what's wrong? I might be able to help you a little."

Despite her diffident tone there was a sympathy about her which reached Miss Withers through her armour of reserve, and Dimsie got through to her as she had a knack of doing. Soon she was sitting down, listening with attention to a confused list of symptoms, and offering such suggestions as occurred to her.

"But much the wiest thing you can do," she finished, "is to see a doctor."

Miss Withers shook her head, and her lips closed in a straight line.

"It would be the best plan," urged Dimsie earnestly.

"I canna," said Miss Withers briefly. "I dinna like the man at Dunkirnie."

"I'm sorry. I wish I could help you more; but there's one thing I know of which might do you good if you care to try it. I make it from herbs, and it won't taste nice, but I'll bring you some tonight, and you can give it a trial."

"I'm no mindin' the taste," said Miss Withers, adding,

120

with an effort at graciousness: "There's no real doctor would tak so muckle interest, and I'll be verra thankful for onything that you think micht benefit me – and for your kindness to the bairn too."

"Oh, nonsense!" said Dimsie. "She's a poppet." She hesitated for a moment, then went on: "I don't want to seem curious, but may I ask who she is? She told us her parents were dead, and that she lived with you."

Miss Withers darted a quick look of suspicion at her visitor. She had a rooted dislike for any sort of gossip, and took a malicious pleasure in baffling any of the neighbours who came to her with questions about Lintie. But this was different; something about Dimsie's sympathetic face disarmed her, and she found herself saying half-grudgingly:

"I wish I kenned. As far as I can tell, the lassie has nae yin but me to turn to, and whiles it gars me fret. It's no the burden o' her keep and clothing, ye ken – yon's naethin' ava – but there's no school here, and I canna just see the sense of sendin' her awa', and her sae young and timid. However, the Lord'll likely provide."

A point on which Dimsie quite agreed, though she was much too shy to say so. Instead she said goodnight to Miss Withers and hurried home through a spattering shower, with a pleasant glow of interest and excitement. Here was an opportunity for using some of her laboriously gained knowledge. After all, it was only what that remote great-grandmother had done with so much success.

Half an hour later Pamela, having returned from golf, was drawn to the kitchen by a strange and fearsome smell for which she could not account. There she found Dimsie intent on a saucepan in which she was stirring a curious greeny-brown brew.

Pamela stood in the doorway and sniffed.

"What in the name of all that's abominable—" she began. "I could smell it as I was coming up the lane!"

Dimsie turned a hot and abstracted face towards her.

"I *know* it's the best thing possible for indigestion," she said. "Several herbalists have said so, but it has to be very carefully boiled and strained. You might go and ask Mother if she has any fine muslin. I daren't leave this."

"I'm only too pleased not to stay," returned Pam cordially. "But you are not preparing this concoction for our supper, I hope?"

"Help! Is it time to get supper? No – I've found a patient, and I am making some medicine for her which I promised to take down tonight. Yes, open the window if you like, but I can guarantee that the smell won't get into the supper."

"A smell of that strength and magnitude would get into anything – *anything*!" declared Pam fervently and fled.

CHAPTER 12

Dimsie Gets Up Early Again

Summer merged uneventfully into autumn, and the household at Twinkle Tap went placidly about its daily business, taking life as it came, and on the whole enjoying it very well.

Mrs Maitland found plenty to do in the house and flower garden, and her interests overflowed into the village below. It was she who had tactfully persuaded Miss Withers that it would be a kindness to them if she allowed the Lintie to come up the hill for her lessons every morning; and though it was beyond even Mrs Maitland's power to cajole any further information about the child from her self-appointed guardian, Miss Withers made no secret of the fact that it was a relief to have the Lintie's education provided for in the meantime.

Mrs Maitland had insisted that Dimsie and Pam must take their share in teaching the Lintie, and – though somewhat alarmed at first – they had entered into it enthusiastically. Pamela taught her music and gymnastics, while Dimsie took her for maths and geography, and the rest was left to Mrs Maitland, though Jean rowed over from Kilaidan twice a week to teach her what she called "the rudiments of English literature".

"Which consists of your telling her stories for an hour on end." said Dimsie. "If they were boiled-down classics I wouldn't mind so much, but half the time you make them up yourself."

"But they're very good and quite thrilling," said Pamela. "I've seen *you* listening enthralled yourself."

"I admit it, but that's not the point," persisted Dimsie. "Can Jean's inventions possibly be classed as English literature, or improving to the young?"

"In this case anyhow the young enjoys herself, and so does Jean. Besides – you never know – her works may be English literature some day. Even Scott and Shakespeare had to start somewhere, remember."

"Humph!" said Dimsie, and went out to cut balm.

The literature lessons had to be suspended when Mr Gordon arrived at Kilaidan, bringing a houseparty for the shooting, and all Jean's time was required as hostess. Erica Innes, her father's secretary and their old school friend, came as well, and shook Loch Shee (according to Pamela) with her energy and her keen interest in all things political. The other three were delighted to have her with them, and secretly much entertained at the respect with which her opinions were treated by the majority of the houseparty. They did not hesitate to contradict her right and left for the good of her soul, and heated discussions raged as fiercely as in the days of the old Anti-Soppist League at "Jane's", when Erica had been its President, and a most autocratic one at that.

"It's such a comfort," murmured Jean contentedly, one day, when words had run very high, "that Eric can no longer quell us with her old slogan: 'Am I, or am I not Head Girl of this school?'"

"But the day will yet come," said Dimsie darkly,

"when Erica in an impassioned speech to the House of Commons, will demand: 'Am I, or am I not Prime Minister of this country?' and Mabs Hunter, up in the reporters' gallery, will burst into tears——"

"What for?" interposed Erica scornfully. "Mabs has too much sense."

"Ah! but old memories will prove too strong for her, and she will become as wet as Rosamund Garth – and Jean will immortalize your speech in a poem which shall ring through the length and breadth of the land, and every verse shall end with the tuneful if pathetic query: 'Am I, or am I not?'"

"I think you talk an amazing amount of rubbish," was Erica's reply, but she was secretly rather pleased.

They spent most of their time at Kilaidan during those weeks. Pamela, Jean, and Erica went out frequently with the guns, but with this form of sport Dimsie sternly refused to have any dealings.

"It's brutal," she declared. "How anyone can *enjoy* going out and slaughtering poor little innocent birds is completely beyond me – especially when you are not very good shots, and may wound without killing."

"But the birds—" began Pamela.

"Oh, don't tell me the birds enjoy it! I know that was your favourite argument about foxes when I told you what I thought about hunting."

And since neither side could convince the other, Dimsie remained behind with her herbs, while her three friends went off to the muirs suitably armed.

"Though at least," Dimsie thought, as she went about gathering seed for the winter drying, "all this activity is making Pam look so much happier. If it would only last!" she added with a sigh, "but she always slips back again when the excitement is over. I wonder if she ever means to tell me about it all. And yet she has said just enough to make it impossible for me to consult Erica or Jean. Poor Pam! it must be very trying not to know whether one is in love or not."

Dimsie had plenty of other things to think about just then. Her garden had flourished, even under her in-experienced hands. Its output was so good that Dimsie had been able to supply all her customers, and the money she earned was to be invested in seeds and plants for next year. She had decided to enlarge her boundaries, and was taking in a piece of the adjoining field (mostly already Twinkle Tap property) in order to fill it mostly with the herbs for which she had found the largest demand.

But all this, encouraging though it was, delighted Dimsie less than the fact that her remedies were becoming known in the village. It happened that her evil-smelling brew had made Miss Withers feel so much better that the dressmaker's taciturn tongue was loosened for once, and she told her neighbours of this extraordinary gift for healing that the "Young leddy up at T'inkle Tap" possessed. The neighbours received the news without surprise; Miss Withers was not a native of Lochside, but those who were assured her that it was only to be expected in a direct descendant of the Grey Lady.

"Fine we kent hoo it would be when Geordie telt us she was delvin' awa' up yonder amang the yerbs and her with the Grey Leddy hersel' to help her," observed Geordie's mother by way of matter-of-fact explanation, and old Grannie Dunn hobbled up the brae, that very evening, to inquire whether Miss Maitland grew a suitable remedy for rheumatism.

The herbalist herself, being very conscious of her inexperience, was rather alarmed at first when all sorts of small ailments were brought to her for advice. Her recent reading, combined with such medical studies as she had been able to take up seriously during the year before her father's death, all tended to impress her with her own extreme ignorance, and, eager though she was to follow in Great-grandmother's footsteps, she shrank from trying rash experiments quite so soon.

"Colds and cut fingers I don't mind having a go at," she told her mother, "if they are not too bad, but when Mrs McAndrew turns up with a cyst on her eyelid, it's really beyond anything I dare tackle. She *must* go over to Dunkirnie and see the doctor."

"She simply won't, I'm afraid," said Mrs Maitland, looking worried. "She is in terror lest he should cut it out, and certainly he isn't the sort of man to whom I should care to go myself, for all his cleverness."

"It would be a good deal better anyway than coming up here to me," said Dimsie decidedly. "An eyelid is a thing I'm quite incapable of dealing with. You must make her go to Dr Beale."

Mrs Maitland did her best, but without success.

"It's no use, Dimsie," she said next day. "As far as I can discover, if *you* can't help her, no one else is to be given the chance. She is very nervous and quite crafty enough to know that there is no question of cutting where you are concerned. Have you really got no suggestion to offer?"

Dimsie looked worried.

"Of course there's appleringie," she conceded, "but I don't know whether it would do any good."

"Try it," Mrs Maitland urged. "It doesn't sound as though it could do much harm, anyhow."

Dimsie went down the garden for a handful of southernwood, which she infused and took the bottled concoction down to Mrs McAndrew with injunctions to bathe her eyelid at frequent intervals; but she first extracted an unwilling promise that if the lotion failed, her patient would consult Dr Beale. It happened however that, far from failing, the lotion proved an entire success, and Dimsie's reputation became more firmly established than ever.

At this time her conscience was weighed down by the weight of her unfulfilled promise to Peter Gilmour. She had not made friends with the Lintie's Ogre, nor helped him in any way, simply because no opportunity had arisen for doing so. It seemed he never left Laurel Bank from one week to another, except on the rare occasions when he boarded the early ferry, and sometimes remained away until the following evening. At these times, according to village gossip, great cleaning operations took place in the house, but as no outside help was ever engaged for it, further information failed to leak out. Neither Orde nor his housekeeper ever attended the village church, and the door had been closed to the minister when he made his duty call.

Peter himself had not been down to the neighbourhood again since that morning when he and Dimsie had rescued Waggles, and she wondered uneasily whether he had really meant it when he said that her promise was a weight off his mind.

"I *must* try and do something somehow," she groaned to herself one day, looking down upon Laurel Bank's chimneys from her stone bench beside the hedge of foxgloves now cut back for the autumn. "But I don't know how I could have been so idiotic as to *promise*. It's worse than Mrs McAndrew's eyelid – unless I can take that as a good omen. Besides, the whole thing is so complicated by Pamela's behaviour at lunch that day. I feel certain he is mixed up in some way with her problems, and if so, she can't possibly want to meet him."

128

Dimsie frowned as she stared down at the roof which sheltered *her* problem; it seemed to become harder to solve the more she thought about it.

"I can't ask Mother to invite him to the house even if I had a good excuse for doing so, because I'm not going to have Pam upset just as she is beginning to cheer up a little. And yet, if he can't be asked up here, how on earth am I to keep that absurd promise? It's high time I set about keeping it if I'm going to do it at all, but I wish Peter Gilmour would come down again, so that I could explain and get him to let me off—"

She stopped short as another difficulty occurred to her, and threw herself back on the bench with a despairing laugh.

"But I couldn't explain to him without giving Pamela away! How horribly complicated it all is! And yet Kenneth Orde must be helped because he is unhappy. Well – difficulties are made to be overcome. I must just try to have an inspiration."

No inspiration came at the minute, but something occurred the very next morning which served to lessen Dimsie's worries a little.

It was glorious September weather, and knowing that she was to spend most of the day at the Gordons', she had got up early, as she often did, to work among her herbs so that she might be free later on. The most urgent job was to cover her peppermint plants with leaf mould, in view of the colder weather which everyone expected to set in soon; but when she had run down the stone steps and through the gate in the yew hedge, she found that Geordie had forgotten overnight to bring up the barrowful of mould which she had ordered.

For a few minutes Dimsie stood still and told herself plainly her opinion of the forgetful George; then she looked about her, and felt more inclined to forgive him. The sun had only just risen, and a lemon glow over the dark mysterious hills at the head of the loch still reflected the eastern glory which must lie hidden behind the woods above her. Dimsie drew a long breath of satisfaction as she inhaled the thousand fragrances which went to make up her garden; then she swung herself nimbly over the dyke and dropped on the dewy slope of the field below.

"There's nothing else I can do," she told herself, "thanks to that lunatic Geordie! so I may just as well enjoy myself."

She paused for a moment, undecided whether to turn right, along the brow of the hill, or left towards the empty high road; not for long, however. Naturally, she always preferred the wild places, and she soon made her way through the fields and along the edge of the hill where it overhung a small coppice fringing the shores of the loch.

"I know!" she exclaimed. "I'll look for mushrooms!"

It was quite lonely here. The shoulder of the hill shut off all sign of the village or of the straggling houses below Twinkle Tap. Even Twinkle Tap itself was hidden behind the hump, and Dimsie had no companions except the larks and rabbits. Growing tired of her unsuccessful search for mushrooms, she clambered on a large boulder and sat there, hugging her knees; then because the birds sang, she sang too in a happy, crooning voice which was not very powerful but sweet and clear as a flute.

Down in the wood below Kenneth Order heard her as he pushed his way through the wet undergrowth, and stopped to listen, his hand raised to hold back a branch obstructing the path. Dimsie's voice reached him as a thin trickle of pleasing melody, and curiosity brought him to the edge of the trees, where he could see her perched on the rock high above him. The early sun burnished into a halo the short chestnut curls clustering round her neck and ears; and her face was tilted to enjoy the morning sun.

"No wonder Peter was impressed!" he exclaimed. "I didn't notice that there was anything unusual about her when she invaded my place, except perhaps her temper! She looks less alarming though, this morning."

Kenneth Orde was far from being a hermit naturally, but he had taken his troubles hardly, and had no wish even yet for human sympathy or companionship, being obsessed by a morbid shrinking from pity in any shape or form. For months now he had lived practically shut up in his house; yet now he was suddenly tired of his self-imposed solitude. Perhaps it was the strong winelike quality of the autumn air, or the singing up on the hillside. At any rate he started to climb up a circuitous path which would bring him upon her before she was aware of him. He could not altogether rid himself of the idea that the sight of him, even with a mask on would be sufficient to make anyone run away.

But Dimsie had seen his tall figure come to the rim of the wood and pause in its shadow; still singing, she watched him disappear behind the bend of the slope, and guessed what he was planning. She had a strong impulse to run away. She wanted this autumn dawn and the beauty of it for herself alone, undisturbed by other people; but remembering her promise kept her there, and once again fates were suspended by a slim thread. If Dimsie had slipped away – if Orde had found her rock empty, the rest of his life (and someone else's) might have been poorer for the loss of an opportunity upon which hung more than either he or Dimsie guessed at the moment.

The song sank down into humming again, and then died away altogether as Orde appeared above the steep dip on her right.

"Good morning," said Dimsie calmly. "Why didn't you come the straight way up?"

CHAPTER 13

Dimsie Tries To Keep
A Promise

For a moment the newcomer looked nonplussed, then he replied honestly:

"Because I hoped to catch you unawares. We got on so badly together at our last meeting that I was afraid you might run away if you recognized me. Please go on singing."

Dimsie had been delighted at this chance of at last keeping her promise to Peter, but with the reference to their last encounter a spirit of contradiction entered her, and she shook her head.

"I don't *sing*," she replied demurely. "I only make a happy noise when I feel moved to do so – which I don't now."

"I see," he remarked with a touch of bitterness, scraping a patch of lichen with his stick from the boulder at her feet. "My coming destroyed your inspiration."

"Oh, no!" answered Dimsie, still perverse. "I don't think that affected it one way or the other."

"I shouldn't have been surprised," he said dejectedly, sitting on a small rock below her, and balancing his stick across his knees. "I can hardly have this depression so badly myself without infecting my neighbours."

Dimsie relented instantly. There was no doubt of his unhappiness – a state of affairs which (quite apart from her promise) was not to be tolerated if she could by any means set it right. There and then she recognized him as a lame dog, and her heart went out to him accordingly.

"You couldn't possibly infect me," she assured him. "I don't get depressed very easily, being naturally cheerful. But I can't sing to anyone other than myself, because that isn't my line."

"I know what your line is," he responded. "One couldn't be long in Lochside, even living a hermit's life as I do, without hearing of 'Miss Maitland and her herbs'. It is very evident that the mantle of the Grey Lady has fallen upon her descendant, judging by the cures you obtain."

"Oh, don't laugh at me!" protested Dimsie hastily. "I am trying to learn all I can about my herbs, and as quickly as I can, but you don't know how ignorant I feel when people come and ask me for things."

He glanced at her curiously.

"But you *believe* in your remedies, don't you? Gilmour – you know Gilmour – tells me you mean to be a herbalist."

"Of *course* I believe in them," she answered without hesitation, "but I know practically nothing at present, though I get hold of all the books I can and study hard. The trouble is that we have no doctor near here, and the village people won't wait for me to learn. They seem to think I am my great-grandmother reincarnated with all the knowledge it must have taken her *years* to learn."

There was a moment's silence during which he studied her in detail from behind his mask, and found her very attractive.

"I should like to see your Garden of Healing," he remarked presently, breaking into the dream which had fallen upon her as she gazed across the quiet loch to the brilliant woods above Kilaidan. "Do you think I could come and see it, and meet your mother, if I'm vouched for by Gilmour?"

The bare suggestion of such a step was a great advance for him, as Dimsie knew, yet remembering Pamela, she grew suddenly crimson with embarrassment, to his astonishment.

"Oh, I'm so sorry!" she exclaimed. "Mother would be delighted – she always enjoys meeting new people – but I'm afraid you mustn't. It's very difficult to explain – in fact I can't explain at all – but you *mustn't* come to the house. It's really rather important that you shouldn't."

His utter astonishment completed her distress.

"Of course I shan't then. I quite understand," he assured her untruthfully, but she stumbled on in embarrassment.

"Oh, no, you don't! You can't possibly. I seem destined always to be rude to you, whether I mean it or not – and just when we were beginning to get on so well too! Why did you suggest coming?"

"I'm extremely sorry," he apologized, more bewildered than ever. "I certainly would not have done it if I had known. But we did seem to be getting on better, and I was curious to see your garden."

Dimsie brightened a little.

"If that's *all,* we could manage it," she said in tones of relief. "You could come up through the field and climb the dyke at the corner behind the summerhouse where it's a little broken – that's how I got out just now. You see, I can't have you coming to the house in the usual way, but tomorrow – no, Thursday—" rapidly calculating that Pamela had arranged to go out shooting that day: "if you will come then at four o'clock – over the dyke – we can have tea in the summerhouse, and Mother will be very pleased to meet you."

134

A struggle was going on in Orde's brain as to how he should receive this curious invitation. Nothing that Peter Gilmour had said had given him reason to believe that Dimsie Maitland of Twinkle Tap was even eccentric, much less out of her mind, yet her behaviour at present was, to put it mildly, unusual, and gave him a faint thrill of curiosity. Looking up suddenly, he caught Dimsie's eyes fixed on him anxiously.

"Do say you'll come!" she begged impulsively, fearful lest the opportunity to help him was about to slip through her fingers after all. "I want you to come rather badly – for reasons of my own. I can see you are wondering if I am quite crazy, but I'm not. I can't explain, but please trust me, and promise that if Mother asks you to the house, you will always make some excuse to avoid going – at least unless you can see by my face that it will be quite safe."

"Oh!" he exclaimed, more and more intrigued by her strange requests. "Then it will be quite safe *sometimes*?"

"It might be," answered Dimsie guardedly. "But you will be guided by me, won't you?"

He hesitated for one moment longer, then threw back his head in the first real laugh he had known for months.

"All right," he cried recklessly. "I'll put myself in your hands, and promise anything which will get me into that garden. This is the most fascinating mystery I've come across for a long time, but I'm prepared to trust you completely. It's very brave of me, when you come to think of it, for that great-grandmother of yours narrowly escaped being burnt as a witch, and Lochside claims that her mantle has fallen on you."

"It wasn't burning she escaped," corrected Dimsie. "They suggested tying her to a stake in the loch, to see whether or not she would drown, but the suggestion apparently was not popular. Talking about mysteries – do you know who the Lintie can be?"

"I? No. She has been to see me once or twice since that unfortunate episode with the dog – I fancy the books are the attraction – but I have not returned the call, so haven't yet met her Miss Withers."

"I wish you would call," said Dimsie eagerly. "It's most puzzling, and Miss Withers doesn't encourage idle curiosity, but she might open out to an author. All the village people are tremendously impressed by your profession, you know."

"I don't call on people casually," said Orde abruptly.

"No," answered Dimsie sympathetically, "I know you don't just *now*, but when you begin again, you might be able to get something out of Miss Withers because you are a novelty. The child *must* have some relations who ought to provide for her."

"I hate going among people – especially village people," Orde confessed abruptly, moved to confide in Dimsie as people who talked with her usually did. "They don't interest me from a professional point of view. I've never attempted rural stories."

"But if you could *help* them in any way," Dimsie persisted, "you would go then, wouldn't you? And I believe you could help poor little Lintie. You must see she needs someone, and it's probably you."

"I don't see how you make that out," he argued, startled at having this responsibility suddenly thrust upon him. "Why should Miss Withers open out to me when your blandishments have been in vain?"

"But I haven't blandished," objected Dimsie quickly. "I couldn't, because I felt it wasn't my business, and I don't suppose it would have been any good if I had."

"I fail to see that it's more *my* business than yours."

"Well, it perhaps isn't – except that someone should do something about it, and you're the most suitable person."

"But why?"

Dimsie shifted her position on the rock, with a sigh for his failure to understand.

"Because," she explained patiently, "almost everyone else in Lochside has tried and failed. Mother, the minister, Mrs McIvor – they've all tried in different ways to get some information out of Miss Withers, and each one has come away defeated. She suspects them of curiosity, when all they want is really to help Lintie. But I can't help feeling that she might confide in *you,* if only because she would be so surprised at your questioning her at all. Moreover, in a small place like Lochside an author is much more awe-inspiring than even a minister."

He looked up at her with a humorous twinkle gleaming through his mask.

"None of which reasons seem to me at all good enough," he remarked drily. "I suspect you, Miss Maitland, of being in league with Gilmour to force me to take an interest in my neighbours, and I don't intend to – not at present, anyhow. Tell me what you were singing as I came up the hill. I didn't recognize the tune."

Neither apparently did he recognize Dimsie's embarrassment at the accuracy with which his random shot had gone home. She hastily welcomed this change of subject.

"It was only a setting of 'Pippa's Song'," she said, "and probably no one would have known it in any case from my performance. But I sang it because it fitted in so beautifully with the morning."

Before either of them could speak again, the bells in the village church below them, hidden by the hill, chimed eight o'clock.

137

Dimsie whirled to her feet, and sprang down with an impetuosity which dispelled all serious thoughts.

"Did you hear that?" she exclaimed. "And it's my turn to get the breakfast! What a blessing it's eggs today, and three minutes will do them! Goodbye – I must run all the way. Don't forget Thursday, and be sure you come by the dyke."

She was gone before Orde had time to protest or say goodbye. But, having no eggs to boil, he stayed where he was long after she had gone, and the bitterness in his heart seemed a little less.

By being extremely speedy Dimsie had breakfast on the table punctually at eight-thirty, but she said nothing of her recent adventure until she and her mother happened to be alone together later in the morning, Pamela having run down on an errand to the village shop. Mrs Maitland heard Dimsie's story to a finish, and then remarked doubtfully:

"My dear, I don't know that I altogether like those early morning rambles of yours. You always seem to encounter some eccentric young man who is not around at other hours."

"Oh, Mother!" exclaimed Dimsie reproachfully. "You can meet Perter Gilmour at any hour when he happens to be in the neighbourhood – and as for the Ogre today – why, that was pure coincidence, though I admit he is seldom seen outside his own garden. He is coming to ours on Thursday though, for I invited him to tea in the summerhouse to meet you, so you will be able to see him for yourself."

Mrs Maitland looked up from the peas she was shelling, and gazed thoughtfully at her daughter.

"I thought he was a complete hermit," she remarked, "that he never went anywhere or saw anybody."

"He doesn't," answered Dimsie, polishing silver,

"but he wants to see my herbs, so I said he might come. You see, Peter Gilmour is very anxious that Mr Orde should be taken out of himself, so I was very pleased when he asked if he might come. Perhaps between us we may manage to cheer him up."

"Another lame dog, eh?" Mrs Maitland asked, with an enigmatic smile.

"That's it," replied Dimsie, rubbing her forks with cheerful vigour.

CHAPTER 14

An Infusion of Marigold Flowers

The Ogre duly came to tea on Thursday (over the dyke as directed) and was introduced to Mrs Maitland, who liked him because she pitied him. Though she chose to smile at Dimsie's passion for lame dogs, Mrs Maitland had a strong preference herself for the lonely and unfortunate, and it seemed to her that Kenneth Orde was both. He on his part was enchanted by the "Garden of Healing", as he called it, and showed great interest in the new piece of ground which Dimsie was taking in from the field beyond, and which was already being dug up and prepared for next spring's planting.

"You will never be able to manage all this by yourself," he declared, as she explained her different arrangements to him, and how the ground was to be divided up for various herbs which required special situations.

"I shall have a clump of larches here to break the wind – oh, yes! I can manage with Pa – with my friend's help, and Geordie's, if I work a bit harder than I have done this summer. But it's awkward at present because the new part isn't half dug, as you can see, and Geordie has inconsiderately sprained his ankle. The gardener hates heavy work like this, and besides, he objects to the herb garden being enlarged, so I can get nothing done just now."

"That's a job I could do," observed Orde, eyeing the rough ground before him. "Would you let me help you?"

"Oh, would you?" cried Dimsie impulsively. "It would be very kind, and I have been so cross about the delay. Now, if you were to——"

She stopped abruptly, remembering Pam who was so constantly with her among the herbs. She didn't want to decline the Ogre's valuable help for his own sake as well as hers; indeed it would be difficult to do so now that she had already half-accepted; yet she was equally anxious to shield Pamela from any embarrassing meetings such as instinct warned her this would be.

"I wonder," she said, coming to a standstill, and looking at him anxiously, "whether you would mind digging only in the morning before breakfast? I can't exactly explain, but – but it would be easier to fit you in then. It's the time when I do a lot myself, and my friend hates early rising, so she isn't there to help at that hour – in fact, if it suited you, it would be more convenient all round."

Orde watched her in amazement, wondering what could be at the bottom of it. He had already seen enough of Dimsie to be sure she was no flirt, but her behaviour was often extremely puzzling. Could it have any connexion with this friend of hers who was absent this afternoon? Probably the friend suffered from excessive shyness, or – was it possible that she might be a little deficient mentally? With this latter idea in his mind the Ogre resolved to be exceedingly tactful.

"As it happens that hour would suit me better than any other," he replied eagerly. "I don't like to be seen about in the daytime with this thing on," touching his mask. "I'm aware that it makes me rather comic, but I should look much worse without it."

"The accident left you badly scarred, didn't it?" answered Dimsie compassionately. "I suppose you wouldn't care—" she stammered a little. "I came across a remedy for that sort of thing – scars, I mean – in one of my herb books lately. Perhaps you might like to try it. It couldn't possibly do any harm—"

She broke off nervously, because it had taken some courage to put forward this suggestion which had been lurking in her mind for several days. Knowing how sensitive he was about his disability, she would never have dared to mention it if he himself had not introduced the subject.

He looked at her keenly through the mask.

"Do you think it would do any good?" he asked.

Dimsie twisted her hands together. She was so eager to help, and so fearful of any false step.

"I can't tell," she answered honestly, "for I've never tried it before, but it might, you know. I got it out of an old recipe-book of Great-great-grandmother's, which I found shoved away behind some books in the library, and I made up some of the lotion then and there, to have it handy. I can give you some this afternoon, if you will only try it."

He smiled at the pleading note in her voice.

"You're keen on your job, aren't you?" he said. "What's in the stuff?"

"Marigold flowers – and other things," said Dimsie. "I could follow the recipe exactly because all the plants (or their descendants) are growing here where Great-great-grandmother left them. Will you try it?"

He hesitated a moment longer, then answered:

"Thanks. As you say, it can do no harm, if it is rather in the nature of an experiment."

"I wish," said Dimsie earnestly, "you'd try to have a little more faith in it, at the same time. You really might, you know. I don't believe any medicine is much good without it."

He laughed outright then.

"Do you go in for faith-healing too?" he asked, but she shook her head.

"It depends on what you mean by faith-healing. I think mind can conquer matter half the time. Now, go back and talk to Mother in the summerhouse while I run in for a bottle of the lotion. But you must be careful to use it in just the way I tell you."

"Mother," said Dimsie, later on, when their guest had departed, "I want you to do me a great favour if you don't mind, without asking why."

They had remained out in the old summerhouse, which was built to catch and hold all the warmth of the afternoon sun. Mrs Maitland looked up from her embroidery, an elaborate piece of cross-stitch, and studied her daughter's flushed embarrassed face.

"Carry on," she answered smiling. "I warn you I shan't undertake to purchase a pig in a poke, but I don't mind listening."

"There's nothing difficult about it," said Dimsie earnestly, "none whatever. It's just that you won't tell Pam we had the Ogre here today."

Mrs Maitland's work fell into her lap, and her thimble rolled under the table.

"Why on earth not? You are the most extraordinary girl, Dimsie!" she exclaimed.

Dimsie bent to capture the rolling thimble.

"I'm not," she protested. "I'm really very simple when people understand me. But helping the Ogre is going to be a very complicated business, for reasons which I can't explain. If I could, it would be less complicated. I just don't want Pam to know he is coming to Twinkle Tap, that's all."

"But he tells me he is coming to help you with these new herb-beds. You can hardly prevent her from seeing him then."

"I have already," answered Dimsie promptly. "I've told him he must only come before breakfast when he will be quite sure of finding me alone. He didn't mind a bit, so you needn't look like that. He said he hated people seeing him in that mask. And you know we shall be perfectly safe from Pamela then; she's never down in time for breakfast."

"My dear Dimsie!" was all Mrs Maitland could find breath to say at first, but presently she added feebly: "I don't want to put foolish notions into your head, darling, but – but I wish you would try not to treat young men exactly as you do your girl friends. After all, they are slightly different when you come to think of it."

"Oh, not much, Mother," argued Dimsie. "Of course the poor Ogre is different from most people, but that's because of his troubles, and they are what make him interesting. Without them he would be just a very ordinary person like any of the men at the houseparty over at Kilaidan, and I shouldn't bother about him at all. I only wish he was, and then I needn't have all this trouble keeping him from Pam!"

"But is that really necessary?" asked Mrs Maitland, still feeling rather weak.

"I'm afraid so. I can't explain, but you will have to take my word for it, Mother dear."

"Well, there is one thing for sure," announced her mother, driving a very firm needle through the canvas on which she was working; "old Sandy must go down and help with this digging in the mornings. He needn't do more than he is able, but he must *be* there."

"He won't be much use," said Dimsie, "but perhaps if he potters about, it will look rather less like taking advantage of the Ogre's kindness by putting him on the job alone."

"It will," agreed Mrs Maitland, "though that was not exactly what I was thinking of. Why, what on earth is wrong now?"

For Dimsie had whirled to her feet, nearly upsetting her mother's workbasket in her hurry.

"I nearly forgot to run down and put that camomile fomentation on Geordie's ankle, and there's barely time before dinner. Goodbye for now, Mother, and thanks for promising not to tell Pam."

It happened, however, that Dimsie's complicated plans for befriending the Ogre were suddenly and unexpectedly simplified next day. Pamela received an invitation from Miss Yorke to spend a fortnight at the old school, and play in a hockey match which was being arranged for Old Girls versus "Jane's".

"Oh! I *must* go!" cried Pam delightedly. "I haven't been back for eighteen months, and I'm longing to see the old place again. Dimsie, you see what Miss Yorke says? If you can come too——"

"But I can't," said Dimsie decidedly. "I mustn't let myself think of it even for a moment, so don't tempt me. You see, there's Mother and the garden, and the expense of that long journey twice in six months. But you go, Pam, and give them all my love. Better ask Rosamund to put you up for another fortnight while you are down in England anyhow. She wanted you in the spring and you couldn't go, so she ought at least to have the chance of you now."

Pamela's eyes shone.

"I shall love it," she said simply. "But I shall miss you and Mrs Maitland, and Twinkle Tap. It's nice to think you are here to come back to again."

"And we shall miss you," returned Dimsie promptly. "I promise that when you return I shall go all the way to Glasgow to meet you. I'm quite looking forward to it already."

"Come up and see me off," suggested Pamela, "you and Jean. It will mean getting up at the crack of dawn to catch the early boat for Greenock, but that will be no hardship for you, though I'm less certain about Jean."

Jean, however, was quite ready to rise to the occasion in both senses of the word, and the three set off in great spirits one shining autumn morning, when the sea-lochs and the open Firth vied with each other for beauty, and the Highland mountains stood clear and blue to the north, with no tantalizing cloud-wreaths to veil their magnificent outlines.

Having waved the traveller off on the London train, Dimsie and Jean went shopping in Sauchiehall Street, and finally had an early lunch in the restaurant to which Peter had introduced Dimsie on a former occasion, though she made no mention of this to Jean. It was during the meal that Jean suddenly leaned across the small table and asked abruptly:

"Dimsie, what's wrong with Pam?"

Dimsie shot a startled glance at her; then lowered her eyes and replied evasively:

"Nothing at all, this morning, I should say. She seemed to me remarkably cheerful."

"Much more so than usual," assented Jean drily. "Have some more salad. I don't mean she has been going about with a long face, but you know as well as I do, Dimsie – and probably better – that Pamela is not happy."

Dimsie gave up her attempt to bluff since it was obviously useless, and admitted soberly that she was afraid Jean was speaking the truth.

"Of course I am," said that astute young lady calmly,

trying to attract the attention of an elusive waitress. "What's more I can tell you what is at the bottom of it – in my opinion Pam's in love."

"I'm very much afraid you're right," agreed Dimsie ruefully.

Jean laughed out.

"Don't look so mournful. (Apricots and cream for two, please, waitress.) That in itself isn't a tragedy, and it's what most of us will come to sooner or later."

"I hope *I* shan't," said Dimsie hastily. "I shall do my best not to at any rate, and I'm well prepared. I feel quite sure it can be avoided."

"What a lot of nonsense you talk, Dimsie!" said Jean compassionately. "I haven't succumbed yet myself, but I know that much. Besides, why should you want to avoid falling in love?"

Dimsie wriggled in her seat, and crumbled her roll impatiently.

"Because it makes people stupid, and spoils everything. Look at Pam."

"That's when it goes wrong," explained Jean with superior wisdom, "which isn't always necessary."

"I suppose," said Dimsie, "being a poet, you know all about such things by instinct, but I'm not, and it seems to me that Pam hasn't gained much by it, if that's what's the matter with her. Perhaps being back at Jane's may do her good. I'm glad you spoke about it though, Jean, for I've been worrying to myself, and it's a relief to discuss it with someone."

"There doesn't seem to be much we can discuss," returned Jean. "It must be pretty bad when she hasn't talked to *you* about it, Dimsie. It's the first time I can remember an Anti-Soppist being in trouble and not pouring it out to you. No? – nonsense! Going to Jane's can't have any lasting effect, though it may divert her for the time being. Who is that man with the nice face? He seems to be heading straight for us, and I don't know him from Adam!"

Dimsie glanced over her shoulder and gave a cry of pleasure.

"Why, it's Peter Gilmour – my train strike man, you know – I told you about him. He is a great friend of mine now, and I haven't seen him for weeks. How do you do, Dr Gilmour? I am glad you happened to come in, for I've got heaps to tell you. Jean and I are going back by the afternoon ferry, and I was just saying – Oh, I'm sorry! I forgot. Dr Gilmour, Miss Jean Gordon."

Her rapid change of note from the unconventional to the severely prim made her companions laugh and broke the ice, though Jean scanned Peter narrowly when he turned to answer Dimsie's questions, and came to the conclusion that he was very attractive. She ate stewed apricots pensively, listened to their conversation without attempting to join in, and learnt from it that Peter Gilmour had at last finished his studies, and was looking for a practice.

"I've heard of one or two." he said vaguely, "but I haven't decided anything yet. It needs thinking over. How's Orde? Seen him lately?"

"Yes, indeed!" said Dimsie cheerfully, pleased that she had a satisfactory answer to give. "He has been to tea with us, and he is coming up in the mornings to help me with my digging. So you see I didn't forget my promise, though it wasn't easy to find a way of making friends with him immediately."

Peter nodded his approval.

"I knew you'd manage it somehow," he said gratefully. "That was why I made you promise. Herbs getting on all right?"

"Yes, thank you. I have started dosing people with them too – in fear and trembling."

"But no one has died so far," observed Jean, laying down her spoon and fork. "You don't deal in poisons, do you, Dimsie? You'd better begin your pudding, or we shall miss that ferry."

Peter accepted this hint to go, and said goodbye, adding:

"I shall be coming over to Lochside one day next week, so I shall hope to see you then."

"Yes, do," said Dimsie. "We shall be delighted to see you."

When he had gone Jean sat in silence for a few minutes, studying Dimsie as she hurriedly finished her meal.

"You are peculiar, Dimsie," she said, as they prepared to leave. "Somehow you're not a bit like other people – not even like the other girls from Jane's, though I always think we are unique!"

CHAPTER 15

Peter Grows Confidential

Pamela being gone, Dimsie imposed no further restrictions on Orde's visits to Twinkle Tap, and they became the best of friends. He had won her heart by his readiness to try her lotion of marigold flowers, because (as she candidly explained to him), though the villagers were almost over-eager to try her remedies, she had not expected anything but scepticism from her friends.

"So you can't think how comforting it is to find an *author* ready to give it a try," she declared triumphantly. "I felt quite encouraged when you took that bottle the other evening."

"But are authors a specially disbelieving type then?" he inquired, with amusement.

"I don't know much about them," said Dimsie, "except Sylvia Drummond, who was head girl at Jane's when I first went there. I suppose you have read her books? And Jean Gordon over at Kilaidan. Not that she's any kind of an author, but she is trying hard to be a poet, and some of her stuff isn't at all bad – though it would never do to let her guess it."

"There spoke the true critic!" he retorted. "And why not, may I ask?"

"You don't know Jean," said Dimsie shrewdly. "If she's given an inch she'll take a mile, and become thoroughly – 'soppy'. Yes, I know that's an old schoolgirl's expression, but I've never yet found a suitable translation for it in the language of grown-ups. To do Jean justice though, she's only 'soppy' in the matter of poetry; with everything else she is perfectly sensible."

"Does she believe in your herbs?"

"I expect she would, but I haven't had a chance to try her out yet. Jean is disgustingly healthy. Ogre, do you think – I know it's rather early to judge – but do you feel as if that lotion was doing you any good yet?"

"I only started it four days ago," he protested. "You mustn't expect miracles. But to tell you the truth – if I'm not imagining it – one scar does seem a trifle fainter."

"Good!" cried the herbalist, with great satisfaction. "No – you would be more likely to imagine the other way, so I think there really must be some improvement. Let me know when you need another bottle."

"And what about your fee?" he inquired.

Dimsie looked rather taken aback.

"I don't know enough to charge fees yet," she said. "I'm only experimenting, and ought really to pay you as a 'guinea-pig' – the villagers too, if they only knew it."

"I shouldn't tell them," he said, his eyes twinkling behind the brown velvet mask. "But suppose your treatment does me good – I must owe you something then."

"All right," she agreed, a gleam of mischief dancing suddenly in her eyes. "If my marigold lotion cures you, then you can repay me by doing something for the Lintie. Is it a bargain?"

"It is," he responded. "With the need for my mask gone, I ought to be brave enough to face even Miss Withers."

The digging of the garden proceeded, and with it the friendship, while Mrs Maitland looked on and listened with a good deal of enjoyment, for the Ogre had travelled widely and was very interesting when he chose to talk. On some subjects he was strangely reserved, and seemed relieved that his new friends respected these. He never referred to the accident which appeared to have made such a difference in his way of life, nor would he discuss his work or divulge his *nom de plume.*

"It's very aggravating," said Dimsie, one day, to her mother, "because from what Peter Gilmour said, he must be rather famous, and we might just as well know it, and enjoy him accordingly."

"Perhaps he will grow more communicative as he gets to know us better," said Mrs Maitland. "We seem to have progressed fairly fast during the past week." She looked up from her mending with a quizzical smile, and went on: "Dimsie dear, I don't know what your reasons are for keeping this young man and Pamela apart, but won't you find it rather hard to manage when she comes back again? He seems to have the run of the garden now, if not the house."

Dimsie frowned.

"I know, but she won't be back for a month yet, and by then the garden will all be dug. We can only go on living one day at a time, and hope for the best in the end."

"That's all very fine and philosophical," remarked Mrs Maitland drily, "but you can't drop the unfortunate man entirely when he has finished digging your beds for you."

"Mother! You know I shouldn't dream of such a thing!" cried Dimsie, horrified. "We shall have to plan some sort of arrangement – I could meet him and take him for walks – but don't you think it would be best to tell him honestly he mustn't come to Twinkle Tap if Pam's about?"

"He might ask why," suggested her mother. "You can't expect everyone to control their natural curiosity as you have trained me to do."

Dimsie looked unhappy.

"I suppose he might. I shall have to think this through. It would be a great pity to stop him coming here when it seems to be doing him so much good. Haven't you noticed how seldom he makes those nasty bitter little speeches now? And his hands have almost stopped shaking, so his nerves must be improving."

"Thanks to hard work in the open air," commented Mrs Maitland, but she admitted later to Daphne, when she came down for the weekend, that Dimsie herself had been a large factor in the cure.

"No one can be melancholy long beside her cheerful, matter-of-fact friendship. She works beside him down there among the herbs, and they have the most extraordinary conversations; but Dr Gilmour knew what he was about when he prescribed Dimsie for his friend."

"But what about Dimsie herself, Auntie?" asked Daphne, a little anxiously. "Do you think it's quite wise from her point of view? She is too good to fall in love with a neurotic invalid."

"You could hardly call him that," answered Mrs Maitland, laughing a little. "Besides, Dimsie is singularly fancy-free. Not for ever, I'm sure, but I don't think Kenneth Orde is the kind of man to attract her, nice man as I believe him to be, behind his problems. And even though there were a risk, how could I prevent Dimsie from holding out a helping hand to anyone in need? I have always believed that Dimsie was born to be a healer."

"But if she gets hurt herself in the process?" objected Daphne.

Her aunt's face saddened.

"Don't you think that is inevitable, my dear? There never was a healer in this world who escaped personal suffering; their own powers are not complete until they know by experience the sorrows they are trying to comfort. It must come to Dimsie as it does to everyone with her enthusiasms and her affectionate character. Her gift of sympathy is natural, but complete understanding can only come through experience."

"So you really think Dimsie is destined to heal other people?" said Daphne.

"I have never doubted it," Mrs Maitland replied, "since first I saw the way she was developing. People are endowed with the qualities which they will need most in their lives. Don't look so regretful, Daphne dear! Whatever destiny awaits her, Dimsie will always be happy – you may be certain of that."

"Oh, I am!" returned Daphne, laughing, though her eyes were suspiciously damp. She had a very special affection for her Dimsie.

Down in the herb garden, meanwhile, Dimsie was entertaining Peter Gilmour, who had announced himself by leaping the low dyke, and very nearly landing on the bed at which she was working.

"Good afternoon," he said with a grin. "I hear this is the route by which you prefer people to arrive when they call upon you, so I instantly adopted it."

"Don't be absurd!" retorted Dimsie, smiling. "You wanted a short cut from Laurel Bank, that was all. When did you come down?"

"Last night – so you see I have lost no time. I wanted to congratulate you upon your patient's improvement. It's wonderful what you have done in a fortnight. What's the secret?"

154

"Oh, I just tried to make friends with him," answered Dimsie placidly. "He seems to like having someone to talk to." She put down the light spade with which she had been sprinkling leaf mould on her peppermint plants against the coming of late autumn frosts, and led the way to the stone bench.

"I'm much more interested in him now," she announced, "because I have begun to like him. Tell me something more about him – the sort of things I can't very well ask him myself."

"What sort of things?" asked Peter, perching himself on the dyke beside her. "Some of Orde's troubles I can't talk about even to you."

"Why *even* to me?" queried Dimsie, her eyes widening.

"Oh, I don't know! You're the sort of person to whom people do tell things. I shouldn't be surprised if Orde told you some himself before long."

"Neither should I. My friends generally do," said Dimsie placidly. "But I don't think he will ever tell me how the accident happened, for instance, because he seems to shrink from referring to it at all. I suppose that's the shock."

Peter turned away his head to watch the afternoon ferry beating her way up the loch; the throb of her engines reached them distinctly across the stillness of the golden October day, and with it an occasional gunshot from the hills opposite, where the remnants of the Kilaidan party were still in pursuit of pheasants.

"No," he said at last, and there was a strange note in his voice. "Orde will never tell you that, but it isn't because of the shock that he prefers not to discuss the affair. You see, the truth is," he spoke jerkily, "it was *my* fault."

"Oh, I am sorry! It must make you feel so – so—" He turned at the sound of her compassionate tone, and she was

155

startled by the look of pain which twisted his face till she hardly recognized it.

"It makes me feel a careless, obstinate pig!" he exclaimed forcefully. "It happened up in Glasgow, one evening, in my little lab. I was trying a certain risky experiment which he warned me was dangerous, but I wouldn't listen, though I knew the risks even better than Orde. He had dabbled a bit in chemistry for his own amusement, and sometimes came in to help me, but he was worried about the job we were on that evening. Well, the upshot of it was that the thing exploded, and he got in the way and saved me at the expense of terrible injuries to himself. We thought he would lose his sight. I shan't forget those weeks in a hurry!"

Peter shivered while Dimsie said nothing, struck dumb by a vivid realization of what his feelings must have been.

"Orde used to be a very good-looking man," Peter went on presently. "You have never seen him without that mask or you'd know how terribly he has been disfigured. No wonder he feels sensitive about it and wants to bury himself down here. Those scars are terrible, and I doubt if he will ever lose them – not for a very long time, anyhow. Now perhaps you can understand why I'd move heaven and earth to help him in any possible way. To think you've wrecked another person's life by your own obstinacy – and that person your best friend——"

"Oh, I do understand!" exclaimed Dimsie quickly. "But after all, it's you I am sorrier for. Only you mustn't reproach yourself too much, for that won't do any good, and he is getting better – you say so yourself. Why must his life be wrecked just by that, terrible though it is?"

"You don't know *everything*," returned Peter. "His spirits are better – thanks to you – but that's only a small

156

part of the problem. You're right though; self-reproach on my part won't do much for him. If I could find his sister – that might."

"Why?" asked Dimsie in surprise. "Has he got a long-lost sister?"

Peter hesitated for a moment, looking at her doubtfully; then he said:

"I don't see why I shouldn't tell you. There's no *secret* about it, though unluckily there's a lot of mystery; and if I could clear up the mystery I should feel I'd paid a small part of my debt to Ken. Yes, he had a sister a year younger than himself, his only relation, in fact. She was very brainy and was at Cambridge, though I don't know what she meant to be when she had finished. Anyhow, she fell in love with a man whom she met, strangely enough, here at Lochside when she and her brother were down for one of their vacations. Orde didn't like the man – thought, for one thing, that he had no right to get involved with a girl when he apparently hadn't a penny to bless himself with – so feeling seems to have run pretty high on both sides, and when she went back to college they didn't part on the friendliest terms. Orde had to go over to America on business connected with his books (he was just beginning to be famous then), and he stayed away a year altogether, working up material for his next novel, the setting for which was to be Canada. He came back to find that his sister had been married nine months before to the man she had met at Lochside, and from that day to this he has completely lost sight of her."

"What an extraordinary story!" exclaimed Dimsie, as he paused for breath.

Peter nodded.

"It is strange, isn't it? Of course Orde could find her if he chose to make inquiries, but his incredible pride would

157

never let him take the first step. I've had a sort of idea at the back of my mind for some time," he added, "that if I could only trace the girl, it might be a small compensation for the damage I've done."

"Was he very fond of his sister?" Dimsie asked.

"Very, but they were both hot-tempered, and neither of them was prepared to give in to the other. Orde broods about it, and it is affecting his recovery, but I can't get him to do anything about it, though I expect he'd be grateful enough if it were done for him."

There was a long pause, broken at last by Mrs Maitland calling them to tea from the house above. Dimsie rose.

"Thank you for telling me," she said earnestly. "It makes me sorrier still for both of you, though I do think he is rather silly. If I can help you in any possible way, please tell me. You will promise, won't you?"

He looked at her serious face, and his own suddenly brightened.

"Of course!" he answered, "I don't know any one to whom I'd sooner turn if I were in a mess."

CHAPTER 16

The Lintie Advertises
For Relations

The snow was falling over Lochside in a soft whirling cloud, blotting out the water and the hills beyond it, and powdering the Lintie's green coat and woolly cap till she looked like a toy figure from a Christmas tree as she trotted home, with the faithful Waggles at her heels as thickly powdered as herself. November was bringing an unexpected foretaste of the winter, which did not usually set in there until after Christmas, but Lintie rather enjoyed it than otherwise. She and Waggles had taken a parcel from Miss Withers to a Mrs McIvor who lived in one of the straggling houses at the opposite end of the village near Laurel Bank, and the Lintie was thinking hard about some of Mrs McIvor's remarks.

She had been invited indoors (without Waggles) while the worthy lady opened the parcel and examined its contents, just in case, she explained, Miss Withers might have forgotten to put in the leftover bits.

"I don't think she has forgotten," said the Lintie seriously. "Miss Withers is always most perticklar about things like that. She says it's commononesty."

"Quite right too," agreed Mrs McIvor, nodding her head as she untied the string, while Lintie watched her hair anxiously; it was built up in an elaborate edifice of curls and seemed in peretual danger of toppling over. "A most respectable woman, Miss Withers! Very openhanded too, as you have good reason to know, for not every woman in her position would have taken in a poor little friendless waif to be a burden upon her. It's quite something to feed and clothe a growing child, these days, my dear, and I hope you are properly grateful to Miss Withers for all her generosity."

The Lintie regarded her with troubled hazel eyes.

"I think I am," she said seriously, "I do try to take care of my clothes and not eat too much. What does 'waif' mean, Mrs McIvor?"

The lady unfolded the parcel before replying, and shook out the garment it contained.

"H'm-m!" she said. "Yes, I think that dress should be quite successful if it fits as well as it looks. Maroon was always most becoming to me. I remember my father noticing my complexion when I was a girl – eh, what, my dear? A waif? Oh, a child who has no relations to provide for her, and has to be looked after by strangers. Yes, you can run along now if you want to, and here's a biscuit to eat on the way."

"I'd rather not take the biscuit, thank you," replied Lintie, though not sure how to explain why she refused; somehow she did not think Mrs McIvor's biscuits would taste good. "I expect I'm not specially hungry," she added by way of explanation, and went off to rejoin Waggles, who was waiting in the porch where he could shelter from the snow.

The Lintie ran home along the loch-road and through the village as fast as her feet would carry her. She was haunted by an uneasy feeling that in some way she was defrauding Miss Withers, and that the matter ought to be set right at once. As she pushed open the door of the dressmaker's cottage, she was guided by the whirr of a sewing-machine to the living-room on the right of the tiny hall but first of all she paused to hang up her damp outdoor clothes on a peg behind the door. Lintie had spoken the truth when she said she was careful of her clothes.

Miss Withers, gaunt and fair and faded, looked up with tired eyes from her work as Lintie came into the room, and a smile flickered over her worn face.

"Come away ben, bairn," she said. "Did you get wet with all yon snow?"

"Not very, thank you," said Lintie seriously. "And Mrs McIvor said the dress was most becoming. Miss Withers, am I a burden to you?"

The dressmaker started, and a flush of indignation rose to her cheek.

"That you are not, my lassie, and never will be! Who's been putting havers like that into your head?"

Lintie knelt on the shabby rug before the fire, and began to rub Waggles down with an old duster.

"Mrs McIvor said so. She called me a name that I don't remember, but it means a person who has no relations to look after her, 'cos I asked. Miss Withers, why am I that thing – a person with no relations?"

Miss Withers's skilful fingers were manipulating a hem before slipping it under the needle of her machine. She did not reply for a moment, but her thin eyebrows met in a sharp frown.

"What for can folk no mind their own business?" she muttered angrily in that mixture of Doric and English which she used to mark her superiority to "the village wives". "I didna send ye to Mistress McIvor's to hear her say such things! Just you forget them, like a good wee lamb, and I'll find you some pieces to dress your dolly."

"They wouldn't be any use, thank you," said Lintie sadly, as she rubbed away at Waggles's right back leg

161

with considerable vigour, "'cos Dolly's dead unfortunately. She died of pewmonia yesterday, and I buried her in the back-green just before the snow came on. That was why I wanted the old shoebox."

Miss Withers shook her head and clicked down the foot of her needle-shaft.

"She was gey old and shabby-like," she admitted, "but no so far gone as all that. Still you can dig her up, the morn's morn, if the snow clears away."

"No, I shan't," said Lintie decidedly. "She's thoroughly dead. Miss Withers, why haven't I got relations like other children? Of course I know Daddy was a relation, but have I got any left on earth? Surely they can't all have gone to heaven. Haven't I got any auntie-sort of relations?"

"I don't know, dearie," said Miss Withers, intent on her seam. "I never heard of any, and there wasn't any letters to show you'd got aunts – or uncles either, for the matter of that. If you had, I'm thinking they'd have looked for you before now. Three years it is, come Christmas, since your poor dear father was taken."

She sighed a little and broke her thread with a sudden snap. Lintie put the damp duster near the fire, and came to her friend's side with a look of anxiety which made her appear much older than her years.

"When you sigh like that," she said earnestly, "it makes me feel just like a burden. What made you sigh, Miss Withers? Please tell me truthfully."

"You'll not be much the wiser when I do," said her guardian kindly. "You see, dearie, it's like this – I canna expect the ladies up at T'inkle Tap to go on teaching you, week in and week out, as they've done for near on five months now. No but what they're willing enough, but it's not just the thing to be aye takin' favours. Yet schoolin' ye maun get, and how am I to give you what's your due? The school-board officer was here again the day, and though he seemed content-like when he heard where you were gettin' your lessons, that is no to last. In the end I'm feared they'll make me send you away to school. That's what garred me sigh, and it's for that reason only I canna but be wishing you had some relations to do the right thing by you."

The Lintie dropped down on the rug beside Waggles, and stared thoughtfully into the fire. That fire was their one luxury, fed all winter by faggots gathered in the woods during the summer months. There were times when Lintie, with the enchanted eyes of her age, saw June sunshine glowing through the flames, or wonderful red-and-gold leaves drifting among the embers.

"I expect," she said slowly, "I have got some if we only knew how to find them. I suppose you don't know how, Miss Withers?"

"No, dearie," said the dressmaker, "or I'd have set about it long before this, though it would be for your own sake and no one else's."

She started her machine again at top speed to make up for lost time, and the conversation dropped. But an idea had grown up in Lintie's mind, which she soon put into execution. Next morning found her, on her way back from lessons, marching up the snowy path to the Ogre's door. The Ogre himself saw her from his study-window, and quickly came to let her in.

"Hullo, Lintie!" he said. "Come to see the books?"

She shook her head.

"How do you do?" she said formally. "I've come on business."

His eyes twinkled down at her through the holes in his mask.

163

"Come in," he said hospitably. "What's the business? You've brought the inevitable Waggles, I see."

"He isn't inevitable!" cried Lintie, quick to flare up in defence of her friend. "He's an angel-dog."

The Ogre ushered them both into his shabby study, where a cheerful fire roared in the grate.

"I'm quite ready to take your word for it," he agreed politely. "And now, what about the business you referred to? What can I do for you?"

Lintie sat down in the armchair he offered her, which seemed to swallow her up completely. Waggles lay down on the hearthrug without waiting for it to be offered to him.

"It's about my relations," she said. "I thought of asking Miss Withers to come with me, but she's very busy, and besides even the best kind of grown-ups don't always understand how important things are."

"I have no doubt," said the Ogre patiently, "I shall understand presently, if you will kindly begin all over again and explain it very simply."

The Lintie rearranged herself in her large chair, sitting very upright with dangling feet, while Waggles shifted his position into line with her, and sat also very upright.

"I want to ask your advice," she began. "I know you don't care very much about being bothered with little girls and dogs, but it's very important, and I thought perhaps it might make a difference to how you felt if we came in politely by the front door instead of through the hole in the fence, as we sometimes do."

"You are quite right," said the Ogre gravely. "It makes all the difference – especially in the case of Waggles."

The Lintie heaved a profound sigh.

"Then p'raps you'll tell me," she said, leaning earnestly towards him, "how to find relations when you need them very badly, and don't know for certain whether you've got any or not?"

The Ogre coughed rather chokingly.

"It's a difficult problem," he remarked in a peculiar and somewhat stifled voice as soon as he had recovered himself, "but I – er – think I should advertise."

"How do you do that?" asked Lintie eagerly. "Does it cost anything?"

"A little initial outlay – yes – but it's sometimes a good investment."

Lintie looked bewildered.

"I don't quite understand all your big words," she told him candidly, "but I s'pose it does cost *something*."

"My fault," apologized the Ogre hastily. "Well, yes, I'm afraid it does a little. I should advise you to read over the notices in the Personal column of *The Times* and compose – I mean make up – one for yourself in the same style. Look here! this is yesterday's paper, and this is the column I'm speaking of. See what you can do with it."

He handed her a sheet of newspaper, pointing to the place she wanted, after which he buried himself behind the rest of the paper and waited, with some silent inward chuckling, which he took great pains to prevent her from detecting. So much dignity in such a small person deserved to be treated seriously and with due respect. Lintie read through the whole column slowly and thoroughly, taking the trouble to spell out difficult words under breath, and at the end she said:

"Thank you very much. It isn't very easy, is it? but I think I see how to do it now." She lowered the paper and looked at him seriously. "I felt sure you'd be the best person to ask 'cos Miss Maitland says you're an author – she says that means someone who makes books, and that they know lots of peculiar things."

"Miss Maitland was pulling your leg," the Ogre said solemnly. "Authors know comparatively little – hardly anything at all."

"Anyhow," said Lintie respectfully, "that must be where you got all your big words. I shan't bother you any longer though, 'cos I must go home and do my notice, and see how much I've got in my moneybox."

She got down from her seat and held out her hand, but an inspiration had come to the Ogre – the first he had had for a long time – and he made haste to act upon it.

"Look here," he said abruptly, "you leave that moneybox alone, because I can get your notice put in for you without that. You write it out and send it to me, addressed as they tell you down here at the foot of the column, and I'll have it put in for you."

"Will you?" asked Lintie happily. "That's very kind of you 'cos then it won't be 'spensive at all, and I haven't got much money in my box – not a very great deal – and it won't buy much. Why will the paper people let you put it in for nothing?"

"That's a secret," he answered promptly. "Perhaps because I'm an Ogre. Run along home now, and write it out. You may come again some day if you like, and bring the animal, but always come through the gate in the usual way. I don't share Miss Maitland's tastes regarding the ways of visitors."

"What do you mean?" inquired Lintie, very interested, but he refused to explain.

"Nothing," he told her. "It's just my silly grown-up way of talking. Goodbye."

But when the Lintie, late that afternoon, handed in her letter, laboriously addressed in her best handwriting, the

Ogre's solid-looking housekeeper opened the door and took it from her on a brass salver, nor did she suggest Lintie came in to see him. In fact, the Ogre was in the grip of one of those black despondent moods which had been much less frequent lately. He sat in the darkened study with his face in his hands, and his mask pushed up on his rumpled hair, nor did he pay any heed to the note which the housekeeper laid on the table at his elbow.

Not until it was time for his solitary meal did he pick up the envelope with a glance at the large crooked characters written on it, and even then no stirring of curiosity prompted him to read its contents, as Lintie had hoped he might do, in case they needed correction. Thrusting his hand into his pocket instead, he drew out some notes, one of which he pushed into the envelope before closing it with a hasty lick.

"That ought to cover it anyhow," he muttered listlessly, "and I suppose the kid will be pleased. Oh well! one must eat to live, but I sometimes wonder why one bothers to live at all in a rotten world like this!"

CHAPTER 17

Dimsie Seeks Advice

Three days later the Ogre climbed the hill again to Twinkle Tap. All trace of the early snowstorm had vanished, and Loch Shee lay still and sparkling under a pale blue sky, while the robins flew busily about the bare woods and hedges, calling to one another with their strange rattling note. His work in the garden was finished, but he felt the need for Dimsie's cheerful company and wondered what excuse he could offer for calling this afternoon. Apparently, however, none was needed. When he walked into the shabby old nursery (which had now reverted to its original style and occupation as stillroom) where Dimsie was writing labels for a formidable row of empty bottles, she greeted him with enthusiasm.

"It seems ages since I saw you," she said with her usual frankness. "I was just wondering what on earth had become of you. By the way, do you want another bottle of lotion?"

"Not yet, thanks," he answered, "but I shall one day next week."

"Well, come and get it when you do. Luckily I made plenty. I sent a sample to a place up in town, and do you know – they've actually ordered a *dozen* bottles. Now, if you'll take that red chair (it has got fewer broken springs than the others) I'll tell you why I've missed you."

"Please do," said Orde, obeying her directions meekly.
"I'm not often missed, so it will be rather interesting to hear
the reason."

Dimsie plunged into the subject at once; it had
evidently been on her mind, for she was very serious about it.

"I want to ask your advice," she explained, laying down
her pen and clasping her hands over the back of her chair as
she twisted half-round to face him. "It's about rather an
important matter."

"My advice is evidently in demand at present," he said,
hitching his chair close to the blazing log fire. "That Lintie of
yours wanted it on Tuesday – came through all the snow to
get it too."

"Oh, *I* shouldn't have gone as far as that," said Dimsie
absently. "But you're the best person to ask because, being
an author, you ought to know."

"So the Lintie assured me," replied Orde gravely. "She
even quoted you as her reference. Really the cases seem very
similar – perhaps you're thinking of advertising for relations
too?"

Dimsie stared.

"Indeed I am not! Was that what Lintie wanted to do?
Poor little thing! I wish I knew how to help her, for I'm afraid
things are very tight just now down at Rose Cottage, and
poor Miss Withers is impossibly proud."

Her face clouded and she gazed sorrowfully at the
flames for a moment or two, while the Ogre cudgelled his
brains for some useful suggestion, but none seemed
forthcoming, and presently she went on:

"No, it's about something different that I want your
opinion. You've heard me speak of my friend Jean Gordon
at Kilaidan – at least that's where she is now, though she

has to live in London most of the year owing to her father unfortunately being a Cabinet Minister."

Orde started perceptibly.

"Is *that* the family she belongs to? Yes, I have heard you speak of her."

Dimsie at the moment was too much absorbed in her subject to notice the peculiarity of his tone.

"Then I must have mentioned her poetry – yes, I remember I did – well, that is what's at the bottom of all this trouble. Poor old Jean is always trying to get herself published; I suppose it's a common enough obsession with writers, but she seems even more set on it than most, and the other day she thought she had a chance at last. Some man wrote to her about her verses, and said that he felt sure that he could come to terms with her about their publication if she would send him a few more poems – enough to make a book. So she did, and some of them were quite good, for Pa – my other friend and I helped her to choose them. But would you believe it?" she paused as though to prepare him gently for the shocking statement which was to follow. "That wretched man wrote yesterday, after keeping her on tenterhooks for months, to say that he could get them produced if she would consent to pay half the cost of publication!"

"Bad luck!" said Orde sympathetically. "Couldn't she get them taken separately in papers and magazines?"

Dimsie shook her head.

"You don't understand," she told him patiently, "though you ought to. What's a stray corner in a magazine or paper compared with a lovely little thin book of your own? Oh, Jean had it all planned months ago, almost as soon as the wretch wrote to her, and though I'm no poet myself, I know just how she must feel."

Her tone implied that the Ogre was failing her

somewhere, and stung him into instant action.

"Does she only write verses?" he asked hastily. "Short stories are a bit easier to place, you know, and I might help you there."

Dimsie's hopes were always buoyant. She looked round at him now with reviving interest.

"Are they?" she queried. "I wonder if the sort of stories she tells the Lintie would be any good. They *sound* splendid."

"At any rate, if she would allow you to show me some of them, I could tell you whether I thought they were likely to succeed. There might be a market for that sort of thing, properly done."

Dimsie brightened.

"I don't believe she ever writes them out, but I shall tell her she must. It will be something to take her thoughts off that horrible man. Have you heard from Peter Gilmour lately? I wonder if he has made up his mind yet about a practice."

Orde gave her a peculiar look.

"Very nearly, I think. He only wants to weigh the pros and cons a bit longer. Old Peter seldom does things on impulse."

"Very wise," said Dimsie gravely. "I often wish I didn't, but I'm afraid that has always been my besetting sin. They used to think at school that I might grow out of it, but I never have."

"I can't imagine," said Orde sincerely, "anyone who knows you wanting to change you at all. Stay just as you are, for there aren't many like you in this wicked world."

"Oh, nonsense!" answered Dimsie airily. "There are dozens, more's the pity! Do you mind passing me the pastepot? It's behind that photo on the mantelpiece – no, not that one – the school group."

Orde obediently rummaged and found the bottle, but in the act of replacing the photograph, he caught sight of one of the netball team on it and stood stockstill, gazing down at it. Dimsie, glancing round to discover the reason for his delay, guessed at once what had happened, and waited rather breathlessly for the questions which she knew would follow.

She had not long to wait.

"Who's that?" he asked abruptly.

"It's the first team at Jane's – the Jane Willard Foundation – my old school down in Kent. At least it was the first team during my last term there."

"But who is that tall girl in the centre?" with a touch of impatience.

"The one with the long hair? That's Pam – Pamela Hughes, our games captain."

He put the photograph back in its place with a hand which shook slightly, and it was a second or two before he turned round again, and Dimsie saw his face. Without appearing to look at it, she noted that what the mask left unconcealed had turned very white. Clearly there must be some connexion between Pam and the Ogre, that each should be so agitated at the mention of the other. Dimsie suddenly took the bull by the horns.

"Why? Do you know her?" she demanded.

But Orde was on his guard.

"I've met her," he answered briefly. "Was she a – a special friend of yours?"

Dimsie carefully applied the paste-brush to a label, and fixed it in place before replying. Something in his tone told her that he wanted to talk about Pamela, and she wondered whether or not it would be wise to indulge him.

"Because I believe he's in love with her, poor thing!" she thought, "and certainly she couldn't possibly care for him. He's not at all the sort of man Pamela would choose – she would want a thoroughgoing sportsman. I can't imagine her throwing herself away on a neurotic author. Besides, it's only too painfully evident that she's in love with someone else, whoever that may be."

Aloud she said:

"I had five special friends at Jane's, but if there were two rather more special than the rest, they were Pamela, and Rosamund Garth. That's Rosamund sitting at the end there, but it isn't a good one of her. This one is much better. It was taken just after she had her hair cut."

But the Ogre evinced no interest in the lovely Rosamund, though the studio portrait which Dimsie handed to him showed her at her best, with her golden hair curling attractively round her ears. He gazed at her absently for a moment; then laid her down on a pile of disordered magazines.

"Very pretty," he said mechanically. "I – I met Pamela Hughes in Glasgow."

Dimsie pasted another label into position, and waited for something more, but nothing followed, so she said, as an experiment:

"She has been staying with us all summer. Did you never see her on the road or in the village?"

"Never!" he answered, with startled emphasis. "You forget that, until I came up here, I hardly left my own garden except for long walks across country after dark, or very early in the morning before anybody was about."

Dimsie's soft heart was diverted at once from the thought of Pamela to her patient's troubles.

"Oh, I know!" she exclaimed sympathetically. "But now that you are better, you won't slip back into those ways again, will you? I want you to come for walks with me

173

sometimes this winter – into Dunkirnie, and all over the place. You mustn't worry about people noticing your mask – they won't look twice when they get used to it. And besides, you won't need it long, for you admit yourself that the marigold lotion is working."

He smiled down at her, softened by her eager sympathy and evident desire to help.

"You are very good-hearted, Dimsie!" he exclaimed warmly, and neither noticed that he had dropped the formal "Miss Maitland". "I said a little while ago that there weren't many like you, and I was right. The only other person who comes anywhere near you is Peter Gilmour. Now he—" he paused abruptly, and then went on: "Would it be boring if I talked to you about something that only Peter has ever even heard me refer to? Sure? There's no earthly reason why you should be bored with my affairs, you know."

"But I *don't* know," returned Dimsie quickly. "If we are really friends, isn't that good enough reason? And nothing ever bores me."

Bending over the hearth, he picked up the poker and balanced it precariously on his fingers.

"It's about Pamela Hughes," he said abruptly. "If she is one of your best friends – if you know her as well as that – you may not be surprised to hear that she is a good deal more to me."

"No," said Dimsie below her breath. "I'm not surprised. I guessed."

"Did you? By my reaction when I saw her unexpectedly in that photograph? One can't hide much from you! I met her a year ago in town. We used to play golf together and that sort of thing. I believe she loved me too – in fact I'm as nearly sure of it as one can be – but we quarrelled over some silly trifle, and then – this happened."

174

"What happened? The accident? But that would have made no difference to Pam," declared Dimsie. "At least, not if she cared about you at all. Pam wouldn't be influenced by an unimportant *outside* thing like that. What did you quarrel about? Perhaps that was less of a trifle to her than your face."

"Possibly," admitted the Ogre, "But do you know, I honestly cannot remember what we quarrelled about. It didn't seem of great importance to me at the time; I thought she would get over it in a day or two. What occurred afterwards put it entirely out of my head. I haven't seen her since, because I could hardly go back to her with a face like this."

Dimsie frowned.

"I don't know why not," she said. "Pamela would only have been so desperately sorry about it that she might have forgiven you for the other thing, which probably wasn't a trifle. I wonder if it's possible——"

She broke off, and studied him earnestly, for she had been on the verge of wondering aloud whether after all, it was Kenneth Orde whom Pam loved. Certainly she had behaved very oddly when she heard him identified with the Lintie's Ogre, and yet he was so entirely foreign to Dimsie's idea of the sort of man Pamela was likely to fall in love with.

"Oh, no! it can't be," she thought, as an unanswerable argument arose in her mind. "Pam *knew* how wretched and miserable and depressed the Ogre was – if she cared about him, she *must* have rushed down to see what she could do, no matter how furiously they had quarrelled. In fact I don't see how she could possibly have stayed away."

This convincing proof as to the state of Pam's feelings made her more careful of Orde's. It seemed too much that he should have the pangs of unrequited love added to his

175

other problems, and in the circumstances she could not decide whether it was wiser to let him talk of Pamela, as he seemed eager to do, or to turn the conversation forcibly into other channels.

"It's terrible," thought Dimsie, "to be so inexperienced in these matters if all my friends are going to fall in love – especially if they are going to fall in love with each other! It will be a terrible nuisance if I find I can't help them without doing the same thing myself. And who in the world could I find to fall in love with, even if I were forced to? I can't think of a single person I could fall in love with."

CHAPTER 18

Dimsie Goes to Town

Depressed by her own inexperience, Dimsie let the conversation drift with the tide, and Orde eagerly made use of this golden opportunity of discussing Pamela with her best friend. He haunted the house more than ever, and even took to waylaying Dimsie on what she proudly called her "rounds" – long trudges or bicycle-rides to outlying farms or cottages where ailing people accepted thankfully the relief which her herbal remedies brought.

Dimsie was slowly beginning to acquire some self-confidence bred of her considerable success, though she still regarded that success as somewhat miraculous. Mrs Maitland, looking on with deep interest, put it down to a different cause; in her opinion it was due to Dimsie's tireless poring over all sorts of herb-lore, ancient and modern, combined with a very real gift for healing which she had perhaps inherited from the Grey Lady. What she studied she remembered, and she appeared to have an almost unerring instinct for applying the right remedy. Frequently her mother sighed for the medical training which had been cut short at its very beginning, feeling that Dimsie, with the advantages which her parents had first intended for her, might have gone far in that profession.

Dimsie, however, appeared to have completely shaken off that disappointment – perhaps because she was too busy to think about it in the whirl of her everyday activities. Though little could be done in the garden at present, the weather was favouring her in another way, for (with the exception of the one snowstorm) the winter was still green and open, which allowed her to put on her boots and search the countryside for roots and plants of various other herbs she wanted for her work. On a good day she would often return with a loaded basket, and though old Sandy turned up his nose contemptuously at the idea of such random transplanting, her spoils continued to grow and flourish, till he was compelled to admit that "Miss Maitland was lucky aboon maist" in her own special line.

She was returning from one of these harvesting expeditions on the first day of December – a clear still golden afternoon which had got left behind from late autumn – a hooked stick in her hand and her basket full of foxglove roots, when she met the Ogre on the road beyond the lochan.

"I was just looking for you," he announced, picking up the basket which she had put down at the foot of a stile she was preparing to cross.

"I know!" groaned Dimsie. "It doesn't matter where or when I go – I always run into you at the end of it. Your intuition is little short of marvellous.";

"Nonsense!" he retorted. "You said on Tuesday that you were going out for foxgloves, and I knew they grew thick in these woods, so I guessed you would be coming back somewhere along this road. I thought of grubbing for some of the plants myself as a little surprise for you, but I wasn't sure if I could recognize them at their present stage."

"I'm glad you didn't, then," said Dimsie ungratefully,

"because I might have had more of a surprise than I bargained for. It would be better if you came and dug with me, where I could see what you were getting up."

"May I?" he asked eagerly.

She remained sitting on the toprail of the stile, her warm brown coat buttoned up to her chin, and a brown woolly hat pulled low over her chestnut curls.

"No," she said slowly, "on second thoughts, you may not. I can't think about what I'm doing, and talk about Pam at the same time. But I'm glad you came to find me today, because I have got something to show you. Jean wrote, this morning – you know she went back to London two weeks ago – and she enclosed a couple of those little stories that she was telling to Lintie."

She dived into her pocket, and produced a long fat envelope which she handed down to him.

"You see how sure I was of meeting you," she remarked. "Will you read them, and tell me what you think? Jean says they are absolute rubbish, much worse than her verses, but I am not so sure."

"I'll look them over with pleasure." His fingers closed on the envelope mechanically, and he thrust it into his pocket. Dimsie, noticing his vague manner, expected their talk to flow immediately into its usual channels, but instead he opened another subject.

"You know the Gordons pretty well," he observed, jabbing his stick into one of the clefts of the dyke. "Do you ever hear them speak of a brother?"

"Oh, yes!" answered Dimsie, rather surprised. "It was very sad, you know. Derrick Gordon died out in the East, three years ago. There is only Jean left now to inherit Kilaidan."

There was a curious silence during which Orde

179

stared into the bare depths of the winter woods, and Dimsie, not for the first time, regretted the baffling mask which hid so much of his expression. She appeared to be always stumbling against mysteries in this strange man. It seemed as though he were on the verge of asking some further questions, but when he spoke again it was only to say gravely:

"So Derrick Gordon is dead? I had not heard of it."

"Did you know him?" she asked.

He roused himself at that, and held out his hand to help her down from her perch.

"I have met him. He knew – a friend of mine. The wind is turning chilly. Shall we move on?"

She said, as they turned towards Loch Shee:

"I've got something else to tell you. Pamela is with Jean just now, and she enclosed a note in hers, this morning, to tell us that her visits are coming to an end. She will be home on Wednesday."

No mask could hide his startled eagerness now.

"On Wednesday?"

Dimsie turned pink, and she gazed straight ahead of her at the gleam of steel-blue water seen through the thinning trees.

"Yes – and when she comes, I'm afraid a lot of this will have to end. Please don't think me horribly rude," she added, turning troubled eyes towards him, "but if you and Pam have quarrelled – if you are not on speaking terms – I can only see you when she isn't with me. You do understand, don't you? It seems better to explain straight out than to – to start being tactful about it afterwards. You might think _I_ didn't want to be friends with you any longer, and you would be quite wrong. Only I don't see how in the world I can combine you and Pam in the circumstances."

He laughed outright at the perplexity in her face.

180

"Rather a difficult position for you, isn't it? But I understand all right, and I'll keep out of your way unless you are alone. By the way," a sudden light breaking upon him, "was that why you made me come over the wall in the early days of our acquaintance? No – impossible! You didn't even know then that she and I had met."

"I guessed something," explained Dimsie, "from Pam's manner when your name was mentioned. But it will be a great deal easier now that I can talk about it openly to you. I'm simply sick to death of mysteries!" she cried, with a sudden outburst of impatience. "As far as I can make out they're all extremely unnecessary, and generally the result of falling in love. Why can't people do it properly or not at all?"

"Depends on what you mean by properly," he replied with a laugh. "It never does run smooth, you know – we have that on excellent authority. But in this case I fear the love is entirely on my side. I don't suppose Pamela gives me a thought."

"I can't be sure," said Dimsie cautiously. "Anyway I must see what I can do, for it's all too uncomfortable and difficult to manage as things are. But I wasn't thinking only of you when I said I was sick of mysteries. There's poor little Lintie too, and that certainly has nothing to do with falling in love. Why can't Miss Withers go and tell everything to somebody who would help her to find the child's relations?"

"Perhaps she doesn't know so very much about it herself," suggested Orde, "and doesn't like to admit it. And that reminds me, I forgot to watch the paper for that advertisement of Lintie's. I bet it was something unique. I wish now I had read it before sticking down the envelope, for she probably meant me to."

"Well, it seems to have brought no results anyhow," Dimsie sighed, as they reached the gate of Twinkle Tap, "and I don't know how they will struggle through the winter at this rate. You'd better come to tea while you still can, Ogre. Mother was going over to Dunkirnie, but she must be back by now."

That evening as Dimsie and her mother sat together over the sitting-room fire, Mrs Maitland asked with considerable interest:

"Have you decided what to do with Mr Orde next week, dear? When Pam comes home again, I mean."

Dimsie looked up from her knitting – a sweater to be presented to the Lintie at Christmas.

"Oh, yes!" she answered at once. "That has worked out better than we expected, Mother. I just told him he couldn't come up when she was here, and he understood at once."

Mrs Maitland's eyes opened rather widely.

"Did he? Well, I think it was very remarkable."

Dimsie retrieved a dropped stitch, and replied, with her eyes on her knitting:

"I don't know that it was exactly. We have been talking about her a good deal lately, because he knows her, you see, and he knows that she doesn't want to be bothered with him just now. Oh, it's all very perplexing, and I wish I could consult you about it, because you know more about these things than I do."

"But you mustn't do that," returned Mrs Maitland quickly. "Confidences can't be passed on. They have to be dealt with to the best of your own ability, and I'm sure you must find your hands full sometimes." She leaned back in her chair and laughed. "Does it never overwhelm you at all, Dimsie?"

"Not very much," Dimsie answered calmly. "Except about the Lintie, and that is weighing on my mind dreadfully just now. If only we were rich enough to adopt her!"

"Or knew someone else who was," added her mother.
"But I fear that's an idle dream."

When Wednesday came, Dimsie, true to her promise,
took the ferry for Glasgow in order to meet Pamela, who was
being driven in from Selkirk by the friends whom she had
been visiting last. There was shopping to be done first of all in
Sauchiehall Street, and Peter Gilmour to be met at the
teashop – by appointment, this time – Dimsie having
summoned him there to a consultation concerning the Ogre.

"He really is improving," she assured Peter with a
beaming face. "His nerves are almost all right again, and he
says my marigold lotion is making the scars fainter. Perhaps,
in time, he may be able to give up that mask."

"He is certainly better," agreed Peter with emphasis,
"and I had proof of that, this morning. Do you know that he
is subletting Laurel Bank, and starting straight away for the
East to work up local colour for a new book?"

Dimsie regarded him with startled eyes, the teapot
suspended in her hand.

"No, indeed! He didn't tell me that, but I have not seen
him for three days – not since he met me coming back from
the woods, and I told him—" She put the teapot down, and
her eyes grew bigger still.

"Do you think," she said, "that may have had anything
to do with it?"

"I should be better able to reply," Peter replied
cautiously, "if I knew what you were talking about."

Dimsie laughed, and resumed her pouring out.

"I told him that Pam Hughes was coming back to us
again – the friend I've come up to meet today. I had
forgotten for the moment that you knew all about that, and
that I can talk to you openly and comfortably. That's a great
relief."

He leaned back in his chair and looked across at her with one of those rare smiles which completely transfigured his face.

"Feeling rather weighed down with it all, eh?" he asked kindly. "I warned you that it wouldn't be long before Orde made a clean breast of his troubles to you, didn't I? You can talk them over safely enough with me. The only fresh item is that you know Pamela Hughes."

"But you must have met her at Twinkle Tap," protested Dimsie, in astonishment.

"It so happens that we were never properly introduced, and I only heard her addressed as Pam, so it didn't enter my head to connect the two. I hadn't met Orde's girlfriend you know, for I was out of Glasgow last year." He leaned across eagerly. "But this is more than mere coincidence – you must see that! I've often thought that if I could get in touch with the girl I might be able to clear up some of the trouble between them, and now she turns out to be your friend! It's a clear case of Providence, of course, and somehow, surely we can put things right, you and I."

Dimsie gazed thoughtfully across the crowded tearoom.

"We ought to be able to," she replied. "Especially if it really is what Providence means us to do; but I warn you I've never understood Pam less than during these last six months, and it's quite possible that I may make an absolute mess of it."

"No fear of that!" he answered confidently. "And think what a wonderful thing it would be if we were only successful. I don't know about *your* friend, but mine has had a pretty miserable time the last year."

"I don't think Pamela has been happy," said Dimsie slowly, "but it may have nothing to do with the Ogre for all that. Have you any idea what they quarrelled about?"

Peter shook his head.

"Not the faintest idea. I only know Orde had a stroke of luck – came unexpectedly into some money – and felt he might go ahead and ask her to marry him; then this trouble arose between them, and before it had a chance to sort itself out, I nearly blew him up through my obstinate stupidity. I've sometimes thought that they might have made it up if they had time and opportunity – but that was where I stepped in. You can understand, can't you, how keen I am to help if it's at all possible?"

"Yes," said Dimsie seriously, "but I expect you'd have been just as keen in any case. Don't you think," she added, smiling suddenly "that it may have been Providence stepping in there too?"

"No," returned Peter. "Taking it all round, I fancy the devil had more to do with that business. You'll try, won't you?" he urged. "I have great faith in your powers of mending matters."

"You are always setting me tasks which I feel are beyond me," she answered ruefully, "but it's like a dare – I feel I can't in honour refuse."

They had finished their tea, and were out in the street again, looking for a bus to take Dimsie back to the station where Pamela was to meet her in time for the boat train to Gourock, when a car suddenly drew up beside them at the kerb, and a hearty voice boomed its greeting. Startled, they turned to meet their travelling companions of the momentous journey in the spring – Barty and Mrs Barty, rosy and complacent, very different from the distraught pair of seven months before, and between them a chubby little girl of Lintie's age.

Perhaps it was the contrast between them which

brought the peaky white face of the Lintie before Dimsie's mind with startling vividness, and she acted as usual on the spur of the moment. Scarcely waiting till the brisk interchange of comment and inquiry had spent itself, she broke in eagerly:

"Oh, Mrs Pritchard – Mr Pritchard – you don't want – I mean you wouldn't like to adopt a little girl who needs a home badly? She's eight years old and an orphan, and I'm afraid she doesn't often have enough to eat. Oh, don't suggest sending her to Dr Barnardo's!" she went on imploringly, as though she read the suggestion in their amazed faces. "She isn't the sort of child who could be sent to a Home. I can't say more than that I'd gladly adopt her myself if I only had the money."

She paused for breath and looked at them expectantly, while Barty exchanged bewildered glances with Mrs Barty, and Peter's desire to break into a roar of laughter was stifled by the earnest look on Dimsie's pleading face.

Mrs Barty was the first to speak, but the words might have been Peter's.

"My dear," she said flutteringly to her husband, "does it not seem to you almost providential?"

Barty shook his ponderous head doubtfully.

"Not yet, my dear, not yet – but I don't say it may not do so presently. The thing is to make some inquiries first. If Miss Maitland will just get into the car – can we drive you to any place, Miss Maitland, where it would be possible to have this out in peace and quiet? Truth is, the wife and I were discussing this very subject only last night – the possibility of finding a companion for Peggy here."

"I've got to meet a friend at the station in half an hour," said Dimsie doubtfully.

"We'll drive you there by a roundabout route,"

declared Barty promptly. "Yes – plenty of time – and you can give us a few particulars as we go along. Must hear about that herb garden of yours too, and how trade's doing. My wife was greatly interested. 'Pon my word, it's the most extraordinary coincidence!"

"Providential!" echoed Dimsie below her breath, with a mischievous glance at Peter, as he helped her into the car. "Then I'd better say goodbye to you, Dr Gilmour."

"For the present," he said. "I shall be down at Laurel Bank within the next few days, and hope to see you then. For sheer nerve and speed in taking occasion by the forelock, you must be pretty hard to beat!"

CHAPTER 19

The Return of Pamela

It certainly seemed something beyond a coincidence which had brought the Pritchards across Dimsie's path that afternoon. As she talked and they listened, even the slow-paced Barty at length caught something of her interest and enthusiasm.

"It may be all right," he said. "She may turn out to be just the child for whom we're looking, but of course you understand, Miss Maitland, we must be careful, and I should have to make very full inquiries – very full. Now, when can I see this child and her guardian? And do you suppose the woman who has her just now would be able and willing to answer all the questions I should have to put?"

Here even Dimsie took fright a little at the speed with which things were beginning to move.

"Oh, I don't know!" she exclaimed. "I hope so. Of course you could go no farther if she weren't – but the truth is that I am speaking entirely without authority. And it would all have to be sorted out officially and legally, I suppose. I don't even know whether Miss Withers would be willing to give the child up. It was only a sudden inspiration which led me to speak to you at all, and I should have to get my mother to suggest it to Miss Withers, and see what she thought. It's sure to be a terrible wrench for her, poor soul! if she has to part with the Lintie, for she is most unselfishly devoted to her. But for that very reason, I don't think she would stand in her way."

"Can't you find out?" asked Mrs Barty's eager voice from her corner of the car. "If your mother were kind enough to sound out this Miss Withers, and you were to let us know – Barty, have you got a card?"

"I'll do my best," promised Dimsie, slipping the card into her purse. "You may be quite sure of that. Perhaps, if it seems hopeful, you could come over and spend a day with us, so as to see Lintie for yourselves? If you like children at all, I don't see how you can help loving the Lintie; she is such a darling, and so quaint."

"Well, even if nothing comes of it," said Mrs Barty, as they drew up at the Central Station to drop their passenger, "I am delighted to have seen you again. My husband and I often talk of you and the young doctor, and your kindness to us that night. We shall never forget it, and it seems as though we ought to be more than casual acquaintances."

"Oh, I hope we shall be!" said Dimsie enthusiastically. "We live at Twinkle Tap, Lochside. I shall write to you as soon as I can, and let you know what happens. Why, I must be late after all! There's my friend waiting for me."

She waved goodbye to them, and ran across the pavement towards Pamela, who was coming to meet her, the light of the frosty sunset on her face. It was six weeks since they had seen each other and Dimsie suddenly realized how pretty her friend was. Was it surprising that Kenneth Orde, or any other man, should fall in love with Pamela?

"If only they'd do it in a ordinary way, and not make such a horrific fuss about it!" thought Dimsie resentfully. "Now, I wonder if she has come back happy."

Pam seemed cheerful enough through the first excitement of their meeting and chatter about old schoolfriends and acquaintances she had met in the south. There were messages to deliver from Miss Yorke and from various girls who had gathered at "Jane's" for the hockey-match, in which, it seemed, Pam had failed to distinguish herself.

"The school won, of course. I know I didn't play my best," she said apologetically, as the train bore them down Clydeside through the gathering murk, "but somehow I hadn't the heart to shoot goals against Jane's – you couldn't have played up yourself, Dimsie. Most of the old girls felt the same. Meg Flynn captained us (I told you when I wrote) and Tony Semple was in the team, and Nell Anderson. Oh! and who do you think drove across from Westover to look on? Fenella Postlethwaite – looking quite human, with her hair nicely cut. She talked plain English too, without any of those long-winded phrases she used to be so fond of. She sent you her love, and hoped you would find time to write to her sometime and tell her about the herbs."

Dimsie chuckled reminiscently.

"I always said there was a lot of good in Fenella if one could only find it out," she observed. "She improved tremendously after that night we spent on the wreck in St Elstrith's Bay. Do you remember, Pam? when we rescued the Vandyck from those Americans."

"Do I remember?" echoed Pam, laughing. "Is it likely I can ever forget? Do *you* remember when we lost ourselves in the smugglers' passages, away back in our Lower Fourth days? There's no doubt about it Dimsie – we used to see life at Jane's."

"We did," agreed Dimsie appreciatively. "Being grown up is nothing to it for a really stirring existence."

Pamela sighed suddenly, and leaned back in her corner as they crashed into a tunnel.

"To be grown up is exciting enough for me at times," she said, "but things don't come right in the end as they used to do in our schooldays. They just drag on and on—"

They had been alone in their compartment since the last stop, and Dimsie crossed over to Pamela's side.

"Pam darling," she said coaxingly, "is the problem no better than it was before you went away? Won't you tell me about it now? You came so near telling me that evening when we rowed back from Jean's, and I've been waiting ever since. Perhaps I could help if I knew."

Pamela sniffed.

"If anyone could help, it would be you, Dimsie, but nobody can – and that's why it's no use talking about it. We've got to learn as we grow older that things don't always come right, that's all."

"But are you *sure,* Pam?" Dimsie's pleading tones went on. "Don't you think, if you've been unhappy about something and brooded over it for months by yourself, it takes on a shape of its own round which it's hard to see? Talk to me about it and let us find out together if there isn't some way to sort things out. Anyhow it may help you to share it with someone else."

"I know it would," said Pamela with difficulty. "I'll try to tell you in the boat, if you're wrapped up warmly enough to stay on deck. We couldn't talk down in the cabin among all the other people. Look! We're just coming into Gourock now."

As the ferry drew away from the brightly lit pier they found a sheltered nook on deck and settled themselves with Pam's thick travelling rug round their knees. It was a frosty evening, but so still that even out on the water they scarcely

191

felt the cold. Beyond the dark peaks of Arran the last of the afterglow still lingered, but the lights were shining out in the little coast towns and villages till they lay like strings of jewels spilled from a broken necklace at the foot of the great black velvet hills. Dimsie and Pam sat in dreamy silence, lulled by the beat of the engines as the boat throbbed its way outwards, and the gates of hidden sea-lochs opened to show more spilt gems on their mysterious shores, before the boat's course closed the passing glimpse again behind the barrier of some steep firclad promontory.

Suddenly the spell was broken by the flash of a white beam lower down the Firth, and Pam spoke.

"That's Toward," she said. "I *am* glad to be back here again," and she began to talk without any further preliminaries.

"You asked me six months ago if I was in love," she said, "and I told you I thought so; but I didn't *think* – I *knew* even then, and I'm doubly certain now! I *am* in love, Dimsie – badly – but the horrible humiliating part of it is that he – the man – doesn't care a scrap for me."

"That's not true anyhow!" exclaimed Dimsie, speaking with the conviction of her secret knowledge. "At least – I mean – any man you cared for would be sure to fall in love with you."

"Unluckily you can't possibly tell!" retorted Pamela very naturally, "but *I* can."

"But how can you?" Dimsie persisted. "Did he say so?"

"Of course not! Is it likely? But there are ways of knowing, let me tell you, beyond any doubt. What would *you* think if a man hung around you for months and then suddenly – just because of a minor quarrel – disappeared without a word of explanation or excuse?"

("Oh!" gasped Dimsie inwardly. "I believe it must be the Ogre after all. I never really believed it before, for all he said.")

Aloud she replied firmly:

"I should simply think that there had been an accident of some sort which had made him very ill, so that he couldn't communicate with me. That's what I should think."

"Nonsense!" said Pam quickly. "Serious street accidents are reported in the newspapers. I never heard anything so absurd!"

"You can have private accidents as well as the street kind," maintained Dimsie, "and those don't often get into the papers."

"As a matter of fact I know he has been ill," admitted Pamela, "though I never heard exactly what was wrong. Still, even when people are ill they recover after a certain time, and then they can write or give some sign – if they want to." She paused, and added in a lower tone: "I told you we quarrelled – not about anything that mattered in the least – but I was wrong, and we parted in anger, and – and he never came back."

Dimsie said with added firmness, being now quite sure of her ground:

"I'm quite convinced there must have been an accident. You may be sure he would have forgotten your silly quarrel next day, and come back again, if something hadn't occurred to prevent him."

Pamela drew herself away a little, and tried to see her friend's face in the darkness.

"But – but what could have happened?" she persisted. "What accident (if it was that) could have lasted all this time? It's – a whole year now, Dimsie."

"You poor thing!" said Dimsie. She was rather

193

at a loss to know what to do next, her natural impulse being to tell all she knew; but for once Dimsie restrained her impulses, feeling that it would hardly be right to betray Kenneth Orde's confidences, even to help him as it appeared to her.

"There's one thing of which I'm perfectly sure," she declared aloud, "and that is that the whole matter is simply a stupid misunderstanding. Don't think he isn't in love with you, Pam, because I *know* you're wrong. I tell you he is – just as certainly as that we are sitting here on the *Caledonia's* deck."

"But, Dimsie," protested Pamela, with a surprise which was not altogether unreasonable, "what makes you so sure about it? It isn't even as though you had even seen us together. Unless you have second sight, how can you possibly tell?"

"Perhaps I have then," Dimsie replied. "Anyhow, I've got a deep internal conviction which is every bit as good. Tell me more, Pam. It will help you now the ice has been broken."

So they sat there wrapped in the rug, and talked in soft undertones while the boat churned its way with a good deal of fuss up to a small deserted pier, where it deposited some mail and two passengers before backing out again, and rounding the point into Loch Shee. High up, as they entered it, they saw the lights of Twinkle Tap gleaming out above the lowlier lights of the village beneath.

"I wonder if the Grey Lady is up there by the dyke, watching to welcome us home," said Dimsie dreamily, but Pamela answered in practical tones:

"She wouldn't bother about me, and you only left her this morning. Besides, it must be too cold even for the Grey Lady on that stone bench tonight."

"I wonder what it is she wants," persisted Dimsie, "which 'naebuddy can jalouse' according to Geordie. I heard a new legend the other day – new to me, that is – which says that she is waiting for love to come into her garden again, as it was when she and her lover spent their happy hours there before he sailed away for ever. I wonder if that is really what she wants. I wish I could 'jalouse', and find some means of giving her troubled spirit rest."

"You needn't worry," said Pam firmly. "If any spirit haunts that garden, it isn't a troubled one. Why, Dimsie, your 'garden of healing' is the most tranquil spot in the world. Just to enter it is to be surrounded by an atmosphere of peace. I felt it whenever I went there, through all my restlessness."

"Oh, Pam!" cried the keeper of the garden, with a glad note in her voice, "what a lovely thing to say! I've often noticed that peacefulness myself, but I thought it was just for me because I loved it so. Imagine if *everyone* feels it who goes in there!"

"I expect they do," said Pamela briefly.

She returned to the subject, that night, when they were brushing their hair beside the fire in Dimsie's bedroom.

"I know I wasn't the first," she said abruptly, "to speak of your 'garden of healing'. Jean told me when I stayed with her in London ten days ago that you said – Kenneth Orde called it that."

Dimsie's heart gave a little jump, but she tried to answer naturally.

"Yes. It sounded so nice and poetical that I thought Jean might like to make verses out of it."

There was a moment's pause while Pamela brushed a cloud of brown hair across her face, as though to conceal it; then she said:

195

"Dimsie, you know so much now, you may as well know everything, because – because I shall have to go away from Twinkle Tap very soon – No! wait a minute, you will soon see why – it was *Kenneth Orde* I was telling you about this afternoon. Now do you understand? It didn't matter before I went away, because our paths never crossed – I never saw him once, not even in the distance – but I know from what Jean said that you and he have become friends, that he often comes to the house, and so – there would always be the danger of meeting—"

Her voice broke suddenly, and Dimsie rushed over to her.

"Pam darling, there is no danger – truly there isn't – and you mustn't talk of leaving us. Why, where could you go, with your home shut up for another year or more? He is not coming to the house again, though I've managed it so that he quite understands, and isn't at all hurt. You see, I guessed you didn't want to meet him. I guessed it as long ago as the day when I first spoke to him, and Jean asked me his name in front of you, though it never entered my head that you could possibly be in love with him. I was careful even then, for he used to come and help me in the garden before you went away, and yet you never met."

"But, Dimsie," Pamela shook back her hair from her pale face and eyes full of unshed tears, "it has been a garden of healing to him – you have helped him in that magical way you have for helping those who need it, and *he* is one of your lame dogs, isn't he? Then how can I drive him out of it all, back upon the kind of morbid seclusion into which he seems to have lapsed before? I *must* go."

"But he is going away himself almost directly," cried Dimsie, playing her trump card. "Peter Gilmour told me today. Kenneth Orde is letting Laurel Bank, and starting for the East, to work up the scene of his new book. So you see you are *not* driving him away, Pam. He is well enough to begin work again, and he is leaving Lochside because of that."

Pamela said nothing for a moment, but sat gazing into the fire with a curious expression, while mechanically fiddling with her soft brown hair.

"So there *was* an accident," she observed at last. "I am beginning to understand. But you see, Dimsie, he has quite recovered from it now, and yet he makes no effort to see me – because he doesn't *want* to!"

"Rubbish!" said Dimsie tersely. "You simply don't understand – that's all. I don't see why being in love should make you so unusually thick. How could you help knowing there had been an accident when you heard he was going about with a mask on?"

"He might have had other reasons," answered Pam vaguely. "I knew he'd been ill, of course – I told you so. Anyhow, the fact remains that he could have come and seen me months ago if he had wanted to, but he obviously didn't."

Dimsie sighed patiently.

"Oh, very well!" she said. "Be uncharitable in your judgements, of course, if you want to, but I warn you it won't make you any happier."

CHAPTER 20

The Lintie's Faith

"Ask and it shall be given you, seek and ye shall find, knock—"

The minister's voice read on through the rest of the passage, but the Lintie's mind was wandering. Not being a very experienced mind yet, it was only capable of holding one great idea at a time, and the one after which it was groping at the present moment was quite large enough.

She looked round the little grey country church, with its clear diamond-paned windows through which could be seen the bare branches of the tall ash trees tossing outside in the kirkyard. She gazed at the choir seated below the high pulpit in their railed-off enclosure, and thought in passing that it was small wonder they looked so important – it was evident that everything depended upon them except, perhaps, the sermon itself. She twisted her head for a glimpse of Mrs McIvor up in the gallery, her hat plastered with feathers, her small gimlet eyes darting to and fro to discover who was not in church, or who – being there – was behaving badly; apparently Lintie came under this last category, for Mrs McIvor gave her a sharp shake of the head, which caused Lintie to twist her head back again hurriedly, and glance in another direction.

Across the aisle in one of the side pews sat the party from Twinkle Tap, and Lintie abandoned her idea for a few minutes, to study her friends. Mrs Maitland sat at the head of the seat, her soft white hair gleaming under her black hat. Beside her sat Pamela, quiet and dreamy, with downcast eyes hiding thoughts which had wandered as far from the sermon as Lintie's own; and next to her was Dimsie, her head tilted back and her brown eyes fixed on the preacher with an eager attention which reproached the little girl back into listening, for Dimsie was to the Lintie a bright and shining example of everything one ought to be if one could only strive hard enough.

"Ask and ye shall receive," the minister was repeating when she began to listen again. "What more simple than to ask for the things we want? The easiest thing possible, yet how many of us do it?"

The Lintie mentally gripped her great idea with both hands and held on tight.

"Why, of course!" she thought, and only checked herself in time from speaking the words aloud. "That's a much simpler way than advertising, and besides advertising hasn't done a bit of good. I never thought of asking *God* before about a thing like that, but perhaps He wouldn't mind. I wonder if the minister would know – he seems to know most things about God."

She was a strange, independent little person, and Miss Withers rarely questioned her movements, having early discovered that the Lintie was always entirely to be trusted; therefore, when she whispered at the close of service that she wished to go and speak to the minister in his vestry, Miss Withers merely nodded and marvelled what whimsy she had got into her head this time, as she watched the small straight figure disappearing through the side door.

The minister of Lochside was an old man and a bachelor, with a very soft spot for the children of his congregation, and especially for the Lintie, with her sad little history. He beamed a welcome to her now, as he turned in his chair to see who it was who had answered his invitation to come in, and put out a hand to draw her to his side.

"Do you want to speak to me, dear?" he asked kindly.

The Lintie looked up at him with clear hazel eyes in which lurked a shade of anxiety.

"Yes, please," she said. "I want to know if I can ask God for anything I like – not just Bible kind of things, but everyday things as well?"

"Why, of course," returned the old man, smiling. "Don't you ask Him for your daily bread?"

Lintie fidgetted from one foot to the other.

"Daily-bread's in the Bible," she answered. "I want to ask Him for something out of my own head that isn't in any proper prayers."

"I understand," said the minister gravely. "Yes, certainly, ask Him. He would like you to do so."

"And will He give it to me?" persisted the Lintie anxiously. "You see, it's terrifically important, and I'm in rather a hurry."

The minister did not reply immediately, but gazed out of the vestry window at the grey waters of the loch tipped with white where the wet wind was raising them into little chopping waves.

"That's often the way, my wee Lintie," he said at last, with a sigh. "I can only tell you for certain that God will give you whatever you ask for if it's good for you to have it, but He may not give it quite as soon as you would like Him to. He sees farther than those big eyes of yours, and He may know that it is wiser to keep you waiting. So, ask for what you want, but don't be disappointed if it doesn't come all in a hurry."

"I see," said Lintie thoughtfully. "I mustn't be impatient. Thank you very much. I just wanted to make sure that God wouldn't mind being bothered by little girls about quite ornarary things."

"You may be quite sure of that," the minister told her emphatically, as he opened the door to let her out.

The Lintie fled home on scurrying feet through the close drizzle which had swept down from the mist-clad hills above Kilaidan. She had a guilty feeling that Waggles, who always knew the time, must have been expecting her home before this. Waggles counted on a run after church, whatever the weather was like, but today he had to wait even a few minutes longer after Lintie's return. Lintie darted up the steep narrow stairs to the tiny cupboard which served her as a bedroom, and dropping on her knees beside the bed, she prayed earnestly:

"Please, God, send me some relations of my own as quickly as ever you can, 'cos this is a very hard winter, and Miss Withers is just at her wits' end, and I'm so afraid of being a waif and a burden on her. Please, God, don't let me have to wait long for them, 'cos we've sometimes been very hungry lately, and there might be enough for Miss Withers if she didn't have to feed me, so let the relations come soon, please – very soon – For Jesus' sake, Amen."

Then she ran down again to attend to Waggles, feeling as though a load had been lifted from her thin little shoulders. She had no doubt that it would be all right now, and only felt inclined to blame herself for not thinking sooner of this solution to her difficulties.

The following afternoon Miss Withers went up to Twinkle Tap to fit Mrs Maitland's new dress, and came home with very red eyes, for which she offered no explanation, and Lintie, with a tact beyond her years, forbore to ask. Deep with in her there lurked a fear that she should hear of some fresh calamity about to fall upon them; so she contented herself with being specially affectionate to poor Miss Withers, and tried not to feel worried when she encountered tearful looks fixed hungrily upon her now and then.

"It's going to be all right in about a day or two," she told herself firmly, "as soon as God sends the relations. It won't take Him very long now."

Next day, however, when her lessons were over, she learned the cause of Miss Withers's depression, for Dimsie said to her, as she put away her pen and exercise book:

"Lintie dear, how would you like to go and live with some nice kind people who have a little girl just your age? They've got a beautiful car and house, and lots of toys and good things to eat, and they want another little girl to share it all with their Peggy. Don't you think it would be nice?"

In a flash Lintie realized that this was the fresh trouble which was hanging over her little household – the possible coming of these kind rich people to take her away from Miss Withers and Waggles. A terrible fear rushed across her mind that this might be the swift answer to her prayer.

"Are they – are they relations?" she asked falteringly. (Surely, true relations would take Miss Withers and Waggles too.)

"Not exactly," said Dimsie, "but they want to be, and you'd find they soon were. I know them, and they're very nice."

The Lintie sat very straight in her highbacked chair.

"If they are not relations," she said firmly, "I'm sorry, but I *can't* go away with them. You see, I'm expecting some real relations of my own almost d'rectly – about the end of the week or p'haps sooner – and it would never do if they came to Rose Cottage and found me gone. It wouldn't seem quite polite to God either, after asking Him most partic'larly to send them quick.''

''Did you ask Him to do that?'' queried Dimsie, hardly knowing whether to laugh or cry at the pathos of the small determined person who was holding herself so extremely upright.

''Yes, on Sunday – so you see, He hasn't had so very long.''

''But don't you think,'' suggested Dimsie diplomatically, ''that He is perhaps sending these people in answer to your prayer. He may mean *them* to be your relations.''

''No,'' said Lintie with decision. ''I asked Him for *real* relations, so I'm perfectly certain He would never send pretend ones. I've only got to wait, and the minister said it might take a little time.''

''All right,'' assented Dimsie. ''But Mr and Mrs Pritchard want to come and see you next week, and if no real relations have turned up by then, you might like to think it over. You know, Lintie dear, it would make Miss Withers happier if she felt you had a comfortable happy home, and everything you needed which she can't give you, however hard she tries. Mr Pritchard wants to come and see her, and hear all about your Daddy, and how he left you with her.''

''There won't be any need,'' persisted the Lintie, with stubborn faith. ''Long before then the real relations will have come, and of course I shall belong to them, and so will Waggles.''

Dimsie let the subject drop for the time being, but her mother had found the dressmaker more amenable, though the thought of parting with Lintie reduced her to mute despair.

"It's no for me to stand in the bairn's way," was her only comment. "I canna provide for her as I would like to do, so if there's others able and willing, it's to them she maun gang. But they'll be good to her, mem? You're able to vouch for it that they'll be good to the wee lassie?"

"I can vouch for nothing," answered Mrs Maitland frankly, "but of course we shall make every possible inquiry before we dream of making any arrangements to hand the Lintie over to them. The minister would be the best person, I should think—"

"Oh, no, Mother!" interposed Dimsie. "He would be too charitable – too easily taken in. Not that I mean for one moment Mr Pritchard would want to take anyone in," she added laughing, "but we ought to be perfectly businesslike about it, oughtn't we?"

"Most certainly," said her mother gravely. "Remember, the responsibility of meddling with the child's life cannot be undertaken in any lighthearted fashion, and you really know nothing whatever about these people. Mr Pritchard himself, in his letter to me this morning, invites the closest examination into their affairs, and gives several references. But if the minister is not to take these up for us, Dimsie, whom can we ask?"

"Dr Gilmour," said Dimsie unhesitatingly. "I know he would do it if we asked him. He would love to help in a case like this, and I have talked to him about Lintie often. Couldn't you write and ask him, Mother?"

Mrs Maitland looked doubtful for a moment, then said:

"If you really think he could find the time, and would not consider that we were asking too much of a comparative stranger——"

"But he isn't a stranger," objected Dimsie; "he's a *friend*. And somehow I don't think anybody could ask too much of Peter Gilmour; he's that sort of person, you know."

So Mrs Maitland wrote, and Miss Withers went sadly about her all-too-scanty employment, wondering whether she would now have been able to keep her charge if she had moved three years ago (when the pinch first began to make itself felt) to the city, where work was more plentiful.

"But I couldn't think to do it," she told herself sorrowfully, "when I minded what the wean's father telt me the night he left her with me. 'Keep her in Lochside, Miss Withers,' he said, 'however many years I may be gone. I have my own reasons for wishing her to be brought up at Loch Shee.' But he never let me ken what his reasons were, and though I've kept by his word as long as is any way possible, I doubt I'll be forced to give it the go-by now. Better she should go with good folk where she'll be nourished and taught as is fitting, than bide on by Loch Shee and be starved."

But tears dropped on the seams of Mrs McIvor's secondbest coat, which had been sent down to the cottage for relining, and Lintie saw them, and took Waggles out into the rain, because the sight of Miss Withers crying made her miserable, and she did not know how to put it right.

"It wouldn't be any good 'splaining to her about the relations," she thought, "'cos somehow grown-ups don't seem to understand. Even Dimsie didn't think that 'Ask and ye shall receive' had anything to do with relations – I *know* she didn't – but the minister said if they were good for me I'd get them, only I might have to wait. And I haven't waited any time at all yet – not really."

Being a reserved child she had not found it easy to mention her prayer even to Dimsie, and the reception her story had met with then did not encourage her to say any more about it. No one alluded to the Pritchards again in her presence. Miss Withers kept silence because she shrank from the painful subject, and the Maitlands avoided it on the principle of letting sleeping dogs lie.

"If you say anything more to her about it," Mrs Maitland warned Dimsie and Pamela, "she will only turn 'thrawb'. Children with as much character as Lintie require such careful handling. Remember this will be a very painful wrench for her, poor little thing! I only hope we are not taking too much on ourselves, but Miss Withers was so obviously relieved by the suggestion, for all her distress at parting with the child – I never knew her so expansive before. She actually confided to me that she had a haunting dread lest anything should befall her, and the Lintie be sent to an orphanage."

"Oh, it's so *sad*!" cried Dimsie, tears springing to her eyes. "But after the first week or so she is bound to be happy with the Pritchards, especially if they let her take Waggles, as they are sure to do. Don't you think we ought to hear from Peter Gilmour tomorrow? It wouldn't take him very long to make his inquiries, and I begin to feel that the sooner it's over the better now."

"I hate to think of Lintie being taken away by strangers," exclaimed Pam suddenly. "She will just eat her heart out, however kind they are. If there was only a way in which we could adopt her ourselves, Mrs Maitland!"

Mrs Maitland shook her head.

"It isn't possible, dear, though I long to do it as much as either of you. It isn't only the present which has to be considered. Whoever takes Lintie now must make himself responsible for her future too. We must wait for Dr

206

Gilmour's report and just hope and pray that things may turn out for the best, and without too much heartbreak for anybody."

CHAPTER 21

Dimsie Puts Things Right

In the midst of all this came Christmas, putting a temporary stop to everybody's plans and arrangements, though the wheels began to revolve faster then ever as soon as the busy week was over. Though chiefly absorbed for the moment in Lintie's affairs, Dimsie had not forgotten the troubles of her other lame dogs, and her heart was set on clearing up the misunderstanding between Pam and her Ogre before the latter started on his trip to the East.

She tackled Pamela first.

"He's going next week," she told her, "and I could wring my hands over you unspeakably stupid pair! It could be put right so easily too. All you need do is to write him a little note, telling him you want to make it up, and he would come here and see you at once."

"Would he?" Pamela's mouth took on a bitter curve. "It isn't quite as simple as all that, Dimsie. If two are needed to make a quarrel, it certainly takes two to mend it, and the first move should come from him."

"Why?"

"Because he is the man."

"But suppose he thinks the quarrel was so bad you can't possibly forgive him?"

"No one but an absolute idiot would think anything of the sort," retorted Pam conclusively. "Besides, he must know perfectly well I was in the wrong. If he really wanted to be friends again, he would have come to see me a year ago."

"But you've forgotten the accident, to which I can now refer openly," Dimsie pointed out. "I don't think you have any idea, Pam, how ill he was after that explosion. Peter Gilmour told me."

"When I heard about that," Pam confessed, "I thought at first it *might* be the explanation of his silence, but afterwards I knew it *couldn't.* If he had minded as much as I did, Dimsie (I don't care if I admit that to you), wouldn't he have come to see me, or written, or done *something* before he left Glasgow? If he was well enough to take Laurel Bank, and travel down here, surely he could have gone as far as Hawthorn Street, first of all. He knew I was there."

"His nerves were all in pieces," objected Dimsie feebly.

But Pamela's answer to that was surprisingly forcible.

"Nerves! Rubbish! You don't know Kenneth Orde if you think that would have prevented him from doing anything on which he had set his heart! His nerves might have spoilt his work for the time being, and caused him to fly from the racket and bustle of Glasgow, but he is not the kind of man to let them get the better of him. Haven't you realized that yet?"

"I've only known him three months," said Dimsie apologetically, "but I must say I didn't think it likely you would care about a neurotic sort of person. It was that which really put me off the scent with you."

"He is not at all neurotic," returned Pamela coldly. "You have only to look at his work to grasp that. All the critics acknowledge that his novels are the sanest, most positive books of the present day."

"I'm sure they do," said Dimsie hurriedly, "but you see, I don't know what they are, for he never will tell me his *nom de plume*."

"Wouldn't he?" cried Pam. "Oh, but I will, because that's ridiculous. He is Timothy Hillier."

Dimsie's mouth and eyes opened wide, for it was the pen name of one of the leading novelists of the day, whose books were devoured throughout the length and breadth of the land from the moment of publication. To think that the Ogre – the man who was in love with Pamela – should prove to be such a famous author! Dimsie's voice was almost awed as she exclaimed:

"Oh, Pam! you are lucky!"

Pamela shook her head with a dreary sigh.

"I thought I might have been – once – but now I wouldn't say as much as that to anyone except you, Dimsie. It isn't very pleasant or soothing to one's pride to feel one has given one's affections where they weren't wanted."

Then, for the first time in her life Dimsie yielded to temptation and betrayed a confidence.

"Don't feel it, Pam, for it isn't true – indeed it isn't," she said earnestly. "I can't see you both making a mess of your lives out of sheer stupidity, and not try to prevent it, though I've no business to tell you – well, what I'm just going to tell you anyway! The Ogre *is* in love with you – he's completely miserable through being in love with you – and he would probably have gone to see you months ago, to try and patch up his side of the quarrel (whatever it was about), but unfortunately he's nearly as silly as you are yourself. It's really extraordinary how falling in love affects people's common sense!"

"Well, get on with it then!" ordered Pamela briefly, feeling with good reason that this was no moment to philosophise.

210

"Well, then, it's because of his face," said Dimsie, plunging headlong into the explanation, lest her scruples should get the better of her before the tale was told. "He has talked to me about you by the hour, whenever he could get me to listen, till I've grown sick of the sound of your name! But he won't come near you because of his scars. I've tried to convince him that you wouldn't mind them a bit, if you really cared for him, but the trouble was that I couldn't be *sure* you did care, and that hindered me from being as convincing as I could have been. I must say," with a sudden sense of grievance, "you didn't behave as though you cared."

"Am I likely to?" returned Pamela, too dazed as yet to grasp the full significance of all that Dimsie was pouring out.

"I don't see how you could help it," said Dimsie. "If I loved anyone – man or woman – and heard they were moping by themselves in a lonely gloomy house, with bad neuralgia and a brown velvet mask on their face, do you suppose I should waste five minutes before I was down there trying to cheer them up?"

"No," said Pam faintly. "I don't suppose *you* would."

"Then will you go down at once, and do it now? He's probably packing right now, but all that will have to be stopped. You'll just have time before tea."

Pamela went red and shrank back.

"Dimsie, you are absolutely impossible! How *can* I do such a thing? Why, I don't even know if he cares—"

But Dimsie had caught her by the shoulders in an exasperated shake.

"*Haven't* I told you he does? Can't you take my word for it? Do you mean to say I've gone and betrayed his confidence – told you things he never meant me to repeat – and it's all for nothing?"

"Dimsie, you don't understand! I – I can't go looking

for him like that. It's not the sort of thing anybody could do."

"*I* could easily," returned Dimsie, and collapsed again on the chair. "I must say I don't understand you, Pam. Here am I doing my very best to put things right for you, and you won't lift a finger to help me, even in your own interests."

But the full meaning of all that Dimsie had told her was at last beginning to take shape in Pamela's mind, confused as it was by the hurricane of argument which was raging over her.

"Oh, but Dimsie!" she cried unsteadily, "you don't know what you've done for me in telling me this! I want to ask you all sorts of questions if you will only listen to me for one moment. You've been absolutely wonderful!"

"Fat lot of good that is!" retorted Dimsie, not in the least mollified, "if nothing more is to come of it than you asking me questions which I probably shan't answer. I've already said a great deal more than I ought to have done, and apparently it's all been for nothing. Tell me this, Pam – if he comes *here,* will you see him?"

"Yes – yes, of course. But he won't come."

"And tell him you love him?"

"Dimsie! Most certainly not!"

"Well, I'm willing to waive that for the moment. You probably will, when you see him. Your own good sense surely must come out in the end. Meanwhile, as far as I can see, the best thing for me to do is to go and fetch him."

She was on her feet and whirling across the room before Pamela could grab her. A protesting cry of "Dimsie, come back!" produced no effect whatever, and a few minutes later the front door banged and she shot past the window. Pamela sank back in her seat before the fire, hardly knowing whether to laugh or cry, and full of half-nervous, half-eager anticipation as to what might happen next. Her talk with

Dimsie had lifted a weight of lead from her shoulders – a weight which she had carried for so long now that she could hardly realize it was gone. Bitter and resentful thoughts melted away in the light of Dimsie's explanation, and it was comforting to feel that she had not, after all, given her affection where it was not wanted – the humiliating fear which had been gradually changing her whole sunny nature during the past twelve months.

Dimsie had set out for Laurel Bank, intending once more to beard the Ogre in his den, though now it was for a very different purpose; but it happened that she did not need to go so far, for at the bend of the road she met Orde himself striding up the brae towards her.

"Hullo!" he exclaimed. "What a piece of luck, for I was just looking for you. In fact, but for my promise, I was nearly coming up to the house."

"And I was looking for you so hard," cried Dimsie impetuously, "that I was – actually – coming down to Laurel Bank. But I'd better hear your news first and get it over, for mine is much more important."

"How do you know that?" he returned, "when you haven't the least idea what I'm going to say. Will you come back to Laurel Bank, then?"

Dimsie paused where an enticing path led off through the wintry woods in the direction of the lochan, with glimpses of violet hills showing between the bare grey stems.

"No," she said. "It's such a glorious frosty afternoon that I want to walk for miles and miles. Let's go up the Lovers' Lane; it's the most appropriate place in the world for what I'm going to tell you."

"Don't raise my hopes too high," he warned her teasingly. "That sounds almost as though you were going to propose to me – Oh, help! if you flash your eyes like that

213

again, I shall run away! Never have I seen such a temper!"

"I know I've got an appalling one," admitted Dimsie, "but I can't waste time arguing about it this afternoon, so I must let your insults pass. Tell me quickly why you were hunting for me on the brae just now."

"Because I have had a note from my publishers," he answered promptly, "from the children's publishers I should say, for whom I do that sort of work. I was so enchanted with those stories you gave me to read just before Christmas that I sent them off to the editor to ask his opinion of them, and the reply came this morning."

"What? Do you mean those stories of Jean's?" asked Dimsie breathlessly. "You *angel*! What did he say?"

"That he liked them so much he was thinking of including them in a new children's annual of theirs, and would be greatly obliged if I could send him Miss Gordon's address."

Dimsie heaved a deep sigh of satisfaction.

"Poor old Jean! She will hardly be able to believe it's true. Success hasn't exactly beaten a path to her door, and now, of course, this is only a beginning; she will go on and do marvels once she has got a start. I must write to her before the post goes."

"Better enclose Heathcote's letter then. Here it is. I am glad I managed to do something about it before going abroad. I'm off next week, you know."

"No, you're not!" cried Dimsie in a triumphant tone which made him to look at her in surprise. "Not if I can prevent it, and I believe I can. When you hear what I've got to say, leaving Lochside will be the last thing you'll think of."

They had reached the stile where he had met her a few weeks before, returning from her search for foxgloves. Dimsie stopped and looked up at him with dancing eyes.

214

"Do you remember what we talked about last time we were here?" she asked meaningly.

He stared at her, getting increasingly puzzled.

"Pamela," he answered. "I'm afraid I've talked of little else to you since that day I found her photograph in the stillroom. Expect I've bored you to tears sometimes."

"Fortunately for me I'm *never* bored," said Dimsie. "But I believe I practically forbade you the house, that afternoon, and now I want to tell you that's all changed. You can come back with me at once to Twinkle Tap, and see Pamela if you wish to – indeed you simply must come whether you wish to or not."

"But why?" was all the bewildered Ogre could find to say, being as taken aback as Pamela herself had been by Dimsie's masterful way of managing their affairs.

"Because she wants to see you, of course," replied Dimsie, leaning back against the stile. "Surely that's obvious?"

"Did she say so?"

"N – no, not exactly, but she meant it all the same. My dear Ogre, I haven't been friends with Pamela for ten years without knowing what she means, whether she says it or not."

He stood in silence for a few minutes, slashing at the withered frozen grasses by the roadside, while Dimsie watched as much of his expression as she could see with rapidly increasing anxiety, which was presently justified.

"I am not coming," he told her, clearing his throat of the huskiness which seemed to have attacked it. "She can't possibly want to see me; you've imagined it out of the kindness of your heart. I tell you we quarrelled at our last parting, and she's just the sort of proud person who would expect me to eat humble pie after that, whether I was right or wrong."

215

"Well?" asked Dimsie. "Surely if you're in love with her, you're not going to make a stupid, obstinate, childish fuss about a trifle like that?"

Silence again, and then the truth came from him in a sort of stifled groan.

"Even if you're right," he cried, "even if she is ready to forgive and forget – how can I go to her like this? She'd shrink from the very sight of me in this hideous mask!"

"Then take it off," replied Dimsie coolly. "I must say I've always thought it was rather absurd. If your face is scarred, what do you suppose Pam will care, except to be sorry? Listen to me, Ogre – I wasn't sure of her feelings before, but now I know them, more or less, and you can take my word for it, she'll forgive you all the faster for those very scars. But you're quite mistaken if you think it's that quarrel she's got to forgive you about, for it isn't that at all."

"Then what on earth is it?" he asked in growing surprise.

"Why, dropping out of her life for a whole year, and never telling her the reason – letting her hear of your accident and illness casually from outsiders months after, and never going near her or writing to her. And I must say," added Dimsie firmly, "I consider she has every cause to be annoyed. You have treated her very badly, and caused her a lot of most unnecessary worry merely (it seems to me) on account of your own personal vanity. I tell you, Pamela will *like* your scars! *Now*, will you go back to Twinkle Tap and say how sorry you are?"

"But – but," he reiterated piteously, "what on earth shall I do if she is revolted by them?"

Dimsie heaved a sigh and turned homewards along the Lovers' Lane.

"Haven't I told you it's the very last thing Pam will

dream of doing? Come along! You really can't waste any more time standing in the middle of the road and arguing round and round in a circle. What you have got to do is to go straight to Pamela, and – well, I'll take all responsibility for what may happen afterwards."

"You're incredibly bold!" exclaimed the Ogre respectfully, but he followed her obediently down the road.

CHAPTER 22

An Unposted Letter

Mrs Maitland called that tea was ready and Pamela rose from her seat by the fire, though hardly yet awake from her daydream. Before she could cross the room, however, she heard the front door open, and Dimsie's voice and step in the hall followed by a heavier tread, at the sound of which Pamela stood still with a startled gasp, both hands twisting the heavy string of blue beads she wore.

She heard Dimsie say:

"In there – the stillroom. You can come in to tea when you are ready. I'll go and tell Mother not to wait, or she will wonder what has happened to everybody."

Then the heavier step came on alone, the stillroom door opened and shut, and Pamela and Kenneth, who had parted in anger a year before, faced each other across a room filled with the conflicting lights of a fire blazing on the hearth, and a frosty sunset, nearly as fiery, blazing along the sky outside.

Pamela faltered and hesitated. Could it be the strange gleams and shadows which made his face look so lean, and showed strange hollows where the mask did not cover it? That hateful disguising mask! Suddenly she stretched out her hands to him with a cry.

"Oh!" she said. "I am sorry – so sorry! You must have

suffered – far more than I realized."

"Did you think about it at all?" he asked eagerly. "I didn't know you had even heard of it. I thought I was too deeply in your bad books for you to care one way or another what happened to me."

A sense of her own grievance came back upon Pamela, aggravated somehow by her intense pity for the big man with his masked features who stood in front of her almost like a guilty child waiting for a scolding.

"So that was why you never wrote or told me? How could you be so unutterably stupid – so unreasonable too, when you knew perfectly well I was in the wrong all through our quarrel! You did know it, didn't you?"

"I – I – yes, I suppose I did – but I didn't know *you* knew it."

Pamela's sense of injury evaporated again as swiftly as it had arisen.

"Well, you know now," she said in a subdued voice, "because I've told you. And – I want to be friends again."

He took a step forward, and gripped the back of a chair with both hands.

"I want to be something more than that," he answered, gaining courage. "Can't we, Pamela? Friendship isn't enough. It's too liable to the kind of misunderstanding which has parted us all this year. Can't you give me something more than that?"

Through her tumult of feelings she noticed with a quick thrill of delight that he had forgotten his scars, and everything else except his love for her.

"Friendship isn't enough for me either," she said haltingly, "and I – can't bear any more misunderstandings. They wasted twelve sickening long months for us, Kenneth, when I might have been helping you through your bad

219

time. Oh, you can't think how badly I wanted to do something for you when I discovered who was the Lintie's Ogre, shut up in that gloomy house down there!"

"I wish you had!" he exclaimed fervently. "Why didn't you?"

She threw back her head and laughed into his eyes.

"How was I to know you wanted me to stupid? You never said you did till this moment!"

It was fully half an hour later that a rather embarrassed couple entered the sitting-room, where Mrs Maitland still mounted guard over the partially dismantled teatable, while Dimsie, seated on a low stool by the fender, scribbled busily on a fat writing-pad.

At first glimpse of the Ogre, both gave little cries of astonishment.

"Has the mask really gone?" asked Mrs Maitland. "That is a tremendous step forward! and are these the marks you thought so terrible? Why, it seems to me you have been making a great fuss about nothing at all."

And indeed the happiness beaming from Orde's face was enough to obliterate the unsightliness of far worse scars.

"Pamela says she doesn't mind them," he answered, "and I've just decided that her opinion matters most, so—"

"Only just?" Dimsie sprang up, and standing in front of the pair regarded them quizzically. "Anyhow I'm glad the mask is gone – in every sense of the word. Masks are things with which I have no patience whatever. Bless you, my children! Mother oughtn't you to say something of the sort too?"

Mrs Maitland looked rather helplessly from one to the other.

"My dear, let me have a few seconds in which to pull

myself together. To use a hackneyed formula – this is so sudden! Remember, that I am practically *in loco parentis* of Pamela at present while she is under my roof."

"Dear Mrs Maitland," Pam said simply. "I shall always feel grateful that it was under your roof such a wonderful thing happened. And don't worry about what my father would say, because, Kenneth says he spoke to him about it before – before things went wrong between us."

"And what did he say?" inquired Dimsie, deeply interested.

"Dimsie!"

"Well, Mother, I should like to know what the Professor would say in such circumstances. Did he tell you it was quite all right, and he would attend to it when he had finished the pamphlet on which he was working at that moment?"

Orde burst out laughing.

"That's a more or less accurate guess," he admitted.

"Though probably – in fact, certainly – he forgot all about it the next minute." added Pamela.

"Still it lends an air of respectability to your present situation," said Dimsie, "which will keep poor Mother from feeling too responsible. Now I shall make some fresh tea, and when you have finished, Pam, we can slip off for a little, and leave her to talk to the Ogre seriously. I expect she will feel happier then."

"I must say I am a trifle oppressed by the *in loco parentis* feeling," said Mrs Maitland laughing, "but it's a great relief if Professor Hughes knows something about it."

Dimsie bent to retrieve her writing-pad which had fallen on the rug at her first impetuous leaping up.

"I was just writing to Jean," she remarked, "about those stories of hers. I must add this news later on. She ought to enjoy this letter. It's *full* of interesting news."

Later on, when they were alone together, Pam said seriously:

"This is your doing, you know, Dimsie. If you hadn't 'barged in', as Erica used to call it at school, Kenneth and I would still be miles apart, and he would probably have started for the East, next week, without knowing how I really felt, and have been feeling all along. Oh, we do owe you a tremendous mount and we are both very aware of it."

"Idiots!" said Dimsie bluntly. "But if you really think you owe me anything (which you don't) let me beg one favour of you. I want you to promise that you will carry our Anti-Soppist principles into your new walk in life. I may be asking impossibilities – I don't know – but when I think of Rosamund and the others – especially Rosamund – I feel that *you've* got a splendid opportunity for proving to them that one needn't be 'soppy', even though engaged."

"I'll try," promised Pamela demurely. "I know your ideals on the Anti-Soppist question have always been rather exalted, and I may not be able to live up to them myself, much less keep Kenneth to it, but we shall both feel that your wishes ought to be respected as far as possible."

She broke off to hug Dimsie.

"Oh, Dimsie!" she cried. "I'm so happy! I shall never be one of your lame dogs any more."

"Don't be too sure," Dimsie warned her grimly. "You may quarrel again at any moment. But you are both off my hands now at least, which is a great relief, and so apparently is Jean. That leaves me free to attend to Lintie, Peter Gilmour, and the ghost."

"You know my theory that the ghost haunts that garden out of sheer happiness," said Pamela. "I don't think you need worry about her. And what's wrong with Peter Gilmour?"

A thoughtful expression crossed Dimsie's face.

"Thwarted ambitions," she said seriously. "They don't show much, do they? He is always so busy helping other people that he probably has no time for being depressed."

"In which he is not unlike you," Pamela looked curiously at her friend's face, and wondered if her own happiness was colouring all her thoughts, since the idea rose unbidden and so swiftly that Dimsie and Peter Gilmour had a similarity of character which seemed more than mere coincidence.

"As though (to use his own phaseology) Providence intended them for one another. Wouldn't that be wonderful! But it would be a case of 'how are the mighty fallen' if such a thing ever happened to Dimsie!"

It was late that evening before Kenneth Orde left Twinkle Tap and strode down the hill towards his own house, but he had no intention of going to bed. Though it was impossible to cancel his trip altogether, he was anxious to make arrangements at once which would shorten it very considerably, and allow him to return to Loch Shee and Pamela before the end of March.

"Though I suppose you will have to find rooms in the village," Dimsie had said, "since Laurel Bank is let. Do you know who has taken it, by the way? Or did you let it through an agent?"

"No, I managed it privately." Orde hesitated and gave her a doubtful look. "I don't quite know what you'll say when you hear that the person who has taken it is a doctor, and that he is coming here with a view to starting a practice. You won't feel that he is poaching on your preserves, till you, Dimsie?"

"How can I? when we have been needing a doctor here so long and so badly. I wonder if he will want to use my herbs."

"I think it's rather hard luck on Dimsie," said Pamela sympathetically. "She can hardly go dosing the new man's patients on her own account, and yet she has been doing a lot of good with her herb medicines and has thoroughly enjoyed doing it."

"Except when I felt out of my depth, and there was no one to whom I could appeal. But you're right, Pam – I shall miss doing what I can. It would be great if he would be satisfied with the serious cases, and leave me to try my hand still on the minor ailments."

"Better enter into partnership with him," suggested Orde, with twinkling eyes. "I imagine you will get on very nicely."

He thought over this conversation now, as he turned into his own gate, and speculated upon Dimsie's first encounter with the new doctor, regretting that he could not be there to see it. There was some correspondence to be tackled which he ought to have seen to earlier in the day, and putting on the light in his study, he slipped off his coat and looked about for the old tweed jacket he usually wore on these occasions. He couldn't find it, however, and realizing that he had left it upstairs, he dived into the cupboard for a yet older and more disreputable garment kept there for such emergencies, which he had not worn for several weeks. As he sat down at his desk, he thrust his hand into the breast-pocket, and pulled out a rather crumpled envelope addressed in large crooked handwriting to the office of *The Times* – Lintie's advertisement till unposted!

Orde laid it down on the table and stared at it guiltily, remembering the child's disappointment that her appeal had met with no response.

"I don't suppose it would have worked in any case," he thought ruefully, "but that doesn't excuse me. I'd better dash out and post it at once, but first of all I'll look at it, this time, if only to make sure that I did enclose the money."

He opened the envelope cautiously, not to tear the flap, and unfolding the sheet of paper which it contained he glanced over the Lintie's straggling characters. What he saw there nearly caused him to drop the paper in bewilderment and dismay. Steadying himself with an effort, he read it over again, the comical wording of it forcing a smile from him even through his distress.

"Wanted some relations for a little girl called Miss Carolyn Orde Gordon, aged eight-and-a-half, who has got no father or mother. Anyone applying to her at Rose Cottage, Lochside, will hear of something to their advantage."

The strange advertisement slipped from the Ogre's hand and drifted under the table, while he sank back in his chair and stared straight ahead of him through the dark window over which he had forgotten to draw the curtains; but he was not looking at the faint black outline of the monkey-puzzle tree's spikey branches through which glittered a few frosty stars. Instead he saw an angry face regarding him with mutinous eyes – his sister Carolyn as he had seen her ten years ago for the last time before he sailed for Canada, having practically forbidden her marriage with Derrick Gordon.

"You have no authority over me – absolutely none!" he heard her angry young voice declare. "I shall be of age in six months and free to do as I choose. You have nothing against Derrick except his lack of money, and your own groundless prejudices."

"Any man who wants to marry a girl on nothing a year is selfish and thoughtless!" he heard his own voice retort with equal heat. "I may have no authority, but I tell you this,

225

Carol – marry Gordon, and you'll see no more of me! I warn you it will be a complete break."

And she had done so, and he had kept his word dourly throughout the ensuing years. Probably only Peter Gilmour knew how much the dourness had cost him, or how he longed for news of his sister, which his stubborn pride would not let him seek. When Peter (who found it hard to comprehend a state of mind so foreign to his own) had urged him to let bygones be bygones, and write to an address which he knew would find her, Orde had retorted that the first move should come from her. Carol had cut herself off from him by her own choice and had made no attempt to bridge the gulf, and he had imagined her pride to be as obstinate as his own. Tonight he learned his mistake. Carol had been dead for many years, and her husband too, and their only child – of whose existence he had known nothing – was living on charity, underfed and poorly clad, at the other end of the village.

Even Orde's new happiness was overshadowed, for the time being, by this shock, and he dropped his head on his hands with a return of the old black depression which had lately relaxed its grip. It was too late to go down to Rose Cottage and claim the child – his chief and overpowering impulse – too late also to take his trouble and remorse to Pamela, as he longed to do. He could only sit before the fire in his study with hands clenched on his knees, staring into the wind-tossed gloom outside, and going over the past in his mind.

Then his thoughts turned to the Lintie and what he knew of her. Half-forgotten items told him by Dimsie came back to him now, and fitted into their place in the puzzle. How the child's father had brought her to Rose Cottage for a month's holiday one early summer in the days when Miss

226

Withers took lodgers, had received a good offer of work in the East and had gone off in haste, leaving the child in her care with a promise of money, which had been lavishly kept up to the time of his sudden death. Orde fancied he could understand the sentimental notion which had moved Derrick to bring his motherless little girl to the place where her parents had first met and loved. He had quarrelled with his family (that much Orde had known for some time), so he had chosen a month when Kilaidan was empty, and had evidently taken precautions not to be recognized – quite easy, since he had never been to the place after childhood, except for the brief visit during which he had met Carol. Derrick Gordon had been a young man for whom the glitter of cities held more attraction than the sunlight on Loch Shee.

Evidently he had kept the fact of Lintie's existence from his own family as from his wife's, and somehow Orde felt he understood the pride which had been unwilling to announce the child to those who had refused to acknowledge her mother. Whatever Derrick's faults – and Orde found himself wondering, with a newborn charity, if after all they had been as bad as his prejudice had painted them – he had been madly devoted to Carol.

At last Orde rose wearily, his letters still unwritten, and putting out the light he prepared to go upstairs to bed.

"Well, Lintie's advertisement has found her relations right enough," he thought, with a sad smile, "though it never reached its intended destination after all. I must see Miss Withers in the morning, and then I shall have to let old Gordon know, for the child is as much theirs as mine. Strange to think that she has grown up for eight years without our knowing of her existence! They say her mother died when she was born. Poor Carol! and I have thought badly of her all this time. If only he had let me know! But

227

probably he was wild with grief, and full of bitterness against me on her account. Ah, well! all the vain regrets in the world won't restore our lost opportunities. Tomorrow I must start doing what I can to make it up to her child."

CHAPTER 23

The Lintie's Flight

But tomorrow brought a very different state of affairs from anything that Orde or anybody else had anticipated. As he came out of his gate after breakfast on his way to Rose Cottage, he almost ran into Dimsie, who was speeding down the road on flying feet, fastening her coat as she ran.

"Hang on a minute!" he protested. "You nearly knocked me down! Where are you off to in such a hurry? Has somebody burned herself or severed an artery?"

"Oh, far worse!" said Dimsie breathlessly. "Come with me – I can't stop to explain, and besides you might be useful. The Lintie's lost."

"Lost, good grief! she isn't? Who told you? She's much too bright a child to lose herself in a neighbourhood where she knows every field and sheep-path."

"Geordie brought the news to us ten minutes ago, and I didn't wait to ask many questions. I thought Miss Withers could tell me better, but I imagine that the child has run away."

"What on earth for?" asked Orde, more astonished still, as he kept pace with her in long strides. "Why should she?"

Dimsie paused long enough for an impatient stamp.

"How stupid you are! It's the most natural thing in the world for her to do, of course. The Pritchards were coming down on the twelve o'clock boat today to see her, and unluckily Miss Withers must have let it out. The poor thing was quite convinced that her own relations were going to appear this week." Dimsie's eyes filled with sudden tears. "It was really rather pathetic, Ogre. She told me they were bound to come in a day or two, because she had asked God to send them as soon as possible."

The Ogre cleared his throat sharply, but nevertheless his voice was still husky as he said:

"Strangely enough the kid was quite right. I was on my way there myself when you ran into me just now. It's a very odd business altogether, Dimsie, but I only discovered last night that Lintie is my sister's child."

"*What?*"

"Fact!" And he told her the story of the unposted advertisement, and how he had come to learn Lintie's real name for the first time.

"So her prayer was answered after all," said Dimsie quietly, as he opened the gate of Rose Cottage. "And she has run off because she had so much faith in it that she wasn't going to be forced into any other arrangement. It strikes me the Lintie is an example to some of us grown-ups."

"I am inclined to think she is," said Kenneth Orde seriously, as he followed her up the path.

For the first time since she had come to live at Lochside, Miss Withers was unable to "keep herself to herself", for it seemed to Dimsie and the Ogre as if most of the village was thronging the shabby sitting-room and narrow little hall, full of suggestions, helpful and otherwise, and hushing their chatter to a subdued key out of deference to Miss Withers's distress. Nobody, however, seemed ready to carry out any of the suggestions, which were each contradicted as they arose by some fresh and more brilliant inspiration; while in the centre of it all sat the gaunt dressmaker, a wooden image of despair, apparently too much overcome to take any steps at all.

"What happened, Miss Withers?" asked Dimsie, with a note of authority, as she entered the small crowded room. "What is all this about Lintie?"

Miss Withers looked up at the sound of her voice, and a gleam of hope flitted across her drawn features.

"Eh, Miss Maitland!" she said beseechingly, all her careful semi-English scattered to the winds, "will ye tell me whaur to go, or whit to dae to find her? The Lintie's awa' and there's them as says she went on the early boat, and I'm fair dithered, no kenning whit way to turn. Dae ye think she is gane on the boat, Miss Maitland?"

"I do not," said Dimsie crisply, disposing of the most popular theory at one blow. "Where would she get the money? Besides, they would know at the pier-head if she had bought a ticket. Run, someone, to the pier, and ask Saunders if he saw her."

One or two volunteers melted hurriedly out of the group, and somebody else spoke of Dunkirnie.

"She might have gone that way," agreed Dimsie, "though I don't know why. Will some of you who can spare the time please go in that direction and make inquiries in the town? if you don't find her before, that is – and perhaps somebody else would go round the loch's head to Kilaidan? Annie Gemmell, will you go to the phonebox and telephone the police at Dunkirnie? Now, Miss Withers, please tell me when you missed her first."

"It would be when I rose, the morn," answered the dressmaker readily enough. "She wasna in her bed, and there was a loaf gane frae the kitchen cupboard, and some money on the table that didna belang tae me, and I'm thinking mebbe the puir bit lassie pit it there in payment-like for the bread, though fine she kent she was welcome tae a' I had!''

"And there was no sign of her anywhere about?"

Miss Withers shook her head despairingly.

"No the ghost o' a sign! Her cap and coat were awa' and the dog tae. And the warst o' it," with a kind of wail, "is that I canna jalouse whaur she can be, or whaur I can be looking for her!"

"We'll think about that," said Dimsie briskly. "Have you had any breakfast? No, I thought not! Well, that comes first, so get out your things while I put the kettle on. And meantime, Mr Orde has a very strange piece of news for you. We have found the Lintie's relations at last, Miss Withers, and when we find Lintie herself again, she will begin to live 'happily ever after'. Do you know that Mr Orde is her uncle, and her father was the son of Mr Gordon over at Kilaidan? I always wondered who it was that his photograph was so like – and all the time it was the Lintie!"

"It's no possible! Yet the bairn's name *was* Gordon – though I never conneckit the twa, for it's a common name eneuch up and doon the country."

"I only discovered last night," explained the Ogre gravely, "that her name is Carolyn Orde Gordon. That was my sister's name, and she married young Gordon of Kilaidan, but no one knew that there was a child."

Under the stimulus of this surprising bit of information, the dazed expression began to clear from Miss Withers's worn face.

"He tell me naething o' that," she said. "Likely he wasna ower sweir for me to ken, seeing he had quarrelled wi'

his ain folk – he telt me that much when he asked me tae tak'
tent o' the Lintie till he cam' back again. I couldna
comprehend why he wanted me tae bide a' the while at
Lochside – I wasna tae leave it, and wi' the money he sent I
had nae need – but I'm thinking noo that he had a kind o'
hope-like that the bairn micht fa' in wi' his friends at
Kilaidan, and matters be strauchtened oot that way."

"I've no doubt he had!" agreed Orde. "He couldn't
have foreseen what was to happen to him, or he would have
left you some clue to the child's identity. And now it looks as
though she is lost again before we had the chance to find
her."

But Dimsie's cheerful tones struck confidently across
this pessimism.

"Nonsense!" she exclaimed. "We haven't begun to
look for her yet. But there's no use wasting time searching in
the wrong direction, because the snow will be down very
soon, and we've got to find her before that happens."

"But which do you suggest is the right direction?"

Dimsie sat down at the table where Miss Withers was
already making an effort to swallow tea and toast. Propping
her head on her hands, she thought hard and vigorously for a
few minutes.

"It's hard to say," she confessed, at last. "I am trying to
think what she would be likely to do. Lintie is a great reader,
and there was a child at school who used to take all her ideas
from the books she read, with horrific results. What has
Lintie been reading lately, Miss Withers? Wait a minute – I
know! I gave her a copy of the *Swiss Family Robinson* three
weeks ago."

"That's it, depend on it!" exclaimed Orde, ready at
once to follow this line of reasoning. "She has taken the loaf
and Waggles, and gone off to live in the woods, since

there are no caves in this neighbourhood. Bright idea that of yours, Dimsie, for it narrows the field of search considerably. I'll go straight away and get some helpers, so that we can start to beat the woods."

"Do," said Dimsie. "Begin with those near the lochan, for they are the largest, and she knows them best. Call in at Twinkle Tap as you pass, and ask Pam to meet me outside the Mavis Wood on the far side of the village. It isn't quite so big, and we might search it together, she and I, working round the head of the loch towards Kilaidan. If you have no luck, come on and join us there. I'll start at once too, for we ought not to lose any more time."

"And I'll be coming with ye, Miss Maitland," said Miss Withers, getting hurriedly to her feet, but Dimsie stopped her, with a glance at her pale exhausted face, for she felt that such strength as the dressmaker possessed would not carry her far.

"No, no!" she said quickly. "Stay here, and keep up the fire. We're sure to find her very soon."

She buttoned her coat up to her chin, and set off along the road with a backward wave to Miss Withers, who went about her household duties with renewed hope and a mind almost eased of its worry, for she felt that the finding of Lintie was in capable hands and could not be long delayed. She had much to think about too in the news about the child's parents and the future which it opened out before her.

"Why, the wee thing 'ull be a Miss Gordon o' Kilaidan!" she said aloud, with a gasp at the brilliant prospect this conveyed. "I doot it's no a wee waif that muckle *wumman*, Mrs McIvor, will be calling her noo! I'll aye think it was Mrs McIvor started a' this steer and trouble wi' her havers to the Lintie, yon day I sent her up wi' the dress."

234

And the stress laid on the word "wumman" seemed to hint that Miss Withers might have preferred a stronger term if her conscience as a kirk member would have permitted it.

But Dimsie, as she swung round the head of the loch towards the Mavis Wood, felt less confident than she had allowed either Orde or the dressmaker to suppose. She was sure that Lintie was not strong enough to go far afield, however early it might have been when she had crept out of the cottage. Given time and fair weather the searchers were bound to find her soon, and probably not much the worse for her adventure; but it was just the weather which was disturbing Dimsie as she looked about her, reading the signs while she tramped on.

The clouds hung over the hills leaden and heavy, pressing on the higher peaks as though some great weight behind were forcing them down, and the north wind whistled through the withered grass by the roadside with a weird and eerie piping. To her right, Loch Shee stretched out towards the distant Firth, a mirror of polished steel reflecting the bare hillsides and the dumb motionless woods which clothed their upper slopes. No birds were twittering. Everywhere was a frozen silence and a waiting, and the atmosphere was charged with a faint indescribable something which Dimsie called the "smell" of coming snow.

As the wood for which she was making loomed in sight on the left of the hard shore road, she slowed down for a moment and looked back. No sign of Pamela, but it was too soon to expect her. Scaling the rough dyke which fenced the wood from the public way, she plunged in among the trees and dead bracken, calling as she went. Plenty of time to go back and meet Pam when she was likely to arrive, but the Lintie must be found before the first flakes fell.

Presently it occurred to her with a pang that the

child might not come when she called; perhaps, indeed, it might only scare her farther afield, since Lintie no longer trusted her friends. If she heard Dimsie's voice she would at once be afraid she would be recaptured and handed over to the Pritchards, who, however kind, were not the "real relations" for whom she craved. Dimsie stopped calling, and moved more cautiously through the crackling undergrowth, depressed by the difficulty of finding a Lintie who had no intention of being caught.

But Dimsie was never depressed for long. She was about to retrace her steps to the road and join Pamela, when a fresh inspiration seized her with a conviction which led her afterwards to regard it as sent in answer to her mute half-conscious prayers. Orde had been wrong when he said there were no caves in the neighbourhood. There was one high up on the slopes of Ben Aidan, of which Dimsie had told the Lintie a week or two before, having discovered it on one of her herb gathering expeditions. She had promised to take her there for a picnic when the summer came, and Lintie had listened with widening eyes.

"Is it a real cave, big enough to sleep in if we wanted to?" she had asked.

Could it be possible that the child was trying to make her way there now, with some wild idea of hiding in it from the well-meaning but officious friends who were trying to arrange her future? Dimsie halted in an open glade where one or two felled trees lay on the shrivelled fern, and a stray flake of snow fell on her upturned face. That decided her. The Lintie might not be on Ben Aidan, but the question could not be left unsettled for a moment longer than was necessary. It would mean a race against the snow to reach the cave while the way to it was yet open, but she might overtake Lintie as she went; anyhow there was no time to meet

Pamela, who must be left to ransack the copse as best she could by herself. Over fallen trees, tangled undergrowth, and boulders Dimsie scrambled, making for the far edge of the wood, where only a strip of shaggy muirland separated it from the lower slopes of the Ben.

At the moment the snow was struggling with difficulty to fall through the frozen air, but Dimsie, weatherwise, knew that the full blizzard could not be long delayed. Every moment was precious, as she sprang from tussock to tussock across the open muir. She dared not call now, and could only hope that the Lintie, if she were anywhere near, might not look back and see the pursuit. As far as she knew, the child had never been on Ben Aidan, but she had asked the way to the cave, and so knew that it led up the side of a small burn, starting from a spot where a great standing-stone made a landmark to intending climbers. Dimsie had told her the local tradition that the saint from whom the mountain was named had once lived in that very cave, coming down to preach by the waters of Loch Shee where had stood the church of St Aidan (Kilaidan), and Lintie had listened with rapt interest.

"Probably she thought," Dimsie told herself with a touch of dry humour, "that a cave which could accommodate a full-grown saint might well shelter one small girl. Sleep there, indeed! It will be a long sleep for the Lintie if she puts herself to bed up yonder in the snow!"

And she hurried on, to reach the lower slope of the mountain as the first white swirl blotted out the wood and water behind.

CHAPTER 24

On the Side of Ben Aidan

At first, though the snow was confusing, Dimsie did not find it impossible to make her way through it in the right direction. The landmarks by which she steered still showed themselves familiarly enough, as she got near them, through the mad soundless dance of the flakes; but by and by, as the ground became covered, the boulders and bog-myrtle bushes were smothered in a whiteness which completely changed their shapes, and the falling snow became so dense that Dimsie stopped and hesitated, uncertain now which path to take, where all paths were of a uniform snowy level.

"I ought to turn off here by that bend in the slope," she thought, "but I'm not quite sure if this *is* the bend, and I can't see the twisted rowan-tree which should be on my right. Anyhow, I'll turn off and risk it, for there's nothing else to be done."

A further scramble, upwards and to the left, continued for some time without bringing her to the standing-stone, and at last she halted again, trying to peer through the thick light darkness, but all to no purpose. She began to realise she was losing her sense of direction. Her surroundings (what she could see of them) had nothing of their natural appearance, and when she hurried forward again, spurred on by the dread of precious time being lost, she suddenly and painfully realized that she herself was lost!

The conviction would have petrified another girl possessing all Dimsie's imagination and less of her courage; for she had no idea how far she had climbed, and she knew that there were parts of Ben Aidan where sheer precipices broke away, forming the sides of deep ravines. Some of these ravines were believed to be impenetrable from below, and she had heard of shepherds being obliged to abandon sheep which had fallen into them, there being no known means of entrance.

Yet suppose the Lintie had slipped into one of these terrible places, and was lying there now, lonely and terrified, perhaps injured, under the blinding curtain of the snow! Dimsie's courage seldom wavered when another's wellbeing depended on it, so she started forward again at once, moving more cautiously now, and testing the ground before her frequently with the crook-handled stick which she carried. Now too she began to call again, feeling sure that no fear of future Pritchards would prevent Lintie from answering now if she were anywhere within earshot.

Dimsie's consciousness of time, as well as distance, was now becoming confused. It seemed to her as though she had been wandering for hours through the storm, and it dawned on her with a rush of horror that she was beginning to feel sleepy, mesmerized by the dizzy twirling of the small soft flakes. Pulling herself together with a tremendous effort, she raised her hands to her mouth and shouted: "Lintie! Lintie! Lintie!" in a mounting crescendo.

For the first time it seemed to her as though an answer came out of the white enshrouding gloom, but it was not Lintie's voice which replied. A long howl, muffled yet penetrating, seemed to rise out of the ground at her feet, and

Dimsie remembered that the faithful Waggles was with his mistress.

Moving forward with still greater caution in the direction from which she believed the sound to have come, she pulled herself up only just in time on the brink of a precipice. She leaned over as far as she dared, trying to see through the thick veil of the snowflakes, and called again:

"Lintie! Waggles! are you there?"

A most discouraging silence was the sole result, and she was beginning to wonder if the howl had been imagination, when it was suddenly repeated just beneath her, ending in a sharp imperious bark. Waggles seemed to know that someone was up there searching for them, and was losing patience over this delay in following his clearly given instructions.

"All right, Waggles, I'm coming! Lintie, are you there?"

This time came a weak but unmistakable response.

"Yes, Waggles and I are here, and we're beginning to be a little bit frightened. Please come!"

"Where are you?"

"I don't know. We climbed down here before the snow came, and we can't get up."

"Before the snow came? Then it isn't rock all the way down?"

"Oh, no! It was quite easy to get over the rocky bit. Who are you, please? Are you an angel?"

Despite cold and danger and anxiety, Dimsie's laugh rang out through the muffling snow.

"Not likely! I'm afraid I'm only Dimsie, so you must make the best of me. I hope you weren't expecting an angel! Now, keep still where you are, and don't wander off, for I am coming down to you."

Holding her stick in her teeth, she boldly let herself down over the cliff, trusting to Lintie's information as to its height, which proved quite correct, for the rock only dropped about four feet, and she found herself standing on a steeply slanting hillside made slippery by the snow. Very cautiously, leaning on the stick, she went downwards crabwise, determined not to risk any false step which might make her incapable of getting Lintie safely home. Fortunately she was very surefooted, or she could scarcely have made the descent without a catastrophe of some sort. As it was, she reached the bottom safely, and paused to reconnoitre her position.

"Lintie!" she called, "where are you? Shout, so that I may know, but don't move on any account. Keep as still as Casabianca till I come to you – though there's not much of the burning deck about this!"

To her relief the rather forced joke met with a faint chuckle of amusement in reply. Lintie was a brave little thing, and her fears had been dispelled by the first sound of Dimsie's voice.

"I'm here!" she answered from somewhere near at hand, and a joyful Waggles bounded through the storm to hurl himself all over their deliverer. Dimsie seized him by the collar, and let him guide her to Lintie, who clung to her tightly in rapturous relief.

"I was just beginning to get lonely," she explained, "though of course Waggles is great company most times. And I couldn't see my way, so I prayed for an angel, and you came! I think," she added candidly, "I'd rather have you than a strange angel I know nothing about. It makes me feel more at home somehow."

"I'm glad," said Dimsie, "for I can't say I feel very much at home myself just now. The sooner we get there the better though. It's much too cold to stand still, so let us see if we can manage to climb up again where we came from. What made you run away, Lintie?"

"I wasn't really running away," explained Lintie, clinging to Dimsie's hand as they turned back to the side of the ravine. "I only meant to live in Aidan's cave for a while, till those kind people had gone away and given up trying to adopt me. You see, I couldn't let myself be adopted when the real relations might be coming at any moment."

"But Lintie, it was a crazy thing to do. Look at this snow – and even if it had been fine summer weather, what could you have lived on?"

"Bread and meat," replied Lintie promptly. "I meant to ask God if He would send it to me by the ravens, just as He did for Elijah. I knew if He did it for a grown-up man, He would do it for a little girl. Wouldn't He, Dimsie?"

Dimsie looked down at the small white face with its confiding eyes through a haze of snowflakes, and made the best reply she could.

"I don't think He would have sent it just that way, Lintie dear, but I am quite sure He would have taken care of you somehow. Perhaps that was why He showed me where to find you just now."

"Then I expect He'll show us the way back," said the Lintie placidly, "'cos I'm afraid it won't be very easy. Couldn't we go to the cave and wait till the snow's off? I got up so early this morning that I'm dreadfully tired and sleepy now."

Dimsie's clasp tightened on the child's hand, and she instinctively quickened her steps.

"Oh, but we can't rest for a second! Think how anxious everybody will be if I don't bring you home at once. Besides, I don't believe I could find the cave in all this. I can't even find the bank we came down, and I thought we were quite close to it."

"Let's try turning the other way," suggested Lintie helpfully. "The snow goes round and round, so we can't really tell which side of us is which."

Recognizing the truth of this, Dimsie struck off at right angles, and they struggled on for a little while longer, but without reaching the side of the gully, till at last it was borne in upon her unwilling mind that, like most snow-wanderers, they were moving in a circle. Desperately she tried to take some sort of bearings, but her senses were now hopelessly confused and she could only plod on determinedly, for she knew well the danger of yielding to the comfortable drowsiness which was stealing over her.

"Dimsie," said the Lintie, with a pathetic break in her brave little voice, "I'm just awfully tired and so cold too. Couldn't we stop and rest only for one minute?"

"Not for one minute," said Dimsie inexorably. "I – I hope we're walking right out of this place, as we haven't come to the sides. We must hurry as much as we can, because I'm afraid we've still a long way to go. But you can wrap my coat round you, and I'm going to tell you something nice and exciting which will help you to forget how tired you are. This morning – not long after you had set out – a real relation came! There! What do you think of that? And you will never guess who it was, if you try from now till we reach home."

"Oh, who?" cried the Lintie, effectively roused from her heaviness by this startling news.

"It was the Ogre! He is your uncle – your mother's brother – and we know all about your other relations now, so you need have no fear of being adopted by any kind people. Mr Gordon at Kilaidan is your grandfather, for your Daddy was his son, and Jean is your auntie. We could never have guessed that, could we, when she used to tell you those lovely stories in the summer."

"I can hardly believe it!" answered Lintie, heaving a deep sigh of content, as they struggled on. "It sounds like one of those stories. Do you think perhaps I'm going to live happy ever after now, and not be a waif any more?"

"Never any more," said Dimsie decidedly. "Why, you have got quite a lot of real relations now, for I have another piece of news for you. Pamela is going to marry the Ogre, which will turn her into another auntie for you."

"How lovely!" said Lintie. "But – but – Pamela is a dear, and I'm es-tremely fond of her, but I love *you* best, Dimsie. Couldn't the Ogre marry you instead?"

"Oh, no!" said Dimsie hastily. "That wouldn't be the same thing at all. What is it, Waggles? What can you hear?"

For the dog, who had been trudging with weary patience at their heels, suddenly stood stockstill, and pricked up his ears. Evidently some sound had again penetrated his keener hearing, and in another minute he threw back his head and gave vent to one of those piercing howls which had attracted Dimsie's attention earlier.

Dimsie felt her heart gave a wild leap of hope. Was it possible that one of the search-parties had thought of exploring such an unlikely neighbourhood as Ben Aidan? At the back of her mind, all the time that she was trying to cheer and distract Lintie, had lurked a dread which she had not dared to face – no one knew where she had gone, nor was anyone likely to guess that she had found Lintie on the mountain only that they might both be lost again in the cold enveloping whiteness of this awful blizzard. Yet she was growing surer every minute that it would be impossible to get the exhausted child home without help.

Circling her mouth with both hands, she shouted

at the top of her voice, seconded by the Lintie's feeble pipe; then both stopped to listen for an answer. Not so Waggles, however, who broke out into wild and frantic barking which it seemed no snowstorm could possibly succeed in muffling, and which lasted for three minutes without a break.

"If there is anyone within earshot," said Dimsie hopefully, "that ought to bring them. Good boy, Waggles! Try again."

But Waggles had broken away from them, and bounded off out of sight in the direction from which he imagined help was coming.

"He has gone to fetch them, as he brought me to you," said Dimsie, turning her attention back to the little girl. "Lintie! what are you *doing*? You *mustn't* go to sleep. They are coming – they will find us in a minute. Wake up, Lintie!"

But it was useless. Completely overcome by the numbing cold, Lintie sank down on the ground, and her eyes closed in the longed-for sleep. Vaguely through her slumbers she was aware that Dimsie was treating her with unusual and surprising roughness. She felt herself shaken violently, even slapped with a vigour which would have been most painful but for this heavy drowsiness which was drugging all sensation. She scarcely felt cold at all now, and anyhow she was too tired to bother, if only Dimsie wouldn't be so nasty to her.

She roused a little presently, at the sound of men's voices and trampling feet, to find herself lifted and carried off by a pair of strong arms, while a scarred face, unfamiliar to her without its usual mask, bent over her compassionately.

"Please, may I go to sleep now?" she muttered and without waiting for permission, slipped back again into a wonderful cosy world of delicious dreams. As it happened the warmth was not altogether a dream-fancy, for, in addition to Dimsie's coat which had been wrapped about her, she was now rolled in the folds of a soft rug which the Ogre had had the foresight to fetch from his own house when the snow began to fall. Some unexplained impulse had made him leave the woods by the lochan to the other searchers, while he himself followed Dimsie's tracks. He had met Pamela fighting her way back through the storm to fetch help, for though Dimsie had not been at their meeting place, she had caught a glimpse of a figure on the lower slope of Ben Aidan just before all views had been blotted out, and had been convinced that it was her friend.

"If Dimsie has gone up the Ben, it must be because she has reason to think that Lintie is there," said Pam. "We must get help and go after her at once, before the snow gets deeper. Run back to the village, Kenneth, at top speed, and fetch anyone who will come, but, above all, try to get hold of the old shepherd, Hamish Campbell; he knows the mountain blindfold. I'll go home and stay with Mrs Maitland."

And perhaps only Dimsie, when she came to hear the story later, fully understood the sacrifice which this involved for Pamela, with her adventurous spirit and constant desire to be in the thick of things.

CHAPTER 25

The New Doctor at Lochside

Dimsie's condition when the rescue-party arrived to relieve her of responsibility was nearly as comatose as the Lintie's. When she realized that the little girl was in safe hands and there was no longer any need to look after her, she relaxed all effort with amazing rapidity, and showed neither surprise nor interest at finding Peter Gilmour among the rescuers.

"If Lintie's safe, I must rest," she told them dully. "I can't help it. I – I can't keep awake."

"You both can and will," said Peter, with some of the sternness she herself had shown half an hour before to the child. "Where's your coat? Oh, I see! Well, take my plaid. Luckily I'd just stepped off the ferry when I met Orde and his gang, and hadn't time to leave my things at Laurel Bank. No, Hamish, it will be better for her to walk – many thanks, all the same. You and the others can push on now with Mr Orde. I'll attend to Miss Maitland – after you've helped her out of this."

Rough kindly hands half-dragged, half-pushed the exhausted Dimsie up the steep side of the gully, and lifted her bodily over the four-foot cliff at the top; then the shepherd and his friends plunged on by themselves through the swirl, which was beginning to slacken a little, leaving

Peter to bring her down the mountain at his own pace – or rather, what he decreed her pace should be. He seemed to have grown surprisingly autocratic all of a sudden, and Dimsie found herself dreamily recalling the way he had assumed the lead on the night of the strike.

"You always seem to be at hand when I get into difficulties," she said, rousing herself to smile at him hazily, as he pulled the plaid more tightly round her shoulders. "But truly I can't walk as fast as this."

"I am quite sure you can," he declared with unfeeling cheerfulness. "It's all a matter of will-power and you're surely not going to chicken out now?"

But the taunt failed to have any effect.

"I don't know that I mind much whether I do or not," she answered candidly. "I won't rest if you'd rather I didn't, but I must go slower."

"Not if I know it! You are all but frozen, and we must get your circulation going again. Besides, I certainly can't go any faster than you, and it isn't particularly good for my gamy leg to stroll along like this."

Had Dimsie been more alert, she would have seen through this crafty piece of apparently selfish information. Never before had Peter been known to complain of his injury. As it was, however, the suggestion took effect, and she braced herself to further effort.

"That's better," he said approvingly. "I believe the blizzard's clearing. It's certainly lighter than it was five minutes ago. You'll be all right if those dizzy flakes stop, you know. That's what is putting you to sleep."

She hung on to his arm without replying, but he was startled by the whiteness of her face, when at length the snow ceased, and there was light enough to see her real condition. They had reached the foot of the slope by now, and were

248

beginning to make their way round the outskirts of the wood, ploughing through drifts at every step; but he stopped abruptly and gazed down at her.

"You poor thing!" he exclaimed. "What a pig I've been to you! Are you any warmer now?"

Dimsie nodded.

"Yes, but so very tired. Never mind. We're through with the worst, and it's clearing up."

"Well, if you are really warmer, here goes!" and Dimsie found herself picked up and carried with a swift irregular motion, as he strode across the rough ground with his limping stride.

"I'm afraid it's not awfully comfortable," he said apologetically. "I'm rather lopsided nowadays when it comes to something like this, but it's better than walking, anyhow, isn't it?"

"Ever so much," said Dimsie gratefully. "And I don't feel sleepy any more now – only tired, and very thankful that Lintie is safe. But I must be a terrible weight for you to carry."

"Oh, terrible!" he answered, with a chuckle. "It's lucky I'm such a heavyweight! Tell me – if you're not too tired to talk – why is Orde going about without that mask of his? What's he done with it?"

"Burnt it," replied Dimsie, with reviving animation, as she realized how much Peter had to learn and she to tell. "At least, Pamela did. It's all her doing, and everything is all right between them now. They're engaged, though it only happened yesterday evening, and we haven't had much time to think about it since."

"Engaged! That's fantastic!" Peter nearly dropped her in his excitement. "Why, it's barely a month since we met in town, and you agreed to take on the case! I'm ready to bet anything you like that it's your doing, but how have you managed to move mountains in such a short time?"

"I just talked to them," said Dimsie, "and explained them to each other, and they did the rest themselves. It was really amazingly easy once I got them started. But it was Pam's doing about that silly mask. What do you think about his scars?" she added eagerly. "Hasn't my lotion improved them?"

"I had neither the time nor the light to examine them. When I heard that you and the Lintie were lost on Ben Aidan, I felt that was the first thing to attend to; but I did notice the absence of the mask. Good for Orde! It's splendid to think he's happy again. Now, if I could manage to find his sister—"

"You can't," said Dimsie. "It's terribly sad, but anyhow he knows all about her now. That too has only happened since yesterday. I'll tell you all about it, but you must put me down, because we have reached the road now, and I can walk easily on smooth ground."

"I doubt it," he said. "Don't imagine I am tired, for I never felt fresher. It's heavy walking even on the road through this snow."

But Dimsie insisted. Her pace was slow and feeble at first, even with the help of his arm, but she forgot her own weariness in recounting the full tale of all that had happened to their friends during the crowded twenty-four hours which had just passed, and he listened eagerly.

"I can't tell you how thankful I am to know things are going to come right for Orde," he repeated when she had finished. "And they owe it all to you."

"But it was you who put me up to it. I should never have bothered about him, to begin with, if you hadn't insisted on my helping him."

"Oh, yes you would! He was too miserable, too down-and-out, for you to have resisted him long once he had crossed your path; but I'm prepared to say that we went into partnership over his case. Have you – er – heard anything about a doctor coming to take up practice at Lochside?"

"Only that he is taking Laurel Bank off the Ogre's hands. Why? Do you know him?"

"Yes – a bit."

"I think he will be rather a nuisance in some ways," said Dimsie frankly. "I want to go on myself doctoring the people who aren't very ill, but he will be sure to think I can't manage it, and really I am learning to help them a lot with my herbs."

"I shouldn't think he'd interfere with any of the cases which you *can* tackle," said Peter. "I hope to tell you more about him tomorrow, but you are too tired just now. I say, that was a bad stumble! You will have to let me carry you the rest of the way after all. There's such a thing as being too determined, you know."

He carried her home, where her mother and Pamela welcomed her with great relief and many exclamations over her soaked garments and weary looks. She was hurried off to bed at once, where Pam administered a hot concoction made from some of her own herbs, maliciously gleeful to see the faces Dimsie pulled as she swallowed it down.

"It's a source of great satisfaction to me to watch the biter being bit," Pamela assured her, "and I know that's specially nasty, for it's the stuff you forced down my throat last time I had a cold."

"It tastes unbelievably horrible," said Dimsie. "I only hope it hasn't gone bad or anything. I put catmint and vervain and yarrow into it, but I had no idea they would blend into a horrible flavour like this."

"Because you never sampled it yourself till now.

251

Perhaps you'll have more sympathy with your victims after this. Now I must pull down the blinds, and leave you to sleep it all off; then you'll wake up fresh in time for dinner."

"I don't feel the least bit sleepy now," said Dimsie rebelliously. "I want to hear about the Lintie. Why can't you stay and talk to me?"

"Because I got my orders about you from Dr Gilmour, and apparently he can lay down the law when he likes. Lintie is all right – in bed too, with Miss Withers and Waggles in close attendance – so good night for the present."

Left to herself, Dimsie did finally sleep, but it was a restless, tossing slumber, full of strange, terrifying dreams in which she wandered through worlds of scorching hot snow, searching for a lost Lintie who wailed perpetually to her from the far side of a bottomless chasm. In the chasm, deep down out of sight, floated Pamela and the Ogre, rising occasionally to the surface only to slip down again as she tried to reach them a helping hand.

She woke at last to find both her mother and Pamela watching her with grave concern, and overheard some murmured reference to the doctor.

"Am I ill?" she asked feverishly, trying to lift her aching head from the hot pillow. "I feel rather – peculiar. But don't send for Dr Beale, Mummy – please don't! Really, there's no need."

"Not for Dr Beale, dear," said Mrs Maitland soothingly, "but I want Dr Gilmour to see you, and he is coming up from Laurel Bank directly. Lie quiet and don't talk till he comes."

"But I don't *need* him," said Dimsie fretfully. "I know just what I ought to have. It's in the second bottle from the far end of the shelf in the stillroom, and it's for stopping fevers. Please get it, Pam."

"I shall do nothing of the sort," said Pam firmly. "I should be held responsible for poisoning you when the worst happened, as it certainly would. Go to sleep till Peter Gilmour comes."

But Dimsie was in no mood for joking.

"I *shan't*," she cried, bouncing up in bed with blazing eyes and cheeks. "I don't want him, and you can quite well fetch me that bottle if you like."

But here Mrs Maitland interfered, pushing her gently back on to her pillows, while she made a discreet signal to Pamela.

"Very well, dear," she said in her placid tones. "Pam will look for the bottle, if she can find it, but you must promise to rest quietly till she comes. Take time and look carefully, Pam, so that you don't bring the wrong one."

And Pamela, taking the hint, crept out of the room, resolved not to reappear until after Peter's visit, though she wondered very much how Dimsie, in her present excited state, would receive him.

When he came, however, the fever was running higher, and Dimsie failed to recognize him. She was babbling of snow in the herb garden, of Lintie and the Ogre, and then – suddenly finding herself back in her schooldays – she talked fast of lessons which must be learned, yet never seemed to be done, of games on the playing-field where she could neither find nor keep her proper place, of the wind on the downs and the waves breaking at the foot of the cliff.

Peter's face was very grave as he felt the hurried fluttering pulse, and watched the big unseeing eyes which stared past him to scenes of which he knew nothing. Turning to Mrs Maitland, he gave a few terse directions and asked permission to go to the stillroom in search of some remedies.

"I shall send over to Dunkirnie for other drugs that

we need," he said, "but I can't wait till the messenger gets back, and I believe I can find what I need at present among her herbs. Keep the room to this temperature, Mrs Maitland, and have a kettle at hand. We shall be lucky if we can stave off pneumonia."

From then followed a stiff fight of many weary days, during which neither Mrs Maitland nor Pam rested for more than an hour at a time, and Peter himself did not leave the house for long at any moment.

"Good thing my brass plate isn't up yet," he remarked once to Pamela with a grim smile. "Gives me a chance to devote myself entirely to my only patient, which I could scarcely have had with a practice on my hands."

She looked at him in wide-eyed astonishment.

"Do you mean to say you are the new doctor? And we never guessed! Kenneth kept the secret well, for of course he must have known what you meant to do when you took Laurel Bank."

"Yes, he knew, but I swore him to secrecy because I wanted to tell Dimsie myself. She has had a free field for her harmless experiments till now, and I was very much afraid she might regard me as an interloper. Indeed I wavered a bit, for that very reason, between this practice and one in Fife."

"Thank goodness you chose this one!" exclaimed Pamela fervently. "Where should we be just now without you?"

"Well, Providence saw to that, I expect," he answered, with a flickering shadow of his old cheerful grin. "I don't mind telling you in confidence that whether I remain here or not depends on one special circumstance."

"Whether you can manage the distances of such a scattered neighbourhood alone I suppose you mean?" said Pamela.

"No – that isn't the condition, but I should have expected you to guess it out of the sympathy for a fellow-sufferer."

He looked at her so strangely that Pamela's eyes opened wider still.

"You can't mean—" she began. "I did think of it once, but it would be so unlike Dimsie. Surely you don't mean—"

"But I do," he assured her. "I mean just that. I can only run this practice in partnership with Dimsie Maitland, if she will allow me to do so, when she is well enough to decide. If she won't – then I'm off to the ends of the earth. I didn't mean to tell you this," he added. "I don't exactly know how it came out, but – since it has – what do you think of my chances?"

"I don't think you have any just now," said Pam frankly. "I mean, you hadn't before she got ill, but perhaps things may be different when she is better. Anyhow, whatever you do, go slowly. Dimsie is a fantastic person, but I don't think she will be easily won. And don't on any account be sentimental with her, because she simply won't stand that. It would do more to put her off you than anything else I can think of."

"I don't see how this sort of thing is to be managed without being a trifle sentimental," he said rather ruefully, "but I shall be as careful as I can. After all, I'm glad I spoke to you, for you've cheered me up somehow, though you haven't been very encouraging. Funny, isn't it? Why don't you go for a walk with Orde? You've had no fresh air for two days, and I am going up now to relieve Mrs Maitland, so you will not be needed. It may be my incurable optimism, but I believe you will find Dimsie better when you come back."

CHAPTER 26

New Vistas

Peter's prophecy was fulfilled, for that night Dimsie began a slow creeping back to health, which extended to the middle of February before he finally pronounced her fit to go away for a change of air.

"Go south," he said, "and you'll return as fit as a fiddle, ready to work in your garden just as the fine spring weather begins. I went down to look at the improvements yesterday. You'll need some help in working all that."

"And Pam won't be here to give hers," added Dimsie languidly. "Why – haven't you heard?"

"I have heard nothing," he said, sitting beside the settee on which she was lying, close to the fire. "You know I've started my practice in good earnest now, and there's a big bout of flu going round the district, which has kept me on the go lately. I wish you were well enough to help me with those herb medicines of yours. People round here take me for a poor substitute. One old body told me, 'Yon stuff o' yours hasna hauf the poo'er o' Miss Maitland's, doctor, but I maun juist tak' it while she's laid by.'"

Dimsie laughed shakily.

"Then you're going to let me help you still?"

"Of course. And meantime I'm running up a good-sized bill with you for various herbs which I've been stealing from your stock. Don't look so alarmed – Pamela has weighed them out for me, and kept a very strict account; but I don't know where I should have been without them sometimes, while waiting for supplies from town."

"Perhaps," said Dimsie hopefully, "I may convert you to herbs altogether. If you took them up – you, with your training and degree – there would be no fumbling in the dark, as there is with me. You would have enough knowledge to go straight ahead and make a great thing of it."

Peter bowed.

"Your opinion of my ability, madam, far exceeds its deserts. But we are wandering from the point. Why won't Pamela be here to work with you in the herb garden this summer?"

"Because she is going to marry the Ogre in the middle of April. I'm surprised he didn't tell you, but actually they only settled it last night, when the cable came from Professor Hughes. You see, the Ogre had to postpone his trip abroad owing to this Lintie business and all its necessary arrangements, so he had an inspiration last week and cabled to the Professor, asking if he might marry Pam straight away and take her with him. It has always been the dream of Pam's life to travel, and she could never persuade her father to take her, so this will be ideal. The answer came yesterday, and everything is being arranged, and they are both very, very happy."

"Fantastic!" cried Peter, his face lighting up as it always did at the news of other people's happiness. "Of course you have heard what happened to the Lintie while you were ill. Her grandfather sent for her, and she and Miss Withers and Waggles travelled up to London together."

"I know. I had a letter from her the other day,

257

weirdly spelt. She is enjoying life immensely with her grandfather and Auntie Jean, and goes to school every day. Miss Withers has been established as housekeeper, and they are all coming up to Kilaidan for Easter and the wedding. Lintie is to be a bridesmaid."

She looked up at him laughing, but there was a suspicious dampness on her lashes. She was still weak, and tears had a tendency to rise for no good reason, a most unusual state of affairs with Dimsie, and one which she herself found hard to understand. This time to her embarrassment, the tears overflowed in earnest.

"There! There!" said Peter huskily, laying his big hand over her small white one, which looked pathetically frail and transparent at that moment. "It's all right, you know – quite all right."

"I'm – not crying!" protested Dimsie.

"No, I'm sure you're not, but it's perfectly natural, and I'm not at all surprised. Just weakness after being ill. Just you let yourself go, and you'll feel better in no time."

"No, I shan't! I – hate – being 'soppy' – and I've got a handkerchief of my own, thanks."

Perhaps the sight of her quivering mouth and wet defiant eyes was too much for Peter, but Pam's good advice went to the winds, and he found himself stammering out broken words of tenderness and comfort, with both Dimsie's hands held tight in his.

For the first few minutes Dimsie let him do it, indeed she hardly seemed to notice anything strange about it at all; then suddenly awaking to what was going on, she drew her hands firmly out of his, saying, as she dried her eyes:

"Don't, Peter. There's no need for you to be silly because I am. Please try to remember I'm a grown-up person and not a baby."

"But I am remembering it – that's just the point. Dimsie darling, can't you see that I'm head over ears in love with you?"

Dimsie's reception of this news was entirely original. Starting up against her cushions, she stared straight at him with a look of something very like dismay in her eyes.

"Oh, Peter!" she cried reproachfully. "How can you say anything so *horrible*? You know I don't want people to be tiresome and fall in love with me. It always leads to problems sooner or later. I have enjoyed being friends with you so much, and never dreamt you would ever want to be anything else. I'm quite sure it's just imagination; you may *think* you're in love with me, but you aren't really – you can't be – because you've always been so *sensible* before."

Peter stood with his back to the fireplace and his hands in his pockets, gazing down at her, a curious mixture of expressions struggling on his face.

"It's not imagination," he said. "My sensible days are done, if that's your definition of being sensible."

"Oh *dear*!" sighed Dimsie.

She had fallen back against the pillows again, and lay looking into the fire with such a forlorn and depressed face that Peter, against his better judgement, began to feel guilty.

"Don't look like that, Dimsie!" he said quickly. "It's altogether my own fault. You've got no reason to blame yourself."

"That doesn't make it any better if you are going to feel miserable about it. Peter, are you quite sure it isn't just imagination – perhaps because I've been ill, and you've felt worried and sorry for me?"

He shook his head.

"Quite sure. It was coming on long before that. But I'm not going to be miserable about it, so don't worry. We can go on being friends if that's the way you want it, and by and by, perhaps—"

"There won't *be* any by and by," said Dimsie emphatically, "so please put it out of your head. Really, it would be much better, because I am one of those people who will never fall in love. I am quite certain of it, and if you only put me out of your head, you will find plenty of girls who would be much better for you. There's Rosamund Garth, for example; she is coming to stay here for Pam's wedding, so you will see her then. Or Jean – you have never met Jean Gordon properly, for you can hardly count those few minutes in the teashop. Either of them would suit you far better than I should."

Peter smiled.

"'Fraid not," he said.

"That's only how you feel just now," Dimsie assured him earnestly, "but after a little it will be altogether different – if you really try to put me out of your thoughts."

"And how's that to be done, may I ask?"

"Well, you know I am going away, next week, first to Daphne's, and then to England, to visit the Garths; that should give you plenty of time to practise forgetting me. Of course I don't want you to do so altogether," she explained seriously, "only to get accustomed to thinking of me just as a *friend*. I shall bring Rosamund back with me, and you'll find that a great help."

"Shall I?"

"Yes, of course! You've never *seen* Rosamund, or you wouldn't doubt it. Peter, you will try not to be silly, won't you? I can't bear to think I've made you unhappy."

He roused himself at that, and met the anxious look in her eyes with a smile which was meant to be reassuring.

"I'm not going to be silly," he answered. "Put your

mind at rest, and turn all your attention to getting better. If you can't give me anything but friendship, my love, let me take that and be thankful. See, I'm not a bit melancholy now, and you mustn't let my feelings upset you, or it may set you back just when you are on the road to recovery. I want you to tell me if there is anything in the herb garden which is likely to require attention while you are away – anything that Pamela can't manage? Her time is sure to be well filled with her own affairs for some weeks to come."

"Oh, thank you!" said Dimsie, slipping back gladly into their old relationship. "There isn't much. The peppermint won't need to be uncovered till I come back again, but some of the roots I put in during the autumn want watching . . ."

She launched out into a number of small directions to which he listened with close attention, jotting things down from time to time in his notebook, and by the time he rose to go all feeling of tension between them had passed off. Even Dimsie, keen-sighted as always for her friends' troubles, failed to discern any sign of the heartache which her doctor carried away with him. But Peter, as he tramped down the hill from Twinkle Tap, told himself firmly that he had only himself to thank.

"Pamela warned me not to rush it, and I should have trusted her opinion. Now I have probably thrown myself back for months through being an idiot, and trying to hustle things."

As it happened, Peter was mistaken. Though Dimsie had turned him down so decidedly, his words and the look in his eyes remained in her thoughts during all the time she was away; gradually and without her own knowledge, these memories began to alter her ideas of him, and their friendship took on a new meaning. Dimsie was beginning at last, and very slowly, to grow up.

Daphne noticed it while her cousin was with her at Stratheager, but knowing of nothing else which could account for the change, she put it down to Dimsie's illness. Daphne had a romance of her own at that time, but such matters do not always open one's eyes to those of others. She petted, coddled, and made much of Dimsie, but she regarded her still as the little girl who had been her special charge during the early days at school, and Dimsie, for the first time, resented it a little inwardly.

"I don't want to be babied, Daph," she protested, one day. "I feel perfectly all right now, and I want to be treated on a footing of equality both mental and physical. I'm not a child any more."

"And I don't want you to be; somehow you seem to have grown up all of a sudden lately, and I haven't kept up with you."

"I think," said Dimsie in all honesty, "it must be due to Pamela's engagement. I've had her affairs on my mind so much of late, and they have been so complicated that probably they have aged me. You see, I hadn't any experience at sorting these things out, and they nearly went wrong altogther."

Her next visit was to Rosamund, who apparently had been having plenty of experience of that sort of thing, but was at first somewhat reluctant to relate it to Dimsie.

"I know you'll disapprove," she said apologetically, "but it's no use pretending I don't enjoy it all tremendously, and if no one concerned takes it seriously, where's the harm?"

"I should think," said Dimsie, with puckered brows, "somebody would be apt to take it seriously sooner or later."

Rosamund laughed cheerfully.

"It's all a game, you know, at present. If it ever grows to be anything more, I believe I shall tell you, Dimsie. Before you came, last week, I used to think I never could, but you are much more sympathetic about such things than I ever thought you would be."

"I've had to learn," said Dimsie, with a half-sigh. "Lame dogs have to be shoved across their stiles, however foolishly they may have lamed themselves. But in your case, I'm more afraid that you may damage others than get lamed yourself."

"I shall try not to," promised Rosamund demurely. "I can't help feeling that Pam's affairs have been very good for you, Dimsie. They've made you more human and less severe than you were a year ago – broadened you, in fact."

"I suppose," said Dimsie, with the first stirrings of a doubt which was to grow considerably before she went home again, "I suppose it *was* Pam's affair which changed me. It couldn't have been—"

"What?" asked Rosamund curiously.

"Oh, nothing!" answered Dimsie.

CHAPTER 27

Deadly Nightshade

Exactly a fortnight before the date fixed for Pamela's wedding Dimsie returned to Lochside completely restored to health, and bringing Rosamund with her. The Kilaidan party were to arrive a week later when Parliament had risen, and they were bringing Mabs Hunter with them for a hard-earned holiday, that the circle of Pamela's schoolfriends might be complete.

"She would never feel properly married," declared Rosamund, "without all the Anti-Soppists being there to see the knot tied hard and fast. Besides, which of us could bear to stay away from our first wedding?"

"Five bridesmaids and the Lintie," observed Pam meditatively. "It sounds a fantastically smart wedding, and it's really going to be nothing of the sort. I expect there will be no one in the church except the villagers."

"Can none of your own people come?" asked Rosamund.

Pam shook her head.

"Most of them live too far away. I had one great surprise though, this morning – Jim will be here! His ship is to refit at Glasgow, and he has managed to get a fortnight's leave, so he is coming straight down to the hotel."

"I wish we had room for him at Twinkle Tap," said Mrs Maitland regretfully.

"Anybody with Mrs Maitland's ideas of hospitality," said Pam, laughing, "ought to live in an expanding house. He will be quite comfortable at the Pierhead Hotel."

"Dimsie," said Rosamund from the window, "the rain has stopped, and I am longing to see the famous garden. Can't you take me now?"

"Yes, do," urged Pamela, "as long as Dimsie is in the room she considers it her duty to help me with my sewing, and though I don't want to seem ungrateful I can get on so much better without her. It will save such a lot of time unpicking if you can manage to remove her before she gets further with that seam."

"Well, really!" cried the outraged Dimsie, throwing down the slip over which she had been bending. "You not only seem, but are, ungrateful! However, I am glad you spoke out, because henceforth I need cast no more of my pearls before swine, and that will be a great saving. Come on, Rosamund! There isn't much to see at this time of year, but I'll explain it all to you, and we'll hunt for violets; they should be out in the bed below the parapet."

"Have you seen the ghost?" asked Rosamund with interest, as they made their way through the wet orchard and down the worn steps to the gate in the yew hedge.

Dimsie paused with her hand on the latch, and gazed dreamily through the low twisted boughs of the apple-trees where they framed a glimpse of Ben Aidan's green braes.

"Do you know," she said slowly, "I can't exactly tell you. It's the strangest thing about Great-great-grandmother. Often when I have been working late in the garden I have fancied I saw someone moving over there beside the stone bench, but when I have looked again I have never seen anything except a little mist gathering over the herb beds. But somehow I always feel as though she were here, waiting for something, and I can't think what it can be."

"There is someone moving over beside the stone bench now," remarked Rosamund drily, "but unless the ghost wears a raincoat and has a limp, I don't think this can be it. And it's certainly made of something much more substantial than mist."

As they passed through the gate and saw Peter coming down the flagged path to meet them, his face beaming with pleasure, Dimsie's heart gave an odd puzzling little jump for which she could not account.

"I was trying to set that corner to rights before you came along," he explained. "I knew you would be here directly the rain stopped, and I wanted to have everything in order. Think it looks none the worse for your absence?"

"No, indeed!" Dimsie's eager gaze ran over the wide brown beds, where clumps and patches of green were showing everywhere. "It couldn't be more spick and span, and I know that isn't due to Geordie's unaided efforts. Mother told me how hard you had been working, but I can't think where you got the time."

"I squeezed it out in half-hours here and there. Besides, it was all in my own interests, because I shall require plenty of your harvest this summer. I have been having one or two very convincing cures with your herbs lately."

He turned to talk to Rosamund, while Dimsie darted from one plot to another, inspecting young growth or fresh shoots on old stems. She returned to them presently with a tiny bunch of early balm leaves, tufts of appleringie, and a sprig of grey lavender spikes.

"There, Rosamund!" she said. "That's your welcome to my garden of healing. It would be a better and bigger one if the spring were more advanced."

266

"It couldn't be sweeter though," said Rosamund, bending to sniff it delightedly. The breeze which had driven off the last of the rain-clouds ruffled the golden curls about her face, which was as pretty and pink as the blossom in the orchard behind them. Dimsie saw Peter glance at her friend admiringly, and wondered why a sudden pang shot through her at the sight. Hitherto she had always revelled in Rosamund's beauty and rejoiced to see it admired, as though it were some special possession of her own, yet somehow she was not sure that she wanted to share Peter's friendship with anyone – not just yet, at least.

"I mustn't be an idiot," she told herself fiercely. "He is only my *friend* – that's all I want him to be – and I can't expect him not to be friends with other girls as well. Only the trouble is that I don't really believe it's possible for any man to be merely friends with Rosamund; they all fall in love with her, if what Jean says is true. Of course," she added to herself with firmness, "nothing would be better, if Rosamund were just as certain to fall in love with him, but I couldn't bear to have her treating Peter as an amusing game."

But during the days which followed, it became very apparent that this was exactly what Rosamund intended to do, while Peter, for his part, seemed to enjoy it. Now and again Dimsie met his eyes fixed upon her with a strange touch of wistfulness, but he sought her company much less frequently than before and never came to work in the herb garden except on rare occasions when he knew her to be out of the way. The Ogre had, of course, abandoned all gardening operations entirely, and Dimsie's chief helper during the ten days before the wedding was Jim Hughes, Pamela's sailor brother, who showed a decided tendency to shadow her wherever she went. And Dimsie found his open devotion pleasantly soothing because of an un-accountable soreness in her heart, which she put down to the coming loss of Pam.

Lintie, of course, had the run of the place, as before, whenever she was able to get across from Kilaidan. Already the three months of comfort and good feeding had made a difference to her; she had grown and filled out, and the unnaturally careworn look had disappeared from her face. She was entirely happy, and seemed to be the light of her grandfather's eyes, while Waggles also appeared quite satisfied with the new state of life to which he had been called.

As the wedding was to be quiet, no elaborate preparations had been made for it, though Mrs Maitland insisted on entertaining the little party afterwards at Twinkle Tap.

"I am still *in loco parentis,* remember," she told the bride, laughing. "My responsibility will not cease till I hand you over to your husband, even though Jim is to do the actual giving-away."

"You have been so kind to me," said Pamela gratefully. "No mother could have done more, and I shall always feel Twinkle Tap is my home."

"At any rate you will always find a welcome here," said Mrs Maitland, touched.

On the day before the wedding, Dimsie, tired with strenuous preparations, had wandered down the garden to watch for the arrival of the afternoon boat. Rosamund and Jim had gone off for a walk together round the head of the loch, meaning to finish up with supper at Kilaidan, and a row homewards in the moonlight; Mrs Maitland, accompanied by Erica Innes (who had lunched at Twinle Tap), had taken the bus into Dunkirnie in search of sundry small items for tomorrow's feast. Pamela and Orde were in possession of the sitting-room, and there was no one left to talk to in house or garden.

"I'm reduced to Great-great-grandmother's society," thought Dimsie, laughing a little at her own thought, "and I'm not even sure that she wants me today. I feel out of tune with her garden of healing, for I want people, not plants, and the people seem all pre-occupied with somebody else. I wonder if Great-great-grandmother ever grew weary of her sweet growing things, and pined for human company. She must have done so often enough during those first years when she sat on this bench and watched for the ship which never came back."

A faint sigh close beside her startled her for a moment, till she realized that it was only the breeze stirring in the junipers which the Grey Lady herself had planted so long ago for the sake of their berries.

"I am becoming absolutely stupid," Dimsie told herself half angrily. "If I weren't so tired I'd go and dig. Hullo, Geordie! Where have you sprung from? What's the matter now?"

Geordie looked white and scared.

"Please, Miss Maitland," he said anxiously, "the doctor's awa' tae Glesgie, the day, and ma mither sent me tae speir if you'd come as fast as you could tae see wee Maggie. She and Wullie was in the woods together, and she's eaten something that's poisoned her – onyway she's gey queer, and Mither said, wud ye come at yince?"

Dimsie sprang to her feet, alert and practical on the instant.

"I'm coming now," she said. "Can you tell me what it was she ate, George?"

"It wud likely be some o' thae red berries," replied

Geordie vaguely. "The woods is fu' o' them yet doon yonder, for the birds dinna seem tae mak' muckle o' them. Ay, it wud be the berries, but I wasna wi'her, so I canna say."

"Nightshade!" exclaimed Dimsie in horror. "And Dr Gilmour away! Here, Geordie! I'll run down to your mother's cottage myself, but you take my bicycle and be off into Dunkirnie as fast as you can for Dr Beale."

"It wudna be ony use," said Geordie, plodding imperturbably beside her. "He's be sayin' that Lochside's got its ain doctor noo, and that he's no coming."

"Do as I tell you!" ordered Dimsie, stamping her foot. "Tell him the child has eaten nightshade berries, and that it's a case of life or death."

And George, accustomed to obeying Dimsie implicitly, disappeared in the direction of the bicycle-shed.

"No that it'll be ony guid ava'," he muttered to himself doggedly, as he wheeled out the machine.

Incidentally, he proved correct, though that was neither his fault nor Dr Beale's; for the front tyre punctured when he was halfway to Dunkirnie, and when he arrived there on foot, having delivered up the bicycle for repairs *en route,* it was to learn that Dr Beale had been called out to a case five miles away in the opposite direction; so Geordie retrieved the mended bicycle after an hour's waiting, and spun philosophically home through the dark with an unlighted lamp.

Dimsie, meanwhile, had hastened down to the village in a good deal of trepidation, aware that she must do her best till Dr Beale arrived, but unhappily conscious that she knew very little about poisons and, above all, was ignorant of any antidote among her herbs for nightshade berries.

The poor mother hailed her coming with a relief which refused to be shaken when Dimsie warned her of how little she had to rely upon.

"Ye'll ken mair nor me, Miss Maitland, onwey, and it's thankful I am tae see your bonnie face! Come awa' ben, for the bairn's awfu' bad. She's been oot o' ane convulsion into anither since she got hame, but she's quiet the noo."

The child lay semi-conscious in the big bed. Dimsie's heart sank within her as she looked at the flushed face and glassy eyes, and she felt that her own ignorance would have scared her less had the patient been a grown person.

"Fill all the hot bottles you can get hold of, and put them round her," she directed rapidly, "but first give me the mustard. We must make her sick at once – I'm quite certain about that."

The woman and a neighbour, who had come in to help, bustled about obeying Dimsie's orders, while she herself tried to persuade the child to swallow the mustard and water which she had prepared. It was not an easy matter, but at last enough of the doses went down to work, and then with a faint memory of something she had learnt before the abrupt ending of her medical studies, she sent out for a lemon, hoping to persuade her patient to suck it.

Before the lemon could come, however, there was another convulsion, and Dimsie, who had never seen such a thing before, did what she could with white face and trembling hands.

"If Mother had even been at home!" she thought, in a frenzy of anxiety. "Or Peter – if only Peter would come! Oh, God! send Peter before it's too late, for I can think of nothing more to do. Oh, please, please, God, don't let the poor mite die! Send Peter quickly!"

Her mind was far too much absorbed in the dangers of the moment to think of such practical details as the coming of the evening ferry, yet she felt no surprise when, on looking up from the child, after what seemed an eternity of struggle,

271

she saw Peter limping into the darkening kitchen. Her eyes met his for one moment in a frantic appeal, but she did not speak, only stepped back from the bed, and leaned against the wall, pressing both her palms back upon it as if for support, while she watched his calm purposeful movements, and tried to read his opinion of the case in the quiet face which bent above the suffering child.

She hardly knew how long she had been standing there, keeping a silent agonized watch, dreading lest even yet (though Peter had come in answer to her prayer) the child might die through some neglect born of her ignorance. At last, however, he settled the bedclothes with gentle hands and stepped back.

"She'll do now," he told the mother gently. "Just keep her warm and quiet – sleeping if you can – and I shall be round again later. Come, Dimsie! There is nothing more we can do just now, and all danger is safely past."

She shuddered a little, but did not speak as she followed him through the low door. Outside, in the gathering dusk, he gave her a keen glance, then drew her hand through his arm.

"It's a pretty terrifying moment," he said gravely, "when there's just one's own faulty knowledge between a human being and death – I know that. This has given you a shock, but there is nothing to fear now. Do you remember what time they sent for you?"

She shook her head, still unable to speak, but he quietly persisted in his effort to dispel the horror – not by avoiding the subject which filled her brain, but by discussing the trivialities of it.

"Where did she find the berries? If it had been autumn, I could have understood it better, but those fruits don't often survive till spring. Either the birds eat them, or they get shrivelled by the winter cold."

272

"Birds don't eat those berries," she answered at last, mechanically. "I know where she got them. There's a sheltered glade in Mavis Wood where some of them have survived the frosts."

"They were probably shrivelled to a certain extent, or the consequences would have been more serious. My love, don't tremble so! Why, Dimsie you would never have made a doctor if you took every serious case to heart like this!"

"It's not that," she said, shuddering again, while she clung to his arm. "If I had known what to *do*, it would have been quite different. Suppose – suppose you hadn't come to Lochside – suppose this had happened when there was only me!"

"No need to suppose anything of the sort, since it didn't. Providence takes care of things like that. Besides, you were working on the right lines, and it would have come right in the end, even if I hadn't come back on that boat. You mustn't lose your nerve for no reason."

"*Did* I do right? You are sure she didn't – didn't suffer more through my ignorance?"

"Quite sure. I happened to have an antidote in my bag, but even without that she would have pulled through on *your* treatment, so don't brood over it any more. Here we are at your gate – run in and talk to Pam or your other friend, and forget all about it."

But Dimsie kept her hand on his arm, and looked up at him, her lips still quivering.

"Please come in and talk to me for a little," she said. "Everyone is out except Pam and the Ogre, and I can't disturb them tonight. Would you mind? Are you too tired? I – don't want to be selfish."

CHAPTER 28

The Garden of Healing

"Certainly I'll come," he answered quickly. "It would never do to leave you alone while you are so tired and over-wrought. Besides, I have plenty of time on hand – no patients expecting me this evening."

He held the gate open for her to go in, and followed her with surprise as she passed by the side of the house and took the path which led down through the orchard and the deep shadows of the windbent apple-trees.

"Not going to rest?" he asked doubtfully. "Surely the garden doesn't need you any more tonight?"

"No – but I need the garden," she returned with a shaky laugh. "It will be lovely there just now, Peter – quite warm, and the moon coming over the top of the hills. Let us stay out in the open, and rest there."

"Very well," he said obediently. "By all means let's do what rests you most."

She led him to the Grey Lady's bench beside the junipers, and they sat together for a while in silence watching the rising moon as it flooded the waters of Loch Shee with silver, making it indeed a "Loch of the Fairies", as its name signified. Opposite them, in the deep shadow of the Kilaidan shore, winked the yellow riding-light of some yacht which had crept to its anchorage early in the year, like a white-winged harbinger of summer. All about them clung a hundred mingled fragrances drawn up by the soft spring warmth from the young herbs.

He drew a long breath and leaned back against the parapet, enjoying the faint southerly breeze.

"Talk about haunts of ancient peace!" he exclaimed. "This place always seems to me almost magically peaceful."

She nodded.

"There's something about its charm which makes me very nearly superstitious – only it's such a beautiful superstition – as though Great-great-grandmother, who spent her life healing all around her, broods over it still like a spirit of tranquillity. One usually thinks of ghosts as being restless and unhappy, but I am beginning to believe that Pamela is right when she says the Grey Lady haunts the garden out of sheer happiness – a wistful happiness which longs to impart its secret to others."

He turned round and, leaning his arms on the low wall, gazed down at the silvered loch below them.

"I don't know," he answered meditatively. "Seems to me Providence would have some better work for such a soul as hers than just to blow about these paths like a whiff of summer mist."

"But don't you think," urged Dimsie, with a touch of pleading in her voice, "she might be allowed to come back here for her playtime? You see, she loved it so. I fancy she must have been one of those people – I'm one myself – who would rather have the new earth than the new heaven."

"Perhaps she was. It wouldn't be surprising, with those hills and that sea before them."

"And then, do you think it would be such unworthy work for her, after all, to come back as a silent messenger of peace for those that can feel her message?''

He glanced at her earnest face, with a smile of gentle amusement.

"So you attribute the whole atmosphere to the influence of the Grey Lady? Don't you think the mantle of her tranquillity may have fallen upon you, Dimsie? It seems to me that both Orde and Pamela have to thank you, principally, for their healing."

"I don't know." Her voice was low and troubled. "There was nothing very tranquil about me this evening. I don't mind confessing that I nearly lost my head."

He frowned sharply, annoyed that the conversation should have strayed back to the subject which distressed her.

"But the point is that you didn't lose it. On the contrary you kept it remarkably well, and did just what you should have done."

She looked at him with eyes which looked very dark and confused in the dim light.

"Nevertheless I was at the end of my tether when you came. If – if you hadn't come just then – the child might have died."

"I think not," he answered calmly. "Providence doesn't run things as closely as that. You see, I *did* come. Why worry about what might have occurred if I hadn't?"

"Because – if it were to happen again—" she said below breath.

He put out his hand and laid it on hers, where it rested on the lichens of the old wall.

"Gently, Dimsie!" he said quietly. "It can't happen again for the simple reason that I shall teach you all you ought to know for such emergencies, and then you will be prepared. It's not like you to be scared by imaginary phantoms."

276

"I know. I'm an idiot," she answered abruptly, but she left her hand in his, and did not withdraw it when he said:

"A very nice idiot! Dimsie – I didn't mean to speak again so soon, but – is there no hope for me yet?"

The silence which followed seemed to him a very long one, as he tried vainly to read her expression in the dim light. Had he blundered again in his impatience, speaking while she was still unready to listen? After all, she was young in these matters, for all her twenty years.

"Dimsie," he repeated sadly, "is there no chance at all?"

She started as one waking from a dream.

"Oh!" she exclaimed. "You sound so unhappy about it, and you mustn't, Peter! I can't bear to think I am making you unhappy. I didn't answer you at once because I couldn't – I can't now. It's all so confusing."

She pulled her hand away, pressing her fingers against her eyes as though to shut out anything that might distract her from the problem with which she was trying to wrestle.

"What is it that you find so confusing, my love? Tell me, and let's see if we can solve it together."

She laughed a little at that.

"Poor Peter! You are so sweet and patient with me! But I must work out my own difficulties. I've done so ever since I was ten years old – and some other people's too. Peter, it's there the rub comes – if I let myself fall in love with you, shall I have time for other people?"

"I think so. Why not? I should do my best not to be selfish or demanding," and he tried to control the eagerness in his voice.

"I couldn't imagine you being either the one or the other. But what about myself? Look at Pamela now – she has hardly a thought to spare for anyone but the Ogre. Jean and I were discussing it yesterday, and Jean says that she is sure Pam will come back to ordinary ways again and make time for all her friends, but I can't feel quite certain about it. She will always have to put the Ogre first – she will want to, and so she should. But if it were I—"

She broke off again, letting her hands fall into her lap, and gazed across the water to the "great black hills like sleeping kings", as though seeking some inspiration from their eternal wisdom.

"If it were you—" Peter prompted gently.

"If *I* were in love, should I become like that – too much absorbed in one person to bother about any of the others? Because, if so, I don't think it would be quite right somehow – not for me."

"I think I know what you mean," he said slowly. "I have been talking about you a great deal with Rosamund lately, and she has told me how much you have been at everyone's beck and call, all through your schooldays – how everyone in difficulty or distress turns naturally to Dimsie. Pam has spoken of it too, and I have seen it for myself. Are you afraid that if you were to undertake one lame dog for life, you would have no time to help others over their stiles?"

Dimsie nodded.

"Something like that. But I think I am chiefly afraid that I might not *want* to. It's impossible to tell, you see, how such things may affect you till they actually happen."

Even in the midst of his anxiety Peter wanted to laugh.

"Quite true," he said, "but somehow I hardly think it would be that way with you. It seems to me the best kind of love is never selfish – it always leaves room for other people; indeed it wants to give out of its own abundance. You would not be afraid of loving like that, Dimsie?"

She turned her face up to him, and he saw that her eyes were shining like stars.

278

"Oh, no!" she replied, with a little catch in her breath. "Not if I could be quite sure it would be like that. It would be altogether different from the ordinary – 'soppiness'."

He laughed out loud.

"I think – since you are you – there would be no danger of 'soppiness'. But, oh, Dimsie darling! all this goes to prove how very far you are from falling in love. When it happens, it isn't a thing to be analysed or discussed – it just *is*!"

"All the more reason to talk about it beforehand," said Dimsie in matter-of-fact tones, "so that one may have some inkling, while still in the possession of one's senses, of what may happen afterwards. But it does seem rather queer that it should be you with whom I am discussing it. Do you mind, Peter?"

"Not in the least. I am rather enjoying it."

"Well, I'd rather it was you, somehow. There seems to be no one else with whom I could discuss it without being misunderstood. You see, I've always been very positive about not giving way to anything of the sort, but there was a poem of Jean's once—"

She broke off and sat in silence for a few minutes; then slipping her hand into the pocket of her jacket, she drew out a rubbed and worn piece of paper.

"This isn't the poem I mean," she said jerkily. "It's another – hers too – and I love the ideas in it, so I've made it a kind of test. When I feel like that for you, Peter, I – I shall know it's all right."

"Am I to read it?" he asked doubtfully, as she held it out to him.

"Yes, please, if you can. The moonlight is quite strong now."

He took the paper from her, and spread it on the top of the wall, where the moon's beams were falling brightest, and Dimsie watched him as he read.

279

"All this thou art to me – the joy of dawn
 In far-off springtimes of my childish days;
The drift of appleblossoms on the lawn;
The rippled clouds across a turquoise sky;
 And, deeply hid within the wood's green maze,
A singing blackbird – happy too as I.

"This too thou art – the soothing and the calm
 Of still seawater lapping on the stones;
 The music of a Covenanting psalm
Sung softly in a little sunlit kirk,
 Or sweetly crooned in tender hushing tones
Above a cradle through the gathering mirk.

"The glory of the everlasting hills,
 The same, yet strangely new from day to day;
And every lovely memory which fills
 My life with sunshine – lo! I find thee there!
But feel thee nearest when I kneel to pray,
 Knowing thy soul kneels with me in my prayer.

"And thus, dear friend o' mine, thou hast a part
 In every goodly joy or hope or dream.
No shaft of sunlight rested on my heart
 But thou wert in it, when I knew thee not;
And now, behold! the very windflowers seem
 Fair visible expressions of thy thought!"

"Oh, Dimsie!" he exclaimed unsteadily, then handed it back to her without another word. She returned it to her pocket and rose, standing beside him half in white radiance, half in the deep shadow of the junipers.

"Do you understand?" she asked, and the wistful

note crept back into her voice again. "Anyone who felt like that, would know it must be all right – that they could only live their life and do their work the better for caring about anyone in that way. I wanted you to know, so that you wouldn't think I was – playing a game as – as some people do. I'm only trying to find out."

He took her hand, and raised it to his lips.

"Go on trying to find out, my darling," he said huskily. "And when you do, you'll tell me, won't you?"

She opened her eyes wide at that.

"Why, of *course*," she said. "It's because of you I'm trying to. Now, I think I shall go in, for Mother must be home again. Thank you for being so understanding, Peter. Will you send Geordie up to tell me how the child is tonight?"

Left to himself, Peter lingered on for a little by the Grey Lady's seat, while the soothing spell of the moonlight and the herb-scent stole over him, and the peace of the garden possessed him once more.

"Possibly I'm prejudiced," he said aloud at last, "but it seems to me there never was, nor ever will be anyone quite like Dimsie. And there were moments tonight when I thought she came nearer caring than she knew, and I almost held my breath. It will be hard for me to live up to her ideals and give her all that her character needs, but with the help of Prividence I'll do it – *if* I get the chance."

CHAPTER 29

Epilogue

"Now, look here, Dimsie! there's no use straining your eyes after a boat which has just vanished round that bend at the foot of the loch. Exit Pamela Orde! who has been absorbing all your attention today – so surely you have got a little to spare for me now."

Dimsie, having changed her bridesmaid's dress, was perched on the great outcrop of grey rock where the Ogre had found her so many months before, and below her, where the Ogre had sat on that occasion, lolled Jim Hughes – a very different person.

"Are you feeling neglected?" she inquired. "Poor little thing! But we have still got two days left in which to enjoy you before your leave is up. It was a great wedding, wasn't it, Jim? even if there wasn't much of it."

"There was more than enough of it," grumbled Jim. "I don't suppose even when I go to bed tonight I'll get rid of all the rice that wretched Lintie kid pushed down my neck. But I expect you liked it. Girls always enjoy weddings."

"I think I enjoy most things," said Dimsie cheerfully. "I suppose it's the way I'm made. But with Pam and the Ogre both beaming so broadly, tears seemed out of place."

"Rosamund was a bit weepy."

"Oh, but Rosamund doesn't count! She always cries on the smallest pretext just from force of habit, not because she's at all unhappy. Didn't Pam make a lovely bride, even if she is your sister?"

"Don't be rude, Dimsie," said Jim reprovingly. "She didn't look bad, but I know someone who would look prettier still if she were dressed up in all that white stuff."

"Who? Rosamund? But her style is quite different from Pamela's. You can't compare—"

"I wasn't," interrupted Jim with determination. "I didn't mean Rosamund. I was speaking of you." His voice grew alarmingly sentimental. "I should like to see *you* as a bride, Dimsie."

"So you shall, Jim. I shan't forget to ask you to my wedding, and you can tell me afterwards if I look as pretty as Pam did."

Jim sat up, threw away the blade of grass which he had been munching, and said impressively:

"I only want to attend your wedding in one capacity, and you know very well what that is."

"I can't promise you'll be best man, because that isn't a matter for me to settle," said Dimsie, looking at him with dancing eyes. She was aware that the sailor, though an adept at flirtation, found it hard to flirt with her, and the fact gave her great satisfaction.

"Dimsie," he said mournfully. "You're a hardhearted little wretch. You always were, even in gymslip and long socks."

"I liked you better then," she retorted. "You were not so idiotic in those days. Look out! I'm coming down. It's time to go home and put the house in order."

"Not just yet. I haven't nearly finished all I've got to say. You don't seem to realize that I'm trying to propose to you. It makes that sort of job so much easier when the girl shows a little kindly intelligence about it."

"But I do realize it, and I've shown a great deal of intelligence in trying to *stop* you. It doesn't amuse me in the least to have you proposing to me, and I'd much rather you didn't. Why should you, anyhow?"

Jim gazed up at her reproachfully.

"Because I'm in love with you, of course."

Dimsie's face suddenly grew serious and she shrank back involuntarily, as though a jarring note had been struck which turned the nonsense into something distasteful.

"Oh, no, you're not, Jim!" she said firmly. "You're only flirting and I don't want to flirt. Go to Rosamund instead. She's much prettier than I am. I'm no good at this sort of thing."

"You'd soon learn," declared Jim hopefully.

"But I tell you I don't want to."

"Nonsense! I never knew a girl who didn't, unless—"

He stopped abruptly, and looked her over with a meditative glance.

"Unless what?" asked Dimsie innocently. "Unless she had something better to do – is that what you mean?"

"Yes, that's it," answered Jim in a peculiar tone, which made her look at him closely.

"I don't believe it is," she said, curiosity aroused.

"Well, I don't mean herb-growing, certainly. No girl wants to flirt when she's serious about someone else – that's what I'm driving at."

"Oh!"

Dimsie sat very still and quiet, her hands crossed on her lap, her eyes on the crown of Ben Aidan, still white with snow though spring had come to all the glens and farmlands. But her mind was far from still; Jim's remark had triggered a flood of thoughts which was taking her very far away from him. She knew (though hardly willing to confess it to herself) that recently her thoughts had been filled with Peter. She had labelled her feeling for him friendship, but Dimsie, for all her wide circle of friends, had never known what it was to be so completely absorbed in any one of them.

Absorbed! The colour rushed in a flood over her face. That was what it had come to after all! Slowly, half-reluctantly, she recognized that her mind had been full of Peter for months now, yet he had by no means cramped or narrowed her sympathies. She had cared as much for her mother, and Pamela's love-affairs, and Lintie's problems; had been as eager to help Jean in her literary struggles, or to study her herb-lore for the good of the sick and ailing. Only, through it all had run like a golden thread the thought of Peter with his ready sympathy and encouragement, his willingness to share with her in all her interests. There had been no monopoly, rather a widening of her powers to help people . . .

"I say, Dimsie!" Jim's voice was part plaintive and part aggrieved. "Am I to understand you refuse to be proposed to, at any price?"

Dimsie awoke with a start.

"Yes – by you."

"And why not? Have I grown horns and a tail overnight – or something?"

Dimsie laughed, and swung herself lightly off the rock.

"Not at all!" she said. "But what's the use, when I've already decided to marry Peter Gilmour? No – he doesn't know it yet, but he will soon, I'm just going to find him and tell him. Why don't you go and propose to Rosamund instead?"